HOCUS POCUS AND PINOT NOIR

MAGICAL MIDLIFE MIXERS

CANDICE BUNDY

LUSIOS PUBLISHING, LLC

To my Mother,
Your boundless inspiration and steadfast support have been
the backbone of my stories. I just know you would have adored
this one.

BLURB

Fleeing her past, Lydia Ash seeks refuge among wolf-shifters in Crescent Crossing, only to become entangled in a murder mystery that leads her to embrace her inner strength and rewrite her destiny.

Running from the haunting shadows of my traumatic past, I seek refuge in this isolated haven, a community of wolf-shifters who've never embraced me, a fae. Amidst towering mountains and whispering forests, I hope to find the peace that has eluded me for so long.

As I wrestle with memories of my bustling city life, the town's mystique draws me into its embrace. Yet, what I thought was a sanctuary soon becomes a labyrinth of challenges when a murder shakes the very foundation of Crescent Crossing.

Within the Howl Away Inn, a haven steeped in history, I confront my own self-doubts and insecurities. The trauma that has haunted me finds its echo here. In a world where wolf-shifters reign and fae like me are outsiders, my journey mirrors themes of self-discovery, resilience, and the power to transcend barriers.

Navigating this new existence, I forge unexpected alliances and grapple with intricate rivalries. The murder becomes a puzzle tied to my own story, revealing layers of deception and truth. Amid Crescent Crossing's rustic charm,

I delve into a world where magic intertwines with the mundane, where my quest for answers mirrors my path toward self-acceptance.

Join me on a journey that proves life after trauma is an opportunity to embrace the extraordinary. With courage as my guide, I uncover ancient secrets, rewrite my narrative, and prove that supernatural second acts are the most spectacular of all.

***

Magical Midlife Mixers is set in the same universe as the Shadow Series. Events begin after the book Shadow Underground.

CONTENTS

CHAPTER 1

The aged station wagon jounced down the pitted mountain highway, its faded teal paint speckled with dust. I clenched the cracked leather steering wheel with a vice-like grip as I navigated the narrow switchbacks, my knuckles bone white. This desolate wilderness was my refuge now, far from the looming memories that had darkened my last few months in Denver. Here, I could pretend I was the only living soul left in the world.

The road unwound like a spool of faded gray ribbon, guiding me away from a past too heavy to bear. It wasn't a journey I embarked upon lightly. My mind wandered, unbidden, to the night before my departure—a living room filled with tense faces and hearts heavy with unspoken fears. Becka, my niece, her hands clasped tightly in her lap, pleaded with a desperation that tightened my throat. "Aunt Lydia, please stay with us. We can keep you safe," she implored, her eyes brimming with tears, a vivid reflection of her dread at the thought of me facing any danger alone.

Quinn, her soulmate, sat beside her, his expression a

mask of understanding veiled with concern. "I get it, Lydia," he said, his voice firm yet gentle. "The fear of being used against Becka again... it's a valid concern. But running might not be the answer you hope for."

And then there was Hamish, whose stoic presence had always been a source of solace. He leaned forward, his voice low, offering a solution that felt like a lifeline amid the storm. "Crescent Crossing might not roll out the welcome mat for you, but it's secluded. Away from the prying eyes and manipulative hands that seek to control your niece. You might not be welcome, but you'll be safe. It's a place where you can start anew, on your own terms."

The room fell silent, heavy with the weight of his words. Becka's refusal to agree, overridden by her adamant wish for my safety and happiness regardless of the path I chose, echoed in my heart. "I just want you to be happy, Aunt Lydia. Safe, but happy. If Crescent Crossing is where you need to be, then... then I wish you all the love and luck in the world." Her voice cracked, a testament to the strength it took to let me go.

With the car windows rolled down to invite the crisp mountain air, I, Lydia Ash, merged into the rhythm of the wilderness while navigating the serpentine road. The hooting of a great horned owl carried on the breeze, a sound so profound it cut through the hum of the engine. Beside the road, a mountain stream played its secretive melody; visible in the occasional clearings, its waters danced over smooth stones. And all the while, the mournful chorus of the late-summer wind sang through the pine boughs, weaving through my hair and caressing my face. In motion, with the wild symphony of nature as my companion, I felt an ephemeral safety—hidden in plain sight, momentarily untraceable within the vast, living tapestry of the wilderness.

At least I hoped so.

My body trembled as memories from my recent past flooded my mind again—the harsh sound of wooden batons hitting my sides, the chilling laughter of my tormentors reverberating as I struggled to breathe through the pain. The paralyzing, icy terror when my suffering became merely bargaining fodder for my release.

I reminisced about my life in Denver, going from farmers' markets to wine tastings, spending weekend nights inspiring others' artwork, and constantly feeling like a background character in everyone else's stories. Helping my niece, Becka, uncover her true heritage and almost dying to protect her had been my only brush with genuine excitement, and then subsequent terror, in years.

Watching Becka find her soulmate in Quinn stirred an ache inside me I'd ignored for too long. I'd been stuck drifting through each day, living for momentary thrills but bereft of passion or purpose. There had to be more to this life than a monotonous existence on the sidelines. Maybe out here in the rugged wilderness, I could rediscover myself after so long spent hiding in the shadows.

Somehow, I had endured that harrowing ordeal by tapping into deep reserves of resilience I barely comprehended. Now I was determined to reclaim some small semblance of normalcy, refusing to let my traumatic experience wholly extinguish the tiny flickering flame of optimism that still burned within.

Yet I couldn't deny the chilling shift in my mindset since those events. That awful experience had instilled a heightened sense of caution and vigilance, as well as a fierce survival instinct that contrasted with my previously easy-going nature. My pulse quickened with a single wish echoing through my mind: that I would remain forever lost to anyone who wished to find me. And maybe, if I was lucky, I would find myself all over again.

I slowed the station wagon as a weathered wooden sign emerged, welcoming me to Crescent Crossing. Population 350. As I passed the carved silhouette of a howling wolf on the sign, an inexplicable chill slithered down my spine.

As the station wagon crested a steep ridge, the tiny, enchanting mountain hamlet of Crescent Crossing unfolded below, an idyllic mirage nestled in the valley. The view was a masterpiece of nature's artistry, with log structures sporting roofs painted in soothing sage green, harmoniously arranged around a dark emerald lake. This jewel of water, mirroring the deep green of ancient forests rather than the sapphire blue of a clear sky, lay cradled by the majestic embrace of snowcapped peaks—a scene of serene beauty under the vast expanse of an azure sky.

However, before I could marvel further at the pastoral scene unfolding before me, the unexpected sight of a large, imposing wolf blocking the road snapped me back to reality. Its fur, a mottled gray that blended with the waning light, bristled with hostility as it stood. An unyielding guardian against my advance. I slowed the car to a stop, heart hammering in my chest as the wolf's amber eyes locked onto mine, a silent challenge issued from its intense gaze as it prowled closer.

With a defiance born from months of facing my fears head-on, I met the creature's glare. "What's it gonna be? You gonna eat me?" I asked, the words laced with a resolve I scarcely recognized as my own. The wolf's response was a low growl, yet there was a moment, a flicker of something in its eyes that hinted at curiosity rather than hunger.

As it leaned closer, the cool mountain air mingled with its warm breath, a tangible sign of its curiosity and power. The distance between us was unguarded, with only the open air of the rolled-down window separating my resolve from its wild scrutiny. Yet, instead of fear, a defiant courage welled up within me. "I've faced worse than you," I said directly to the beast, my voice steady and clear in the open night. "Going back is more terrifying than any set of teeth you have."

At those words, the wolf's ears twitched, its demeanor shifting from aggression to a surprising attentiveness. After a tense moment, it chuffed softly, a sound that might have been laughter in another world, and with a final, assessing glance, it stepped aside, nudging its nose in a gesture that seemed to say, "Then pass."

As the wolf slinked back into the dense forest that bordered the road, a part of me felt an odd sense of respect from the creature. Shaking off the surreal encounter, I pressed the accelerator gently; the car moving forward as I left the wolf, and my hesitation, behind me.

Steadying my breath, I retrieved the rumpled, hand-scrib-bled map and directions given to me by Enforcer Hamish Bittersweet from the passenger seat. With a gentle turn of the steering wheel, I guided the station wagon left down a narrow row of storybook arts-and-crafts style houses and shops. Their faded painted signs and riotously overflowing window boxes brimming with plump crimson begonias and climbing pink roses in full late-summer bloom painted a scene almost too picturesque.

Everything about this remote haven nestled within the mountain's embrace radiated a deep sense of serenity, as if stepping into a landscape painting alive with color and texture. As I veered down a side street lined with quaint cottages, each small home encircled by a picket fence and teeming with aromatic heirloom lavender, globe thistle, and sage, the knot of tension wedged between my shoulder blades began to unfurl. With each turn deeper into this picturesque setting, the distance I put between myself and my past seemed to ease the weight from my shoulders, bit by bit.

Perhaps in this isolated, rugged mountain sanctuary so different from the gleaming Denver metropolis I once called home, I could cautiously build myself a simple life, far from the dangers and painful memories that continued to haunt me. A place where I might finally feel safe again and, over time, allow my lingering wounds to slowly mend, re-learn to breathe fully, and sleep untroubled through the night after enduring so many restless weeks of hypervigilance.

Yet, as idyllic as it seemed, Hamish had warned me that the locals held a strong wariness toward outsiders, especially those lacking the wolf-shifter ability. Normally, my fae blood would make entering impossible. But I was a fae born without magic, so nobody should be worried about me disrupting their peace. Still, prejudices ran deep against fae, which was, ironically, why I'd chosen this isolated town. If I wasn't welcome, neither were other fae.

Three ancient packs of wolf shifters called these mist-veiled valleys home and guarded their territory fiercely. Hamish said the town had a mediator who secretly controlled nearly everything here, from shop hours to the monthly moonlight gatherings.

As I navigated the sleepy town square, my gaze caught on an intricately carved wooden sign for the Crescent Crossing Trailhead. Its elaborately painted image of a glittering brook evoked scenes of dappled sunlight filtering through whispering aspens. But when I glanced again, the sign appeared weathered and worn, the once-vibrant paint faded and flaked like a crumbling artifact from a forgotten age. A prickle of unease crept down my spine. What mysteries lurked beneath this town's idyllic veneer?

Across from the now-faded trailhead sign, the main bakery announced itself with a brightly painted banner strung between two second-story windows. "The Sugared Spruce" was proclaimed in swooping copperplate script, catching the eye with its promise of sweetness. From within, the rich scents of cinnamon rolls and maple donuts wafted out, drawing passersby closer. Despite the early hour, a few locals were already queued up, drawn by the irresistible smells I was sure, chatting quietly as they anticipated the indulgence of freshly baked goods.

Further down sat Willem's Wares, the rambling general store run by a whiskered old-timer whittling on the porch. He conjured fond memories of my grandfather teaching me to carve forest creatures in my wooded childhood home in the fae territories, patiently guiding my small hands as I learned to coax animal shapes from the yielding wood.

Despite its remote mountain location, Crescent Crossing radiated a sense of community and belonging. The weathered wooden facades of shops and meeting halls hinted at the town's hidden histories and secrets waiting to be discovered.

I rechecked Hamish's map, and when I looked up, there was the inn, right where he'd marked the spot. The inn was made of gray stone, had two floors, and featured a steeply sloping roof and abundant windows. A beautifully carved cedar sign read "Howl Away Inn — Est. 1924" in ornate calligraphy.

I couldn't restrain a tentative smile. Even the fanciful name awakened flickers of optimism I had feared were extinguished.

Stepping outside into the radiant late-summer warmth, a pine-scented breeze rippled through my hair like a loving caress. I stood, closing my eyes and embracing the solitude, interrupted only by the rustling trees that whispered among themselves of secrets unknown.

When I opened my eyes, the lovely grounds lay before me, a vision out of a forgotten fairy tale. Pink roses blanketed the weathered stone exterior, releasing a sweet perfume into the crisp mountain air. A bench overlooked the sloping alpine meadows that gave way to unbroken evergreen forest stretching toward distant peaks that jutted into the sky like stone sentinels. An ancient oak stump had been made into a vibrant flower planter, with golden marigolds bobbing in the morning breeze.

After slinging my faded backpack over one shoulder and grabbing my tote bag, I made my way up the uneven stone walkway lined with pansies and coneflowers. As my hand met the elaborately forged door handle, I hesitated, doubts creeping in. Could this place really be my refuge? Or would my past find me, no matter how far I ran? I tamped down the worries and pushed forward.

The moment I stepped into the inviting lobby, I was met

with honey-colored beams, a gently crackling stone hearth that smelled of cedar smoke, and plush leather furniture that exuded a sense of coziness and comfort. My eyes instinctively darted around the lobby, assessing the other patrons. I spotted a few flannel- and leather-clad men conversing in hushed rumbles near the great stone fireplace, their voices fading to silence as they caught sight of me, their penetrating stares following my every move. In the worn braided rug's center, a curly-haired toddler with a wooden train giggled cheerfully until his mother scooped him up hastily, glancing my way with unease.

Just beyond the hearth stood a polished oak front desk. To the right was a well-stocked bar and dining area where a few early diners savored steaming plates, the irresistible aromas making my empty stomach rumble. I spotted a few patrons in the restaurant, including a brooding man in a leather jacket who eyed me warily from the corner and a smiling woman with chestnut curls chatting animatedly with patrons at the bar.

At a corner table, an elderly woman with long silver braids sat sipping chamomile tea, her inscrutable expression shifting to a questioning look tinged with suspicion as I lingered anxiously by the door. A ripple of disquiet passed through the room, with muttered words I couldn't quite catch adding layers to the unfolding drama around me. These whispered exchanges, though indistinct, amplified the atmosphere of intrigue, suggesting a complex tapestry of stories and secrets woven into the fabric of this little haven.

Before I could approach the front desk to inquire about vacancies, a side door behind the counter creaked open and an imposing figure emerged, causing me to freeze in place.

Despite his long, thick hair being shot through with strands of gleaming silver, he carried himself with the vigor and vitality of a much younger man. His rugged features and piercing tawny eyes set deeply beneath a contemplative brow etched with decades of wisdom gave him an undeniable air of quiet yet indomitable confidence. This was clearly no ordinary mountain innkeeper but a man who commanded attention and respect.

As he strode toward me with fluid grace, I sensed a strange energy radiating from him, setting my nerves on edge. Though he moved with ease, I detected a slight limp, slowing his pace only minimally. As I approached, I noticed the intricate details of his aged face—the piercing eyes gleaming with insightful knowledge.

A shiver slithered down my spine, despite the fire's warmth. What secrets lurked behind those assessing eyes? I tensed, ready to flee from their penetrating gaze.

"Welcome to the Howl Away Inn," he rumbled, his resonant voice filling the lobby. "Name's Ryder. I'm the owner of this fine establishment." His scrutiny lingered on my anxious face and stance. Just remain calm, I told myself, attempting a timid smile despite feeling unsettled by his aura of knowledge beyond my grasp. He couldn't possibly know what had brought me, haunted and hollow-eyed, to this remote refuge. Yet the depth of his gaze suggested he was no stranger to mysteries, his eyes seemingly able to pierce through the facades to uncover truths not readily visible.

"And you are?" His polite inquiry caught me off guard. I sensed him carefully evaluating not just my uncommon attire, but also my nervous stance and my shadow-ringed eyes. I composed myself and managed a timid smile.

"I'm Lydia Ash," I replied, cringing at my hoarse, wavering voice. I cleared my throat. "I was hoping you might have a room for me to stay awhile."

The innkeeper nodded slowly, his craggy features impassive yet his gaze still fixed on my face. I couldn't dispel the uncanny feeling that those sharp eyes glimpsed echoes of my harrowing journey here, seeking refuge.

I sensed kindness and protectiveness in Ryder's imposing presence, though I felt he was likely guarded with newcomers. His eyes softened almost imperceptibly at my disheveled appearance and wariness, hinting at compassion within his hardened exterior.

"Well, Miss Ash," he said after a weighty pause, eyes crinkling subtly, "seems you've found the right place."

Reaching beneath the counter, he retrieved an enormous leather ledger and set it down heavily, sending up swirling dust. "The inn has welcomed many seeking refuge over the years."

His words should have been reassuring, yet I detected a probing note in his voice, gently assessing what had brought this haunted, skittish stranger to his remote haven.

Uneasy under his patient but astute scrutiny, my pulse inexplicably quickened. I turned to a faded painting above the hearth, murmuring some excuse about needing solitude after the city's chaos. The evasive half-truth curdled in my mouth. What did this innkeeper discern in me with those keen eyes?

Ryder studied me pensively before nodding and flipping open the substantial ledger, revealing an intricate triskele tattoo on his forearm.

"Solitude can certainly be found here," he affirmed

gently, his eyes reflecting a depth of understanding, as if he recognized my need for a respite rather than solitude, despite my cautious approach. His perceptiveness, both disarming and reassuring, kindled a hope within me. I might have encountered someone who, despite knowing my name, would honor the silence I needed surrounding the reasons that drove me to seek refuge in this secluded haven.

After inscribing my name in the ledger, Ryder retrieved a tarnished brass key from the desk drawer and passed it across the counter to me.

"You'll be in room 212. It's just at the top of the stairs and down the hall on the right." He tipped his head toward a narrow staircase tucked against the back wall. "Young Barnell here will help get your bags on up there and give you the lay of the land."

Right on cue, the office door creaked open and out bounded an eager gangly teen with a fiery shock of unruly orange hair. Though rather scrawny, with oversized hands and feet that seemed borrowed from a larger frame, an air of cheerful helpfulness radiated from the boy's crooked grin.

"No problem, Mr. Ryder. I'll get her bags and show her around straightaway," Barnell offered brightly as he moved to heft my belongings, his enthusiasm outpacing his slight build.

Before I could protest, he had already slung my faded denim backpack over one bony shoulder and snatched up my woven rainbow tote with the other hand, flashing a positively gleeful, gap-toothed grin.

"C'mon this way, miss! I'll give you the full tour and show you all my favorite secret spots."

As he guided me up the creaking staircase, chattering enthusiastically about secluded swimming holes and stunning mountaintop vistas, his boundless exuberance hinted at a spirit hungry for connection and fresh faces in this remote haven.

I made polite murmured sounds in response to his lively prattle, though my doubts soon drowned out his cheerful banter. What had possessed me to believe I could outrun my past by fleeing to this isolated inn? Even miles from the dangers I sought to escape, I felt the icy fingers of memory clawing at my shoulders, heard chilling echoes of laughter reverberating in my mind.

At the end of the hallway, Barnell dramatically flung open the last door with a flourish. "Here we are! What do you think of your new home away from home?" Barnell proudly gestured to the cozy bedroom before us.

I managed a timid smile, taking in the tranquil details. A hand-stitched quilt with interlocking rings of robin's egg blue and ivory adorned the sturdy oak bedframe, the fabric whispering tales of quiet evenings before the fire. Plump goose down pillows beckoned, promising restful slumber. Sheer champagne curtains filtered the early morning sunlight streaming through the wide mullioned window overlooking the pine grove below, where a raven's croaking call echoed up from the valley.

The cushioned reading chair tucked in the corner with its carved oak frame seemed the perfect haven for losing oneself in a book. A beautifully stitched sampler above it read "May the moon guide you home." The polished pine floors glowed amber, leading toward the inviting clawfoot tub in the quaint bathroom.

After so many restless weeks adrift, the cozy room felt like a long-awaited harbor, resonating safety. For a moment, I allowed myself to exhale, releasing the knot of tension that perpetually gripped my shoulders. Perhaps here I might finally find some small measure of peace.

I managed a timid smile at the cozy room. "It's lovely, thank you."

Barnell grinned, seemingly satisfied, as he dropped my bags. "You need anything, you come find me!" With an exaggerated bow, he left, whistling down the hall.

Finally alone, I sank onto the quilt, exhaling shakily. I'd made it here, despite my doubts. For now, I asked only for this simple sanctuary.

I moved to the window, gazing at the swaying pines as birds chirped in the distance, their melodies harmonizing with the soft rustle of leaves. The serene sounds brought a sense of calm over me, even as I marveled at nature's song.

Perhaps here, away from past troubles, I could let go of old fears and embrace a new beginning. Imagine a life not dictated by worries or pain.

Exhausted from the drive up, I wrapped my shawl tighter around my shoulders, my newfound hope wavering. I collapsed into the bed, nestling myself in the layers of soft warmth. I drifted off, lulled by the whispering pines outside my window. But sleep did not come easy. I jolted awake frequently, senses prickling with unease.

Perhaps coming here had been a mistake. Could I ever outrun the looming ghosts of my past? Would the mysteries of this tiny mountain town swallow me whole?

CHAPTER 2

$\mathcal{A}$ restless disquiet stirred me from my dreamless slumber, the first undisturbed rest I'd known in ages. Yet as I lay there, thoughts swirling, an unsettled feeling needled at me. Something ominous lurked in the whispering night, chasing away any hopes of peaceful sleep.

I rose, wrapping my ivory crocheted shawl tight around my shoulders against the mountain chill, my stomach gnawing with hunger. Bare feet muted on the wide pine boards, I eased open the window, breathing deeply of the bracing night air. Above, a waning crescent moon gleamed like a slender sickle amid a sea of stars. All seemed tranquil, the fir boughs still, the inn's lamps darkened in slumber.

Resigned to wakefulness, especially after having slept the day away, I splashed cool water on my face and plaited my hair. If I couldn't sleep, perhaps tea in the dining hall might settle my jittery nerves. Tucking journal and pen into my pack, I crept downstairs, only to halt as flickering firelight and hushed voices drifted from the shadowy lobby. Curiosity overcame me. Who else stirred at this hour? I moved closer.

Around a large table, three strangers sat with Ryder, the innkeeper, engrossed in a solemn game of cards. Glasses of amber liquid punctuated tense exchanges, some iced, some neat, disappearing down throats between terse words. No coins sat upon the table, only a single hand played out with import I couldn't grasp. My entrance went unnoticed, attention narrowed to their cards.

Unease prickled my skin as I studied these sharp-eyed players. The strangers' eyes glinted with cunning, their expressions unreadable masks that set my nerves on edge. What stakes compelled such intensity? They gave no notice as I hovered in the doorway, watching one lean forward, lips barely moving as he uttered something that elicited a scowl from Ryder.

My breath caught at a soft creak overhead. Imagined footsteps, or something more? A shiver traced my spine. This charged scene held an undercurrent of danger that whispered warnings no one heeded. Perhaps I should turn away and retreat upstairs before being noticed. Yet curiosity rooted me in place.

Ryder's next play drew a hiss from the fair-haired man to his left. Eyes blazing, the stranger glared at Ryder, fingers visibly tightening on his glass. Across from him, a raven-haired woman shook her head subtly, a silent caution ignored. Her wary focus flickered briefly to me as I lingered just beyond the ring of firelight. Our gazes locked, but whatever unspoken message she tried to convey was lost as Ryder spoke.

"The inn is mine," Ryder rasped, tone etched with weary resolution. His opponents stirred, exchanging unreadable looks I longed to interpret.

The shadow-veiled player leaned in and chuckled without humor, his voice chilling in its calmness. "Ryder, you've held the upper hand before, but the winds of fortune are shifting. Let's see what fate decides tonight." His words, smooth yet laden with an ominous edge, sent a shiver down my spine. Gripping the door frame tighter, I contemplated escaping to the safety of my room, away from the unsettling undercurrents of this encounter. Yet curiosity held me captive, my feet refusing to move as the room's silence became as heavy and foreboding as the darkness outside.

The burly man who'd spoken had a massive, thickly muscled frame that strained against a battered leather vest. His jet-black hair fell to his shoulders in messy waves, contrasting with startling gray eyes under the deep creases lining his craggy brow. Everything about his imposing presence seemed designed to intimidate and dominate the room. Yet as he reached for an unlit cigar clamped between his teeth, the motion revealed a strange gentleness in those calloused hands, belying his gruff exterior.

The blond man was lean yet muscular, with a lithe, athletic build beneath his red flannel. Though he appeared focused on the game, there was a cunning gleam in his ice-blue eyes which continuously scanned the table. I sensed his strategic movements and groomed appearance suggested he was a dangerous opponent.

Next to him sat the raven-haired woman, assessing her hand with a calculating gleam in her steely gray eyes. Dressed in practical attire, she radiated a quiet wisdom.

Just as I concluded my observation and prepared to slip past them toward the bar, a resonant voice called out from the table of four.

I hovered uncertainly in the doorway as Ryder's gravelly voice called out, "Lydia! What are you doing up at this hour?"

My cheeks flushed at the sudden attention as all eyes turned to me. I opened my mouth, but no words emerged. The imposing strangers stared with inscrutable expressions that set my nerves jittering.

"I..." I faltered, unnerved by the strangers' sudden attention. "I hope I'm not intruding on your game."

"Not at all." Ryder nodded reassuringly.

"Speak for yourself," snapped back the man in the red flannel.

Leather vest's gray eyes suddenly flicked to me, and his face twisted into a scowl. "You're allowing fae to room now, Ryder?" he spat, his voice dripping with disdain. "What's next? Entertaining every stray rat that wanders through the door?"

I felt my cheeks heat, but I quickly raised my chin, refusing to let his rudeness ruffle me. "I assure you, my presence here is neither your concern nor your decision," I replied coolly, meeting his hostile gaze with calm defiance.

His eyes narrowed, and he let out a derisive snort. "Mighty bold words for a fae. You'd be wise to remember you're not in a city or in some fae territory anymore," he growled, clearly unimpressed by my retort. "You're surrounded by wolves now."

Ryder's eyes flashed, and he held up a hand to silence the gruff man. When he spoke, his voice was low and stern. "Drake, I know you're seldom in town, but you'd do well to remember that I make the rules here." He paused, glancing at me and then back at Drake, his voice tinged with a warning. "I won't have you threatening my guests."

Did he mean just at his inn, or in the whole town too? I was curious to ask, but I didn't want to get in the middle of their testosterone-fueled moment.

Drake grunted, clearly unhappy but unwilling to challenge Ryder further. He turned back to his cards, his shoulders still rigid with tension.

Ryder continued on, his voice returning to its usual warm gravelly tone as he addressed me. "The big cranky guy is Drake, pretty boy is Kai, and the lady is Harper." They each nodded to me, but I could tell their interest was on getting back to the game, not exchanging niceties with me.

Just then, I heard a buzzing coming from Ryder's pocket. He pulled out his phone, brows scrunching. "In fact, Lydia, your arrival is fortuitous. I'm afraid I have to take this... it's an urgent matter. I need you to take my seat and hold my cards till I return."

Before I could protest, Ryder steered me into his vacant chair with a gentle hand. I perched awkwardly as he disappeared, intensely aware of the strangers' speculative looks boring into me. Apprehension gnawed at my composure. What had I stumbled into? These were no casual players. Every line of their bodies dripped with cunning and restrained power. And I now held the focal point—Ryder's hand.

Before walking away, Ryder added under his breath near my ear, "Whatever you do, don't reveal your hand or fold. Understood?"

I nodded mutely, unnerved by the gravity in his tone. With a brisk nod of satisfaction, he limped toward a side door leading out of the lobby, his uneven gait echoing on the wooden floors until the door creaked open and heavy stillness fell once more over the room.

An uneasiness settled upon the table. It seemed the game was on hold until Ryder returned. I could feel Drake's searing gaze burning into me though I refused to meet his eyes. I cleared my throat awkwardly and attempted a timid smile.

"Lovely night for a game, isn't it?" I began hesitantly, trying to break the tense silence. My weak attempt at congenial small talk was met with only a continued hush. "What are you four playing for?"

Drake leaned back and fished a lighter out of his vest pocket, bringing it up to his mouth to light his cigar.

Harper spoke with a crisp, authoritative voice. "Take it outside; not in here! We're not playing until Ryder comes back, anyway. No hard feelings," she said, turning to face me.

I didn't let her words get to me. I had no idea how to play the game. I was here only because Ryder had been so welcoming and had given me no choice. So far, he'd been an excellent host.

With a string of unintelligible muttering, Drake stomped outside and slammed the heavy wooden door behind him.

Kai seized the chance and rose gracefully from his chair. "I'm off to use the facilities. I trust neither of you will peek." He sauntered away toward the restrooms at the back, long legs eating up the distance.

Now it was just Harper and me at the table. She glanced at her cards again and sighed but made no move to leave like the others.

Just then, the young bartender with a name tag which

read 'Briar' walked over with a friendly smile. "Can I get you a drink while you wait, hon? Whiskey? Beer?"

I shook my head, my stomach feeling too unsettled for anything strong. "I'll just have a glass of Pinot Noir if you have it. And maybe something to eat? I seem to have slept away my day and evening."

"Travel can really take it out of you. I know just what you need!" Briar headed to the bar and returned swiftly with a generous glass of garnet wine and a steaming bowl of stew. "Our hunter's stew is really hearty and delicious, and that chunk of bread is fresh sourdough. We make it daily. Let me know if you need anything else!"

As I sipped the fragrant wine and sampled the savory stew, Kai returned from the restroom and took his seat. Only once he was back did Harper stand abruptly.

"I need to pop up to my room quickly for something. I trust you won't get up to any shenanigans?" she asked Kai pointedly.

He flashed her a grin, but Harper didn't seem charmed. "Who, me?" he asked with amusement.

I focused on enjoying my meal, the savory stew momentarily distracting me from the undercurrents of tension. Ryder's cards, a tangible reminder of his abrupt departure, lay beside my plate on the table, their presence adding to my growing perplexity at the strange dynamics unfolding around me. With each bite, my unease deepened, a knot of apprehension tightening in my gut. I found myself glancing at the door repeatedly, wishing for Ryder's swift return to reclaim his mysterious hand.

These shifters were playing for far more than just money,

I sensed. What had I stumbled into? Where was Ryder, and why had he been gone so long?

Harper returned and slumped back into her chair, her gaze fixed on the floor. Meanwhile, Briar collected my empty dishes, the clinking of silverware reverberating through the room.

"You want another glass of pinot?"

I nodded, although I was debating if something stronger might steady my jittery nerves.

We all watched in strained silence as Drake stumbled in, trailing a thick cloud of cigar smoke. He planted himself down in his seat with another muttered curse. Without so much as an apology for his behavior, he growled, "Where the hell is Ryder?"

"I'll go check on him," Briar replied, heading out the way Ryder had gone. A moment later, a blood-curdling scream pierced the night.

We all jumped up from the table and we rushed down the dim hallway after Briar, our footsteps echoing like frantic drums. I had scooped up the innkeeper's cards and now clutched them. A sense of sick dread crept over me as we reached the back door Ryder had exited through earlier.

"No! It can't be!" Briar cried hysterically.

We crowded around the doorway, and the sight knocked the breath from my lungs. Ryder lay lifeless on the ground, eyes vacant, reflecting the moon. His shirt was soaked through with inky blood still spreading in a sinister pool around him.

Kai uttered a choked gasp, all his polished composure vanishing. Drake let out an anguished bellow, like a wounded animal. Harper pressed a trembling hand to her mouth, muffling a sob.

Ryder's blood triggered vivid flashbacks of my trauma, transporting me back to that horrific night, leaving me frozen and mute. I couldn't breathe, couldn't think, couldn't move.

Drake gently helped a hysterical Briar to her feet while she clutched at him, tears streaming down her cheeks. Though my own eyes remained dry, guilt and grief warred within me. I wished desperately to comfort her, to offer some solace, but the words lodged in my throat.

Harper squeezed my shoulder, her eyes shadowed with pain. "Come away," she murmured. "There's nothing more we can do for him now."

I let her guide me back down the hallway on unsteady feet, unable to tear my eyes from the tragic scene until we turned the corner. Leaning against the wall, I struggled to slow my ragged breathing. "What happened to him?" I finally rasped.

Briar's delicate features had blanched to an ashen hue, her emerald eyes wide with shock and sorrow. "Murder," she rasped hoarsely. "Ryder's dead. There's blood everywhere." She shuddered, fresh tears sliding down her cheeks.

I swallowed hard, wrapping my arms around myself. Nothing could have prepared me for this.

My heart stuttered to a stop as the barkeep's grim words sunk in. Murder? Here? Impossible. I'd just fled from murderers and violence. Surely I hadn't stumbled into more tragedy here. But the awful reality slowly sank in. Ryder, the innkeeper who had welcomed me kindly just hours ago, now laid dead, murdered brutally.

"Ryder was the most respected man in town," Drake

replied, his voice rough as gravel. "What kind of monster would do this?"

The hollow expression on Briar's face tore at my soul. For several heartbeats, the world seemed to spin around me. I clutched the wall to steady myself, gripping Ryder's cards to my chest.

Kai spoke carefully, a hint of panicked alarm in his tone. "I did not see this coming."

"The game is over," Harper declared solemnly. She moved to the table and flipped her cards face up. "I hate to take away from the gravity of this moment, but we have no choice. Let's see what fate dealt each of us."

At her words, the agony in Briar's features hardened into icy resolve. She drew herself up, bracing her shoulders back. "You can't just go on like nothing's happened!"

"No, Harper's right. We must finish this hand," Drake replied, his eyes hooded. He turned over three kings.

Kai revealed a decent hand, but from their expressions, there was no clear winner. All eyes turned to me. I reluctantly showed my mediocre cards, a run of diamonds, but no pairs. Surely one of the others had me beat.

"Well, well," Kai murmured, "seems fortune favors you tonight."

I swayed unsteadily, paralyzed by shock and confusion. My arm itched fiercely, but I could hardly focus on the strange sensation.

Briar turned to address the players, raw anguish in her voice. "The game has ended. Lydia, as stand-in for Ryder, is the winner."

Harper spoke solemnly. "Lydia will take Ryder's place as keeper of the Howl Away Inn and town mediator."

Her words fell sharply, piercing the dense silence that had enveloped the room. I stared at her, utterly staggered. Me, the keeper of the inn? The mediator? The weight of the titles seemed surreal, anchoring me to the spot as I grappled with the sudden shift in my fate.

What the fuck?

"There must be some mistake," I managed faintly. I was no leader. Just a woman seeking refuge from her own demons. How could I possibly fill Ryder's shoes? "Who the hell bets an inn on a single hand of cards?"

Before I could gather my scattered thoughts, Briar came up beside me, grasping my shoulders urgently. Her blazing eyes reflected desperation.

"You must listen closely. Dangerous forces have been unleashed tonight. But you must have the courage to restore balance." Then she pulled up my shirt sleeve, revealing the cause of the itching on my arm. Adorning my left forearm now was an elaborate triskele tattoo, an exact replica of the one I had noticed on Ryder's arm.

As I struggled to absorb her words, a small part of me wondered if maybe this unexpected duty was just the thing I needed. Back in Denver, I'd felt so aimless and adrift. Perhaps managing this inn could give me renewed purpose. It was a terrifying prospect, but also held a glimmer of long-overdue change I realized I craved.

Harper's expression was sharp as a razor's edge. "I'll honor fate's choice, but don't think I won't seek any way out. Know I'll be challenging again as soon as possible, which is a year from today." She strode upstairs without waiting for a response.

"And you two?" Briar asked Drake and Kai.

"Who am I to challenge fate?" Kai replied lightly, but the humor didn't reach his steely eyes.

"I'll do more than challenge it," Drake growled. "But for now, I'll abide."

"Well, that's something," Briar said, a weary hand brushing her forehead as she turned slightly to address me directly, recognizing my unfamiliarity with the community's ways. "After what has happened to Ryder, I must contact Silas, our local coroner and mortician. He handles both roles, a necessity in our small town." She offered me a brief, sad smile, an implicit acknowledgment of the unusual circumstances I found myself in. "Now, if you'll excuse me, I need to make that call and go watch over him until Silas arrives." Her resolve to fulfill this duty, despite the shock, underscored the depth of their communal ties.

She brushed past me, tears streaming down her cheeks. Her uneven steps echoed hollowly until the door creaked shut, leaving a heavy silence in her wake.

I swayed, lightheaded from the torrent of revelations. Murder. Victor. Innkeeper. Briar's words swirled in my mind, devoid of sense.

A humorless chuckle jarred me from turbulent thoughts. Kai regarded me with unveiled disdain twisting his patrician features.

"What a dreadfully disappointing outcome," he remarked. "To think the venerable Ryder Shadowfang's legacy now rests in your hopelessly unqualified hands." His scornful gaze raked over me. "Still, I suppose the old man's foolish adherence to tradition must be honored, no matter how ludicrous."

With that ominous parting shot, he gathered his jacket and strode briskly out, leaving me reeling.

I slowly turned to face Drake, still lingering at the room's edge. My heart stuttered as I met the intensity of his penetrating gray gaze, now tinged with disbelief and grudging curiosity. He took one step closer, and I drew a sharp breath, overwhelmed by his formidable presence.

When at last he broke the silence, his voice rumbled like gathering thunder. "Never met a fae I'd wager on in a test of will or worth. Yet here we stand." He moved nearer, eyes hooded. "Know that winning was the easy part. The real challenge lies before you."

Before I could respond, he, too, disappeared out the front door, leaving me trembling in his wake.

His ominous words echoed in my mind, raising far more questions than answers. I knew only that an unexpected twist of fate had landed me in uncharted territory, with mysteries and perils lurking in every shadowed corner.

Somewhere, a lone wolf's mournful howl echoed through the silent hills. Shuddering, I wrapped my arms tight around my middle, unsure what the future would hold but knowing the worst was yet to come.

CHAPTER 3

In the early hours of the morning before the sun had begun to make an appearance over the mountains, I drifted back downstairs, more phantom than flesh, still unable to accept this new reality. The dimly lit lobby seemed cavernous and ominous; the oak panels and stone hearth, formerly so welcoming, now took on a sinister cast. Briar sat slumped on one of the lobby couches, her face buried in her hands. At my whispered greeting, she glanced up, her eyes bloodshot and cheeks streaked with tears.

Before I could offer any hollow words of comfort, a brisk knock shattered the uneasy silence. The sharp sound made us both jump, as if our raw nerves couldn't handle even the slightest disruption. Briar bolted up, arms wrapped around herself. I crossed the worn rug, each step feeling leaden, and opened the carved oak door with reluctance. An imposing yet refined figure stood haloed in the dim porch light.

"Good morning. I'm Silas Blackthorn, the local mortician and coroner," he introduced himself with a somber tone. His presence on the threshold, framed by the night, emphasized the solemnity of the task which brought him here.

A question surfaced amid my turmoil. "Silas, if you don't mind me asking, who handles law enforcement around here? In cases like these, I mean."

Briar, edging closer, answered before Silas could. "In our town, the innkeeper not only manages the inn but also serves as a sort of... local authority, especially in matters concerning the supernatural community."

Silas nodded in agreement. "Yes, traditionally, the innkeeper acts as the mediator and, to some extent, the peace-keeper among the enclaves. With Ryder gone, those duties fall to you, Miss Ash."

I absorbed this new information with a mix of disbelief and a dawning sense of duty. "So, I'm expected to... what? Step into Ryder's shoes as the local law?"

Briar's gaze was sympathetic yet firm. "It's an unconventional system, but it's how things have always been done here. You'll find the community respects the innkeeper's authority, especially in resolving disputes."

Silas's expression was earnest as he added, "We're a close-knit community, Miss Ash. Ryder was much more than an innkeeper; he was a guardian of sorts. And now, you are too."

The realization settled heavily upon me, a mantle I was yet unsure how to bear. Yet, as Silas and Briar outlined the expectations and traditions that now encompassed my unexpected role, a reluctant resolve began to form within me. If this was my path, then I would walk it, for Ryder's sake and for the peace of the town he loved.

Though undoubtedly accustomed to death, traces of

sorrow marked Silas's stoic countenance. With chilling efficiency, he followed Briar outside to where Ryder lay. I drifted behind them, disconnected from the scene unfolding before me.

This couldn't be real. Surely at any moment I'd wake in my bed, the horrific visions of the night fading away with the darkness. Yet the truth confronted me with unrelenting clarity in the silver moonlight. Ryder was gone. And the sun would continue to rise and set in the valley he'd called home, heedless of his absence.

Wrapped in the chill of the predawn air, I clasped my arms tightly around myself, a futile shield against the onslaught of memories from that harrowing night at the mercy of the Shadow Dwellers. In their cruel grasp, I was nothing but a tool meant to shatter my niece, Becka's, resolve —her screams, the sight of blood, the merciless beatings, all haunted me anew. My eyes snapped shut, a desperate attempt to banish these vivid, terrifying flashes, even as my heart thundered against my ribcage. History was repeating itself, a vicious cycle, but now, the weight of unraveling this nightmare had inexplicably shifted to me.

I took a deep, shaky breath, trying to fortify my resolve against the onslaught of my own fears. The first light of dawn was on the horizon, bringing with it the undeniable reality of my new, heavy burden. The safety of the shadows was no longer an option; I faced an inevitable confrontation with whatever lay ahead.

As time slipped by unnoticed, Silas, with his practiced solemnity, began the grim task of preparing Ryder for transport. Briar, overcoming her initial hesitation, stepped forward to assist him. Together, they gently lifted Ryder's body onto a stretcher with a care that spoke volumes of their respect for the departed. Their coordinated efforts, a silent testimony to the communal spirit, ensured Ryder was treated with dignity. They then carefully loaded the stretcher into a nondescript black van, their movements synchronized in a dance of mournful duty. This shared responsibility, borne out of necessity and respect, underscored the gravity of the moment and the deep bonds within the community.

Briar kept her face turned away whenever possible and now stood back, arms crossed tightly over her chest, clearly overwhelmed by the heartbreaking scene. My own limbs felt numb and leaden, my breaths shallow as potent sorrow and dread constricted my chest.

After a moment, Silas returned to us, his stoicism replaced by sincere empathy. "Did you notice any weapon?"

A shudder passed through Briar. "No. The murderer must have taken it with them," she said, her composure shattered.

Silas nodded. "I promise to take the utmost care with him. And I'll examine everything thoroughly for any evidence." He met my gaze. "We'll speak soon, Miss Ash. I wish you strength in the difficult days ahead."

With those ominous words, he turned and headed for his van. The taillights faded into the distance, leaving Briar and I alone again. I sensed she had more to say about my new role here, though it would have to wait for the full light of day.

"I'm going to try to get some sleep. If you can, you should as well."

Briar managed a choked, "I'll try," as she muffled a sob.

My heart shattered watching her pain, and I instinctively pulled her into a hug. Briar melted against me, and I gazed up at the brightening sky, drawing slow, steady breaths. I knew all too well that no words could comfort such bottomless grief. Only time might gradually dull the aching edges of this tragedy.

How could I possibly fill Ryder's shoes? I was no mediator or leader. In Denver, I'd never managed more than drifting from day to day in my own aimless life. But to steward an entire community of shifters? The task seemed insurmountable. I didn't even know where to start.

Oh Ryder, I lamented silently, Why did you give those cards to me? I'm utterly unqualified for this role. Anyone in this town would be better suited to uniting the enclaves and keeping the peace. What do I know of shifters, magic, or balancing precarious politics?

I'm just... me.

The early morning breeze coming off the mountains carried no answers, only the echo of my own jagged breaths. I had no choice but to face the unknown path ahead, woefully unprepared as I felt. But I didn't have to walk it alone. Briar believed in me. And for now, her faith would have to sustain me.

When Briar pulled away, we shared awkward, half-hearted smiles.

"Sleep it is," she replied, heading back inside.

Squaring my shoulders against the chill, I turned and followed her in, my heart heavy but resolved. I had to at least try though each step made my doubts swell.

After a couple of fitful hours of sleep, I found Briar aimlessly cleaning already spotless glasses behind the bar, hands trembling. She quickly set down the rag when she spotted me approaching.

"How are you holding up?" I asked.

"I feel like I should be holding myself together better," she said, and her reddened eyes were testament to the struggle behind her calm facade. "Ryder would want me to rise to the challenge."

"Nonsense. You've suffered a tremendous loss," I replied gently. "I imagine Ryder would understand."

Briar's composure crumbled as fresh tears welled up. "Oh, Lydia, I just can't believe he's actually gone! What will we do without him? I feel so lost."

I enveloped the distraught girl in yet another fierce embrace, blinking back my own tears. "We honor him by carrying on his legacy," I said, trying to inject conviction into my voice. But inside, my chest tightened with anxiety. I pulled back to meet her tearful gaze.

"Which is why I want you to tell me everything about this inn and what's expected of me now. Don't leave out a single detail. I know nothing, so consider me your pupil."

My request was an attempt to fortify Briar, offering a much-needed focus for her energy. She dabbed her eyes and nodded firmly. "Of course. We have much to discuss." She gave me an appraising look. "It won't be easy, Lydia. But together, we will weather this storm."

I managed a thin smile in return, wishing I shared her confidence. She bustled off to fetch us some chai, while I sank onto a bar stool, trying to ignore the dread coiling in my gut.

I was woefully out of my depth in this new role, but refusing the duty would only lead to chaos and strife between the enclaves. For Ryder's sake, and for Briar's, I had to at least try to fill this position until another to take on the role, unqualified as I felt.

Soon, Briar would unveil all the secrets of this place and what fate had in store for me. I feared the truth would confirm my worst suspicions about my inadequacy. Whether I'd crumble beneath the weight of expectations or somehow rise to meet the challenge remained to be seen. But I would face it with eyes wide open, however overwhelming the prospect felt.

Over steaming mugs of chai, Briar began unraveling the complex history of the Howl Away Inn for its reluctant new owner.

"So what exactly is the purpose of this inn?" I asked, trying to keep the worry out of my voice. "It seems like more than just accommodations for travelers."

Briar nodded gravely. "For generations, the Howl Away Inn has served as neutral territory where the wolf shifters of the three regional enclaves gather to conduct trade, settle disputes, and maintain a fragile peace."

I tensed at the word "shifters." Supernatural politics were murky waters I knew nothing about navigating, and they'd never been fond of the fae.

Clearly noticing my unease, Briar continued gently, "There are three ancient shifter enclaves in this region: Bittersweet, Elk, and Flat Top. The owners of this inn have served as mediators between them since the town was established."

My thoughts spun as the enormity of my new role hit me. "And now they expect me, a stranger, to fill Ryder's shoes?" I asked shakily. "Because of a card game?" How could I now be responsible for an entire community?

Briar squeezed my hand, her eyes filled with compassion. "I can sense you carry wounds from your past, Lydia. But fate chose you as the new steward here. Have faith in yourself, and I promise your path will become clear."

I swallowed hard, clinging to her encouragement even as doubt shadowed my heart. Briar showed me to Ryder's private office, unlocking the door to reveal the cozy, tranquil space filled with ancient tomes and artifacts.

Briar handed me an ornate iron key. "As Ryder's successor, this office and all its contents now belong to you," she intoned solemnly.

The edges of reality seemed to blur as the weight of her words hit me. I drew a steady breath, pushing down the doubts swirling within. With time and dedication, I would prove worthy of this immense responsibility entrusted to me.

I held the key in my hand, the metal cool and heavy in my palm, before sliding it into my pocket. "Well then, we'd best get started."

I drifted a hand over the leather-bound books. These repositories of knowledge were now mine to master. The task felt overwhelming. But as I gazed out the window at the snowcapped Rockies, I vowed to honor Ryder's legacy of wisdom and impartiality to the best of my abilities. For now, all I could do was take the first step forward.

I turned slowly, overcome by the sheer volume of information surrounding me. Nestled between the shelves, I discovered a lacquered wooden box. Unlatching the tarnished bronze clasp revealed a medallion inside bearing the same triskele symbol engraved on Ryder's forearm. Three interconnected spirals gleamed silver against a background of obsidian stone polished to an ebony sheen. I started to lift it, then paused, unsure if removing it would be overstepping. For now, I simply traced my fingers over the identical mark which now adorned my skin, its presence still mysterious and unsettling.

As if sensing my unease, Briar said gently, "The triskele tattoo marks you as the owner of the inn. All three enclaves will recognize its significance."

I nodded, stomach tightening. For better or worse, this mark bound me to my duties here now. I would bear it with the honor it deserved.

Next, my gaze landed on a thick, faded tome titled "Histories of the Enclaves."

"Let's start there," I suggested, hoping education would temper my doubts.

As I laid the ancient tome on the desk, unease prickled across my skin. How could I possibly mediate peace between these ancient groups when I remained an ignorant outsider? Briar gave my shoulder a reassuring squeeze. "Don't fret. Just trust in fate and the path ahead," she encouraged gently.

Bolstered by her faith, I focused on absorbing her first history lesson about the tranquil Elk clan. Their world sounded idyllic—solitary packs dwelling in harmony with nature, gathering under the stars for joyful solstice celebrations full of artistry and song.

Yet the overwhelming weight of this sudden life change pressed relentlessly on me. I was no guardian or supernatural diplomat. But walking away wasn't something I could do. Even if I did, who could I pass on the ownership to when I had no idea who was responsible for Ryder's death? However unready I felt, this was the path fate had laid before me.

"I'm just worried, Briar. The weight of this responsibility, of keeping the supernatural peace... I don't know if I'm cut out for it."

Briar leaned back, regarding me thoughtfully. "It's natural to feel overwhelmed. But you have a strength in you, Lydia—a fierceness I've seen in few others. You'll need to draw on that now."

Her steadfast tone ignited a flicker of indignation within me. "You speak as if I have a choice in this burden," I replied bitterly. "Yet, in truth, I'm trapped, am I not?"

Briar's expression softened with empathy. "Ryder was intuitive, almost magically so. Perhaps he discerned your destiny was intertwined with this place, and that's why he bid you take his spot."

A chill ran through me. What might Ryder have seen in me? When I remained silent, Briar continued gently, "I cannot claim to understand the forces that brought you here. But since Ryder trusted you to hold his cards, you were destined for this role. Otherwise, it would not have worked out as it did."

At the mention of the murdered innkeeper, melancholy pierced my simmering frustration. Whatever mysteries Ryder had known would be buried alongside him, leaving me adrift. Sorrow for his tragic end vied with trepidation over the chaotic future looming before me.

Once we finished reviewing the Elk clan's history, Briar leaned against the desk and flipped the pages to the battle-hardened Flat Top shifters. "Their territory lies along the Continental Divide. They defend the pass from outside threats," she explained. According to Briar, lately mining companies had been trying to gain access to Flat Top lands, causing unrest. As the mediator, I would need to broker a fair compromise.

After covering the proud Flat Tops, Briar described the

most isolated and secretive clan—the Bittersweet shifters, who dwelled deep within the snowy peaks. As she described their ancient rituals and bond with nature, I sensed a deep complexity beneath the surface. Of all the enclaves, the Bittersweets seemed most shrouded in mystery.

"Far less is truly known about the Bittersweet clan, as they shun outsiders," Briar explained in a hushed tone. "Their remote territory lies amid the highest, most treacherous mountains. Some say they possess mysterious seers and healers among their ranks."

Briar leaned in close. "There is another matter we must discuss," she whispered. "Legend claims the inn's keeper gains access to certain mystical powers tied to this place."

I stared at her, stunned. "Magic? Me? Impossible. My fae lineage never blessed me with such abilities. That's why I've lived separately from other fae since my teens. I know nothing of spells beyond childhood tales."

"I confess I know little of these powers myself," Briar admitted. "But on a few occasions, Ryder implied the inn's magic responds to its guardian. I doubt the inn will care about your lineage or whether you had other magic before now."

I shifted in my seat, deeply unnerved. What use could I have for powers beyond my grasp?

Briar gave an encouraging smile. "Try not to fret. I'll help as much as I can."

I nodded slowly, far from put at ease by the thought of unfathomable powers potentially stirring within me. For now, I needed to focus on learning my role here and solving Ryder's murder. If magical talents did manifest, I would confront that bridge when I came to it.

Though I tried to absorb everything Briar shared, my mind swam with the torrent of new information about customs, history, and mystical rumors. As though sensing my overwhelmed state, Briar suggested gently, "Perhaps a break to clear our heads would be beneficial?"

"Yes, a break sounds perfect," I readily agreed, stifling a yawn despite my nervous energy. My concentration was fraying rapidly under the torrent of new information.

Briar smiled and stood, stretching her arms overhead. "Wonderful idea. Let me pull together some breakfast."

I sagged back, exhaling shakily. My mind spun, trying to absorb all I'd learned about the clans, their customs, and histories. A respite to refresh was just what I needed before diving back into my crash course on this unfamiliar supernatural world.

In the kitchen, tantalizing aromas made my empty stomach rumble. Between spoonfuls of Briar's simple but delicious oatmeal with fresh peaches and cream, I remarked on how nice it was to see a hint of her smile return.

"It helps to focus on something useful," she admitted. "But the inn feels so empty without Ryder." Fresh tears shimmered in her eyes.

I gently squeezed her hand. "We'll honor him by carrying on his legacy together."

She nodded, dabbing her eyes. "Maybe we should both clean up?"

After Briar left, I went to my room, yearning for rest. But sleep eluded me. As I lay staring at the ceiling, panic remained strangely at bay. In its place flowed a fragile sense of purpose. My life could never follow its old worn tracks after this night. For inexplicable reasons, I'd been granted an unexpected new path forward, away from past traumas. I now had to find the courage to discover where it led.

When sleep refused my call, I cleaned up and drifted back downstairs, seeking solace in a hot cup of coffee to energize my flagging focus. But as I entered the dining hall, the scent of brewing java was overridden by pipe tobacco and worn leather. Drake occupied the corner table, scowling over a worn map.

At my entrance, he glanced up, gray eyes gleaming with disdain beneath his furrowed brow.

"Well, if it ain't Ryder's stray fae," he growled, pipe smoke coiling around him. "Come to claim a throne that ain't yours?"

I bristled, hands clenching at his contemptuous tone. "Morning to you too, Drake. I see your manners haven't improved."

He let out an insolent snort, shoving aside his barely touched plate. "Ain't nothin' good about it. This town's gonna fall to pieces with Ryder gone, especially now that we've got a fraud like you playing leader."

His candid disdain ignited my simmering grief into indignation. I crossed my arms, holding my ground. It was one thing to doubt myself. It was something else for this lout to doubt my capabilities. "Clearly you prefer casting blame to taking action. What exactly are you doing to find Ryder's killer?"

Drake's eyes blazed with fury, and he slammed his fist on the table, making the dishes rattle. Lurching to his feet, he strode over until he loomed above me, his imposing figure blocking the light filtering in through the window.

"Don't pretend you give a damn about Ryder," he spat.

"No outsider can waltz in here and replace him." Drake stepped even closer, his wood smoke and leather scent enveloping me. "Hand over your mantle and walk away now, before you destroy everything he built."

Refusing to be intimidated, I glared up at him unflinchingly. "Fate chose me as Ryder's successor. Dare you question its wisdom?" I raised my chin defiantly.

Drake clenched his jaw, eyes blazing. "Mark my words, you'll fail, just like all your pointy-eared kind," he growled. "These enclaves will never accept an interloper, much less a fae, as one of their own."

I held his blistering gaze, keeping my voice low and steady. "We shall see. Now, if you'll excuse me, I have duties to attend to." With that, I stepped around him and made my way out of the dining room, my back rigid, refusing to let Drake's contempt shake my resolve. The path forward was fraught with uncertainty, yet I was determined to navigate it, for Ryder's memory and for my own peace of mind.

Finding a quiet corner, I sank into a chair to collect my thoughts. Just then, the balcony door creaked open, and a rumpled Barnell appeared, rubbing the sleep from his eyes. Catching sight of me, he waved and made his way downstairs with a tired shuffle.

"Rough night, huh?" he remarked sympathetically, plopping down into the chair beside mine.

I managed a wan smile, the weight of our shared unrest briefly uniting us. "I don't think any of us will find peace in sleep for some time after..." My voice faltered, the words catching in my throat as the reality of our situation settled heavily around us.

Barnell's face crumpled in sorrow, tears pooling in his

earnest eyes. "Briar woke me up and told me last night. I can't believe old Ryder's gone. He was always so good to me." He swiped at his sleeve. "Who could do something so evil?"

I had no comforting words, my heart also shaken. On impulse, I wrapped an arm around his skinny shoulders. We stood in silence, drawing solace from one another. I wished I could unravel this injustice for the boy who had welcomed me so warmly. If my role demanded anything now, it was to bring meaning to the chaos and justice for Ryder. I prayed my untested abilities would prove sufficient for the trials ahead.

After a time, Barnell pulled away, dashing at his eyes. "I should start getting to my duties. Folks will be up soon and there's cleaning to do." He glanced back, a spark reigniting behind the tears. "We'll get through this together. It's what Ryder would expect."

I watched him go, marveling at his resilience. However long the road ahead, I would not walk it alone, despite doubters like Drake. For now, it was enough to take things one day at a time.

CHAPTER 4

The grandfather clock's hollow chimes announced two o'clock in the afternoon, a grim reminder of how little time had passed since last night's horror. I nursed black coffee as my temples throbbed; the dining hall's chatter and laughter veiling the unease poisoning Crescent Crossing's spirit. Word of Ryder's demise had already spread through the town, but the sinister truth that he'd been murdered had been kept quiet pending the coroner's report.

I pushed away my half-eaten plate when a familiar deep rumble called my name. Relief surged through me at the sight of Enforcer Hamish Bittersweet striding in through the front door, Saige Stormborn at his side. Her piercing green eyes and short brown pixie cut contrasted with Hamish's hulking frame and grizzled auburn hair, though both had grave concern etching their faces.

"Lydia, thank the stars you're okay," Hamish hugged me and said in his distinctively clipped voice, his relief obvious. "When we got word of the incident, I feared the worst."

I quickly led Hamish and Saige to a secluded corner

booth with a view of the back garden, where we could speak freely away from prying ears. I was eager for news from Denver and my niece, yet anxious about the uncertain situation here, which weighed heavily on my mind.

"How is Becka recovering in Denver?" I asked first.

Saige squeezed my hand reassuringly. "She's regained her strength and is back to her cheerful self. Mostly. Quinn said to tell you not to worry."

Her encouragement helped steady me. "Well, I hoped for rest here, yet it hasn't worked out like that, has it?"

Hamish's sympathetic chuckle eased the building tension. "Yes, it seems your path took an unexpected turn. But we're here for you, Lydia. Now tell us what transpired last night."

I nodded, taking a deep breath before delving into the alarming events surrounding Ryder's demise. Despite the uncertainties that troubled me, the assurance of my loved ones' safety provided me with the strength to face the unknowns that awaited me here in Crescent Crossing.

"We came as soon as we heard about poor Ryder's murder," Saige added grimly. She hesitated, then said in a low voice, "Was Kai Wilder one of the last to see Ryder alive? Rumor has it, he's gotten mixed up in some shady business lately to pay off his debts."

"He wasn't the only one at that game, or the only one to last see Ryder alive," I added.

Hamish and Saige exchanged surprised glances as I described Briar's belief that Ryder had planned the inn specifically for me.

"I cannot fathom why Ryder would entrust the inn's fate to a stranger, especially me, given my own troubled past," I admitted. "Not to mention I'm a fae in a sea of shifters."

After a weighty pause, Hamish spoke in his deep, rumbling voice. "Do not underestimate your strengths, Lydia. Fate's call came unexpectedly but remember that the inn must have chosen you for a reason."

I bit my lip, craving certainty to calm my swirling doubts.

As if sensing my skepticism, Saige interjected in her typically blunt manner. "We cannot know why Ryder made the choices he did. But his actions have set you on a meaningful path, difficult though it may seem right now."

I drew a shaky breath, bolstered by my friends' steadfast faith. My mind still swam with uncertainties, but I knew I could not wade through this precarious path alone.

"Will you stay awhile then and help me get my footing here?" I asked tentatively. "It's hard when I don't know who to trust."

Hamish gave my shoulder a reassuring squeeze, a hint of protectiveness glinting in his eyes. "Of course. We shall assist you however we can."

I let out a breath I didn't know I was holding. Having these two by my side, and them being wolf shifters at that, it felt like I could finally see a light at the end of the tunnel, even with all this darkness around.

"Good. Then you can help me solve his murder," I whispered. Then I caught Briar's eye and motioned for her to join us, quickly introducing my friends.

"I know you might want to focus on solving this crime quickly, but to do that, you first need to understand the inn and what it means to this town. Ryder trusted very few with knowledge of the inn's magical history," Briar explained in a hushed tone. "So I don't know how it came to be, but he hinted at a legacy spanning centuries, one now tied to you as his successor."

I shifted uncomfortably in my seat. Magic? Me, who had never demonstrated even the faintest spark of power in all my life? It was just my luck that I'd inherited a power that didn't even come with a manual.

Hamish and Saige didn't bat an eye at the news, as if such revelations were commonplace in their world. With a lean forward, Hamish's voice dropped to a rumble, sharing whispered tales that danced on the edge of myth. He spoke of ancient places, hidden from the unseeing eyes of the mundane, where the earth itself could awaken and magnify the latent supernatural powers of those deemed worthy to guard them. These sites, he suggested, were intertwined with the very essence of wolf-shifter lore—sacred grounds that tested and bestowed gifts upon their caretakers in ways that the uninitiated could scarcely comprehend.

"I've also heard of buildings imbued with spirits or spells that are tied to each owner," Saige added. "From Briar's description, it sounds like the Howl Away Inn is such a place."

I listened to their speculation with growing unease. Surely they were mistaken.

Briar gave an emphatic nod, her voice dropping to a whisper as if sharing a confidential secret. "I can't claim to fully grasp the extent of it. But since last night, there have been unmistakable signs that the inn is resonating with you, adapting in ways both small and profound."

She leaned in closer, her gaze intense. "For instance, the quilt in your room. Yesterday, it was a simple, plain fabric, but this morning, I noticed it's now adorned with patterns of ivy and iris—I have to assume these complement your tastes. And the tea assortment in the kitchen, it's suddenly stocked with varieties that weren't there before."

Pausing, she scanned the room as if to ensure no one was eavesdropping. "Even more telling is the painting that hangs by the staircase. Remember the one you admired yesterday for its serene landscape? This morning, I swear the scene was different—now it features a moonlit forest, eerily similar to the description of a dream you shared over breakfast."

Briar's examples sent a shiver down my spine; each detail she mentioned was indeed an aspect I held dear, preferences I hadn't realized I'd disclosed. The inn's sentient response to my presence, altering its environment to reflect my subconscious likes and comfort, was both astonishing and unsettling.

"I know it sounds incredible," Briar concluded, her eyes searching mine for skepticism, "but these changes, they're too specific to be coincidental. It's as if the inn itself is attuning its spirit to yours, making itself a sanctuary not just for you, but of you."

I exhaled slowly, glimpsing for the first time the enormity of the destiny Ryder had set in motion by drawing me into his orbit. Whatever mystical inheritance now flowed in my veins, I prayed it would prove enough for the trials ahead.

Just then, Briar's phone beeped, and her expression turned bleak as she read a message. "It's Silas, the coroner," Briar explained breathlessly. "He said he's ready for us to come review preliminary findings." She blinked rapidly, clearly struggling to maintain composure.

While tragic, focusing on the grim task at hand felt far

less overwhelming than speculating about inexplicable magical destinies.

I turned to Hamish and Saige, aware of their unique skill sets. Hamish, with his years as a city enforcer, possessed a detective's keen eye, while Saige's experience as a bodyguard had honed her instincts for detecting danger and deceit. "Your expertise could be crucial in examining the evidence," I suggested. "Would you join us?"

"Of course," Hamish affirmed with a nod.

"We'll examine everything closely," Saige promised, her tone determined.

Upon our arrival at the Eternal Slumber Mortuary, Silas, with a demeanor that blended professionalism with solemn respect, guided us to where Ryder lay under a draped sheet. He donned gloves, signaling us to prepare for the grim reality beneath. With a careful hand, Silas revealed the extent of Ryder's injuries, the sight arresting our breaths with its brutality.

"Multiple deep stabs are present, concentrated on the torso—three penetrating the abdomen, two directed upward through the heart," Silas explained methodically, his voice steady despite the gruesome details. "The nature of the wounds suggests a serrated blade, twisted with force," he added, allowing us to draw closer.

Before he could proceed, I interrupted, feeling the weight of my next request. "May I examine him myself?" I asked, aware of the unusual nature of my inquiry. Silas hesitated, his gaze meeting mine. Clearly recognizing the determination there, he gave a slight nod of assent.

I leaned in, my examination revealing not only the

savagery of the attacks but a disturbing precision behind them.

"There's more," Silas continued, turning Ryder to reveal another wound—a puncture between the shoulders. "Likely the first strike, intended to immobilize," he theorized.

Hamish, taking a step forward, inquired, "Can you surmise the attacker's dominant hand, and possibly the dimensions of the blade used?"

"Given the angles and depth, the assailant was likely right-handed, using a blade approximately seven inches in length, dual-edged and serrated," Silas concluded after a moment's careful consideration.

As Silas concluded his preliminary findings, I found myself fixated on the puncture on Ryder's back.

Silas straightened. "I'll run additional toxicology tests on his blood for potential injection agents. That will take about a day."

After we returned to the inn, I decided to spend some time alone to clear my head. I slipped outside into the inn's tranquil garden while Hamish and Saige settled into their room, promising to find them later.

I sank onto a stone bench beneath the sprawling oak, its gnarled limbs casting dancing shadows on the mossy ground. So much had happened in the short time since I arrived at the Howl Away Inn.

As the leaves rustled overhead in the breeze, my mind drifted back to life in Denver—my eclectic and unpredictable routine, often focused on finding joy in the moment while avoiding any sense of direction. I realized how much my inner spark had dimmed. Where once I would have seized an unexpected adventure, now fear and uncertainty paralyzed me.

Cradled in the garden's stillness, I hoped discovering my purpose here might reignite that dormant fire within. This role, so foreign and daunting, might be the key to unlocking a deeper meaning that had eluded me for so long back home.

I knew the road ahead would be strewn with mysteries, yet I refused to shrink from the unknown. With courage and care, this new path could help me rediscover my passion and purpose. I would face the future with an open heart, come what may.

Barely two days ago, my only goal had been a quiet haven to heal old wounds. Now, suddenly, I found myself at the center of clan intrigues haunted by murder and magic.

I shuddered, drawing my shawl tight against the mountain chill. Had I been naïve to think I'd left danger behind in Denver? It seemed fate had merely redirected my path into new peril.

As the leaves rustled overhead, I noticed a tiny white blossom at my feet, its delicate petals perfectly intact. I reached down and ran a fingertip across its petals, admiring its resilience. Like this fragile flower, I would endure the dangers ahead. Crescent Crossing was my home for now, and I would see my purpose through, wherever it led.

Over dinner, Hamish and Saige regaled me with amusing tales of Denver, their fond reminiscing kindling homesickness yet also deepening my appreciation for these loyal friends.

When I returned to my room to fetch my fuzzy slippers, at first nothing seemed amiss in the cozy space. But subtle changes leaped out—the quilt's new burgundy hue, my favorite tea bags in the cupboard, the painting's moonlit forest.

Were these more of the changes Briar mentioned earlier or was exhaustion eroding my reason? No, these things, however minor, were definitely different from yesterday.

Frowning, I crossed to the window, which I'd left open yet now it was firmly shut. Had Briar or Barnell taken it upon themselves to shut it? I rushed downstairs, questions about the mysterious life I now found myself in swirling through my head like leaves in the wind.

I sought Briar, who I found working behind the bar. "Did you shut my window?"

She looked baffled. "No, I haven't even been up there. Why?"

A chill went through me. The inn truly must be reshaping itself to suit me. How sentient was this place? I turned to glance out the lobby window and froze. Through the distorted antique glass, a shadowy figure stood motionless beneath the oak tree, half-obscured in darkness. Though the silhouette was featureless, an icy dread told me it was the killer watching me. I blinked rapidly, but when I looked again, they had vanished. I knew if I sent someone out to check, whoever it was would be long gone.

Later, as I sat by the fire, Briar, Saige, and Hamish joined me, and our conversation quickly turned reflective.

"We've seen your courage before," Hamish said. "You'll navigate these rough waters now too." I dropped my gaze, shying from those memories still.

Saige squeezed my shoulder, her eyes intense. "Your past

doesn't matter to Crescent Crossing. These people are your responsibility now."

I nodded slowly, unsure if her words were a comfort or a curse. Both maybe? My old life felt lifetimes away. All I could do was move forward, one step at a time.

"It's not just the murder on your hands," Hamish said. "I heard from a friend that the Elk clan is furious over Flat Top encroachments on prime hunting grounds out west."

"Meanwhile, the Flat Tops want more mountain access that the Elk refuse to grant," Saige added. "Tensions are escalating."

I sat back heavily. "So there are simmering conflicts even without Ryder's murder inflaming things further."

Hamish nodded grimly. "Your task as mediator just got exponentially harder. From what I hear, this could boil over any day."

I exhaled slowly. Uniting feuding factions seemed like an impossible feat for a fae newcomer like me. But the alternative—open conflict—was unthinkable. However steep the path, I had to try. The future of Crescent Crossing depended on it.

"It looks like I've got my work cut out for me," I sighed. "But there's no way I'm just sitting around while things go south."

Hamish and Saige gave each other serious looks. I knew we could all feel big storms brewing over Crescent Crossing. Whatever happened though, we were going to stick it out together.

I raked a hand through my hair. Uniting the packs seemed like an impossible feat, but I had to try before violence erupted.

"We need to determine the next steps in investigating Ryder's death," I said gravely.

Briar set her teacup down with resolve. "Agreed. As much as I'd like to take my time grieving, we can't let the trail grow cold."

"Interviewing everyone present at the time seems like a wise start," Hamish suggested. "Their insights could prove invaluable."

"We can help conduct them," Saige added. "Assuming you approve?" she asked me.

I exhaled, energized to have a plan shaping up. "Excellent idea. Let's list potential witnesses." I fetched my notebook from my bag.

Together, we compiled a list. Besides Briar and me, Harper, Kai, and Drake—the card players present when Ryder met his tragic end. Also Barnell, though I doubted the teen was strong enough to harm Ryder. Still, he might have seen something.

Tomorrow we would begin unraveling their tangled threads of memory, seeking any clue that could expose the killer's identity.

As the embers faded to crimson, exhaustion claimed me. I bid them goodnight, profoundly grateful for their presence. Upstairs, I prepared for bed with a strange sense of being watched. I shook off the feeling as fatigue-fueled fancy. But slipping between the cool sheets, the prickling sense of unseen eyes persisted.

Uneasily, I peered into the shadows gathered in the corners of the room, seeing nothing yet unable to shake the uncanny sensation of not being alone. A creak from the hallway sent a chill down my spine.

"Hello?" I called out shakily. "Is someone there?"

Only silence answered my query. The inn was wrapped in slumber's embrace. With effort, I closed my eyes, willing my uneasy dreams away.

CHAPTER 5

The sun's harsh morning glare pierced through the lattice of branches outside my window, assaulting my eyes like an interrogation lamp. I stood frozen, staring into the oval mirror as if facing a stranger, absently tugging a fraying thread on my blouse hem. The hollow-cheeked woman gazing back appeared haunted and weary.

What had happened to the daring adventurer who once laughed freely and embraced each day with wide-eyed wonder? The old Lydia had lived for languid weekends, wandering bustling art fairs downtown, sampling cheeses while chatting up the local artists as they created chalk scenes along the sidewalks.

I had relished gathering friends on a whim for evenings spent sipping flights of spicy Rioja and crisp Pinot Grigio on my favorite wine bar's patio. Our spirited debates over books, art, and music would stretch deep into the starry night.

I yearned for that woman, the one who met each morning with optimism, believing the world brimmed with possibilities awaiting discovery. Before the troubles in Denver dimmed my spirit, I'd faced every day with resilience.

Now, here I stood, a timid specter of my former self. Denver had snuffed out that buoyant light from my eyes, violent as a gale extinguishing a flickering candle. I slowly raised my eyes to meet my reflected gaze, a realization dawning of all that had been lost: my optimism, resilience, and passion for life. My sense of self had been shattered, leaving only dull shards glinting in the ashes.

If I continued to passively accept this diminished existence, I may as well flee into the mountains to live out my days in solitude. Yet anger stirred deep within at this thought, fanning the lingering embers.

I refused to surrender and leave the light within me to be smothered. This winding road to the inn set me on a path to wholeness and would not leave me broken. I must reclaim faith in a brighter tomorrow, nurturing my ripened potential patiently. The Lydia who'd arrived here just three days ago could never have envisioned leading a murder investigation among formidable shifters. Yet today I would open my eyes to every possibility instead of shrinking away. With each probing interview and every hard-won truth unveiled, I would take another step on the winding trail to rediscovering myself.

Having resolved not to retreat from the challenges ahead, I finished preparing myself and headed downstairs. My nerves still pulled taut as a violin string, yet I endeavored to project calm confidence. Last night's conversation had kindled a fragile spark of optimism within, as delicate as a newborn fawn. Only time would tell if it flourished or faltered.

I found Hamish and Saige tucked into a corner booth, mid-breakfast. Briar sat beside them, face wan and eyes haunted, clutching her tea. My heart ached seeing grief dimming her vibrant spirit. I gently squeezed her hand before sitting down. She managed a faint smile.

"What can I get you?" Barnell breezed by, nearly tripping in his haste.

"Eggs and toast, please. And Irish breakfast tea."

He quirked a brow. "Not the Earl Grey type, then?"

"Never," I affirmed. Soon I had a steaming mug cradled in my hands. "Any suggestions on where to begin with the suspects?"

"Let's begin with Kai," Hamish suggested. "He's too slippery. We should question him before he has time to come up with lies."

I hesitated, anxiety fluttering at the thought of facing the cunning man so soon. "Wouldn't Briar be better first? I think it would get me in the swing of things."

"Wise idea," Saige concurred. "Get your feet wet with an ally. Kai can wait."

Hamish bent his head in agreement. "Practice with Briar first. But we interrogate Kai next, no delay." His approving look heartened me.

I exhaled in relief at their input. Briar first would bolster my courage.

I turned to her and asked, "Can we talk today? I know it might be difficult, but we need to keep moving forward."

Spine straightening, Briar met my gaze resolutely. "I'll do whatever it takes to get justice for Ryder. Ready whenever you are."

With her unwavering bravery, I swiftly finished my meal, and the shadows dissipated from my thoughts.

I probed deeper into the tense interactions Briar had witnessed that night between Ryder and the others before my arrival. "Did you notice any rising tensions or arguments?" I asked. "Even subtle barbs or insults?"

Brow furrowing, Briar thought back. "Drake was more sullen than usual with Ryder. Real hostility simmering underneath."

"Over what specifically?" I pressed gently.

"Territory disputes, from what I gathered," Briar replied. "Drake was furious that Ryder denied his clan the requested winter hunting grounds. He said it wasn't fair that Elk got preferential treatment. But Ryder refused to budge."

This potential motive gave me pause. I jotted notes as Briar continued.

"And Kai kept making jabs about Ryder losing his edge, suggesting it was time for new management." Pain flickered in her eyes. "I wanted to slap that smug grin off his face."

Saige gave Briar's hand a bracing squeeze. "Steady on now," she murmured. Briar took a slow, cleansing breath.

Pain flickered in Briar's eyes again. "Kai kept making sly comments to undermine Ryder's authority and wisdom, implying that Ryder was biased and no longer capable of making sound decisions."

"You've given invaluable context, Briar," I said. "Now, Ryder's demeanor before stepping outside—what do you recall?"

Briar inhaled deeply, delving into memories.

"Ryder rarely left games unfinished, but he got that

urgent call and asked you to take his spot," she began slowly. "I figured he'd return shortly."

I nodded encouragement as she went on.

"But minutes dragged on. The others grew impatient and distrustful. Especially Drake."

"What gave you that impression?" I asked.

"I heard him muttering, 'Where the hell is Ryder?'"

I quickly jotted down notes. "Crucial details, thank you. Now, please, can you recount when you went outside and discovered Ryder?"

Briar paled slightly but nodded, inhaling deeply. "I expected to find Ryder in his office or room. But he wasn't there."

She paused, blinking back tears. "That's when I went outside and saw him just lying there. Blood everywhere. His eyes were staring up at nothing." Briar squeezed her eyes shut against the horrific memories.

I clasped her icy hand in both of mine. "You're incredibly brave. Take your time."

After several moments, Briar regained some composure, but that gruesome sight would haunt us both forever.

After giving Briar time to recover from reliving her trauma, I decided we had gleaned enough insights from her for one day. Though I still had questions, I thought it best to proceed deliberately rather than risk re-traumatizing our ally. Briar's courage today deserved careful handling.

"Briar, could you call Kai and ask him to come by?"

She nodded. "When do you want him?"

"As soon as he'll grace us with his presence," I replied.

Barnell was diligently bussing tables nearby when I beckoned him over with a gesture. His eyes, rimmed with the tell-tale signs of a restless night, lifted in response.

"Morning, Barnell," I greeted him, my voice softened with concern. "Are you prepared to discuss Ryder?"

He nodded, the anxiousness palpable in his movements. "Of course, happy to assist in any way I can." His gaze dropped, and he began to compulsively wipe his hands on the cloth that dangled from his apron.

Taking a seat with a nervous shuffle, Barnell seemed to draw a measure of comfort from sitting across from me. I knew he possessed no direct knowledge of the events, having retired early on the fateful evening.

Before I could begin questioning him, Hamish cut in, his question sharp. "Notice anything unusual the next morning?"

A spark of recollection ignited in Barnell's eyes. "I meant to show you something!" he exclaimed. With a flurry of movement, he rummaged in his pocket before producing a small, peculiar object.

It was a raven amulet, masterfully carved from dark wood and suspended on a braided cord. The tiny obsidian eyes set into the carving caught the light with an ominous gleam.

"Where exactly did you find this?" I inquired, curiosity piqued.

Barnell swallowed, his voice lowering. "Under the steps near where they discovered Mr. Ryder." He paused, his next words laden with gravity. "I was cleaning off some blood stains on the back deck when I noticed something glinting beneath the porch. It seemed... important."

I turned the amulet over in my hands, its weight made

more significant with potential implications. "You did well to keep this," I affirmed, nodding appreciatively. "It might just be the clue we need."

The raven, enigmatic and foreboding, had indeed introduced a compelling new element to our unfolding mystery.

Hamish, Saige, and I moved into my office, anticipating Kai's arrival. It didn't take long before an arrogant voice called out, "What a cozy scene here!"

I looked up to see Kai sauntering through the door, a confident, sexy smirk in place. My pulse quickened, despite myself. I would need to be on top of my game to handle this charismatic man.

"Kai, thanks for making the time," I managed tightly.

Kai slid onto the couch next to Saige, casually draping his arm behind her. She shifted sharply away.

"How could I resist, Innkeeper? Besides, I assumed you'd seek me out about dear Ryder's nasty demise, so I didn't roam far," he remarked breezily. "Poor man deserved better."

I studied him closely, but I saw only polite regret on his face.

"We need you to walk us through that night," I said carefully. "Even minor things could prove useful."

Kai nodded. "I am happy to assist however I can. My memory remains painfully vivid..."

I paid close attention, searching for any signs of dishonesty as he told his story.

"After Ryder rushed off, we were all quite confused," Kai began, smoothing his blond hair. "Drake grumbled about the interrupted game. Harper kept sighing and checking her watch. I tried lightening the mood, to no avail. I mentioned needing to use the facilities, but really, I went out front hoping to catch a glimpse of whatever was so urgent Ryder left so abruptly."

I leaned forward intently. "And did you see or hear anything unusual while you were outside?"

Kai hesitated for a beat before replying smoothly, "No, I'm afraid not. It was all quite uneventful. I didn't smell any blood in the air or hear any arguing."

His quick denial felt rehearsed, but I couldn't quite pinpoint the deception. I made a mental note to press harder.

Then Kai paused, looking contemplative. "In hindsight, I wish I'd checked on Ryder before I came back in. But who could have predicted such horror was unfolding under our very noses?"

He lowered his gaze with convincing remorse, but his glib words still bothered me. I decided to press further. "In the past, have you witnessed any incidents or altercations between Ryder and the other clan leaders that might have escalated to violence?"

Kai's eyes widened briefly before he regained his composure. "Well, there have been heated disagreements, of course. But nothing that ever came to blows, as far as I know." He shrugged, his expression unreadable.

I changed course. "What exactly did you do when you returned inside?"

Kai pursed his lips. "Let's see. Just you and Harper were waiting. She stepped away to go to her room. You were holding onto those cards almost as tight as you gripped that glass of pinot. We kept waiting for Ryder. I tried to keep the conversation light, but there was an undeniable tension in the air."

"Before I arrived, did you and Harper discuss anything noteworthy?" I asked, watching his expression closely.

"Oh, nothing of consequence," Kai replied breezily. "Just idle chatter to pass the time."

His vague answer and casual dismissal sent up red flags, but I kept my tone neutral as I continued my line of questioning.

"And then chaos struck when Briar went out back to check."

His tale seemed convincing, but I sensed hidden depths beneath the affable facade.

Flashing a pained smile, Kai concluded smoothly, "So, you see, I'm afraid I can add little to the overall picture. I wish you the best in bringing Ryder's killer to justice."

He rose to leave, but I spoke quickly. "Just one moment more, if you would. I'm curious what you make of this." I held up the raven amulet.

For the first time, Kai's urbane mask cracked. Shock registered briefly across his features at the sight of the talisman.

Interesting. This trinket seemed like a promising thread to unravel. I met Kai's suddenly wary gaze evenly. "Anything you can tell us about this piece would be most helpful."

Kai cleared his throat, eyes locked on the amulet. "I can't say I know anything useful. Doubtless, it's just some random curio." But the tremor in his voice suggested otherwise.

"Well, please let us know if you recall anything pertinent," I said smoothly, pocketing the carving again. "One more thing, Kai. Briar mentioned you made comments suggesting Ryder had 'lost his edge.' Can you elaborate on what you meant by that?"

Kai's jaw tightened almost imperceptibly. "Ah, that. It

was just a harmless observation, really. Ryder had made some questionable decisions recently, and I merely pointed out that perhaps he wasn't as sharp as he used to be. It was all in jest, of course." His smile didn't quite reach his eyes.

With flawless composure, Kai turned and took his leave, but I sensed a new wariness in his stride.

After Kai's departure, I sank onto the plush couch next to Saige, resting my head in my hands. I felt unqualified to match wits against Kai's glib evasions and half-truths.

"Don't lose heart," Saige said, patting my shoulder. "These skills require practice to hone."

"I've seen you both interview with such savvy. I feel like I'm bungling along," I sighed.

Saige shook her head firmly. "Our experience can assist you, but your unique perspective is critical." She gripped my hands. "Blaze your own trail here. Have courage."

I hesitated, biting my lip. Could I really hope to develop such discernment alone? It's possible that there are some skills I could never attain. Yet I knew relying overly on their methods would only lead me astray. I must find my own way to unravel truth from deception, giving myself the grace to stumble along the way.

I lifted my head, my resolve renewed by Saige's steadfast faith in me. With patient practice, I would gain confidence in my fledgling skills. I just had to rise to meet the moment.

An uneasy silence hung over us as I turned over the interview in my mind, seeking clarity amid the chaos. Kai spoke with such eloquence that it was easy to get drawn into his web of words. Yet something indefinable still struck me as off-key.

"He's clearly committed to his version of events," Saige

said, tapping her fingers impatiently. "He revealed just enough to seem cooperative while hiding real motives and movements."

Hamish nodded, jotting down notes. "Agreed. He kept his responses vague. It is difficult to establish anything with absolute certainty."

I worried at my lip. "When he saw the amulet, his poise slipped briefly. I think it rattled him, but why?" A thought struck me. "Hypothetically, who do you think might have had the most compelling motive or gained the most from Ryder's death?"

Saige leaned back, considering. "It's hard to say. Drake and Ryder's territorial dispute could be a factor. And Kai's comments about Ryder losing his edge suggest a potential power play. But we can't rule out other motives we might not be aware of yet."

"A nice catch," Hamish approved. "We must be cautious with Kai, but that amulet is a promising lead."

I exhaled, glad for Hamish's confidence in me. Perhaps I could pierce Kai's veil of deception if I stayed focused.

"I can confirm some of what he said about waiting for Ryder, but we need more details about what happened before I arrived," I said, frustrated by Kai's evasions.

Hamish leaned forward intently. "Ryder's call logs could provide context. Do we have his mobile phone?"

I located Ryder's phone in the bag of personal effects Silas had handed off and tentatively pressed the home button, relieved to find it unlocked.

"Examine his calls around the time he was killed," Saige suggested.

I checked the logs and saw only an unknown blocked

number near the time Ryder died. I showed them the screen, and we exchanged solemn looks.

"Not very useful," Hamish admitted.

On impulse, I opened Ryder's contacts and found Harper's number. Before overthinking, I called her.

After two rings, Harper's crisp voice answered. I quickly explained why I was calling.

To my surprise, she seemed to have expected my call. "I assumed you'd be in touch and stayed nearby in case you needed to talk."

I sagged in relief. "That's very helpful. Thank you. Could you come by the inn this afternoon?"

"I can," Harper replied. "I'll see you in a couple of hours."

I thanked her and hung up, cautiously hopeful that this interview might move us forward. While I had momentum, I steeled myself to call Drake next, despite my nerves. I could not let my fear of the surly man stall this investigation.

With a bracing sip of coffee, I shakily dialed his number. After four rings, his gruff voice barked, "What?"

I forced my voice to be steady. "Drake, it's Lydia Ash. I'm following up on Ryder's case and need to speak with you."

He cut me off with a derisive snort. "The interloper's giving orders now? Why should I talk to your kind?"

I summoned my last shred of courage. "I may be an outsider, but I've inherited Ryder's role. I must speak with you in person."

After a weighty pause, Drake spat, "Fine. I'll stop by later. But don't expect me to play nice with your kind." He hung up without saying another word.

Exhausted by the morning, I collapsed into the chair and

let out a heavy sigh. This entire process felt futile. If I couldn't successfully persuade a witness, how would I go about unraveling this situation?

I tossed my notepad down in frustration. "I have no idea how I'm supposed to handle that man."

Saige and Hamish shared a look, and Hamish discreetly excused himself.

After he left, Saige came up behind me and briskly started kneading my tense shoulders. I exhaled shakily at the bracing contact.

"Doubting yourself is natural when facing new challenges," she said. "But you have deep inner strength, Lydia. I know. I've seen you endure so much worse. This will reveal that, not crush you."

I shook my head wearily. "I don't feel strong. I feel like a scared girl playing pretend. Maybe Drake was right—I'm in over my head."

Saige clasped my hands with a reassuring strength. "The strongest hearts are forged through adversity. Let this experience sharpen your courage rather than fuel your doubts. Confidence will come with time."

As I wavered, still ensnared by uncertainty, Saige tightened her grip, her eyes searching mine intently. "Listen to your intuition. Set aside logic for a moment—what does your heart tell you?"

I quieted my doubts to listen within. Under the cacophony, a small flame of conviction flickered. I clung to its light like a lifeline.

Opening my eyes, I managed a shaky smile. "It says I can do this. I just need to trust myself."

Saige nodded approvingly. "Exactly. With time and care,

you'll find your footing. For now, be patient and keep listening within."

Saige's wisdom reignited my inner spark. By holding onto its faint glow, I would manage to progress through the darkness, even with unsteady strides, until my path became clear again.

CHAPTER 6

The soft afternoon sunlight streamed into the office, bathing everything in a peaceful glow as I carefully examined the innkeeper's detailed records. Unease gnawed at me as I searched for any clue amid his leather-bound books and tidy stacks of parchment that might unravel the tangled threads leading to his demise. My half-eaten sandwich sat abandoned, my hunger focused on other nourishment.

My fingers traced the cool, worn leather spines chronicling generations of the enclaves' complex histories before coming to rest on Ryder's weathered calendar. As I turned each densely scrawled page, the sheer volume of disputes and negotiations penned in the weeks prior was astonishing.

Nearly every day held meetings aimed at quelling rising tensions over territorial boundaries, hunting rights, trade route access, and other recurring clashes stemming from the enclaves' ancient roots.

According to the histories Briar had reviewed with me, the peace-loving Elk clan first settled Crescent Valley over a century ago, establishing the original village that, in time, became Crescent Crossing. Their numbers and influence grew rapidly during those early, prosperous decades of plentiful game and fertile farmland.

Yet in recent generations, the formidable Flat Top warriors had pushed increasingly beyond their traditional mountain domain along the Continental Divide, pursuing more hunting grounds to supplement the meager resources on their own harsh, rocky slopes.

At the same time, the secretive Bittersweet shifters had ventured down from their cloud-veiled strongholds high in the snowy peaks, lured by prospects of increased trade and collaboration with the nearby enclaves.

This influx strained resources and brought intensifying competition and clashes. As mediator, Ryder tirelessly brokered compromises and settlements to maintain equilibrium. But an uneasy peace reigned, repeatedly threatening to boil over into open conflict.

Skimming the densely detailed calendar pages, I felt certain that someone among the divergent wolf packs must have harbored a deep resentment toward the man tasked with maintaining their precarious balance. But which of the enclaves had gone too far in seeking revenge?

Equally troubling was the question nagging at my own restless thoughts. Would I, as Ryder's untested successor, also become a target for whoever silenced his unwavering voice? The weight of the unknown pressed down on me, as heavy and suffocating as the afternoon shadows.

When Hamish and Saige knocked on the office door, I called them in.

"How was lunch?" I asked.

"Better than yours, it seems," Hamish arched a brow at me as he eyed my half-eaten sandwich.

I waved off his concern. "I suppose I'm too distracted. Still getting my bearings."

Hamish and Saige exchanged a glance. "If you want us to stay with you for the interviews this afternoon, we can. But we're both feeling the need to stretch our legs," Hamish said. "We can have a walk around and try to find out more information. Maybe one of my friends in town knows something that could help us."

I nodded in agreement, sensing their wolves must not be looking forward to being cooped up in a musty office all day. "That sounds like a good idea. Maybe you can get some more leads on who might have been behind this. You two go ahead and look around town for clues. I can handle the meetings today. Besides, Briar will be around if I need help. We'll need all the information we can get if we're going to figure out who did this."

"All right then," Saige said after a moment of solemn contemplation between her and Hamish.

Hamish squared his shoulders and met my gaze steadily before nodding curtly in agreement. "Let's see what we can dig up."

With Hamish and Saige dispatched on their discreet mission around town, I awaited Harper's arrival alone, steeling myself for another fruitless bout of verbal sparring. However, I was resolved to uncover her hidden secrets.

A brisk knock heralded the raven-haired woman, her sharp gaze scouring the room the moment I opened the door.

"Tea?" I offered blandly.

"No, thank you," she replied, already moving to the chair opposite my desk, spine ruler straight.

I hid a sigh, wishing the woman would easily thaw for me. Still, I had to try coaxing something useful from her inscrutable depths.

Settling behind the heavy oak desk, I folded my hands and met her flinty stare. "Let's review the timeline of events leading up to Ryder's disappearance that night."

Harper arched one sculpted brow fractionally. "I doubt I have anything new to add."

I leaned forward intently. "Humor me by walking through it. Your perspective on the night could prove invaluable."

After an impassive stare, Harper shrugged in acquiescence. "Very well. The Elk and Flat Tops were at odds. Both were convinced Ryder favored the other regarding territory." She paused, her eyes focusing on another time. "With Ryder gone, I imagine things will only worsen. Those brutes understand only strength."

I filed away this insight about the building tensions. "Did these challenges to Ryder's authority happen frequently?" I asked.

Harper cut a curt nod. "Periodically, yes. I can't remember a time where more than a year went by without the enclaves challenging his authority, but he always endured. Frankly, your appointment worries the Bittersweets most," Harper continued candidly. "An outsider replacing Ryder feels dangerous to all of us. And we don't know your intentions."

Her words sent a chill through me. Not only did I have to mediate disputes, but the Bittersweets already mistrusted me before we'd even met. I sensed this simmering animosity could easily boil over if I wasn't cautious.

"I appreciate your honesty," I replied evenly, keeping my voice neutral. The insights from Harper shed light on a bleaker landscape than I had initially realized. It finally dawned on me how vulnerable my situation was.

"I'm surprised they allowed Ryder to act as a go-between. For some reason, I'd expect wolf shifters to fight things out."

"Within our enclaves, that's how it's done. But in Ryder's role as a mediator, he was ever reassuring that he wasn't here to challenge our rights to lead our packs, but to get us working together."

"Are you, Kai, and Drake pack alphas?"

"No, our alphas are in charge of our territories. The additional role of mediator would be too much strain for any alpha. Each of us are delegates, handpicked by our respective alphas."

"Ryder wasn't from one of your packs?"

Harper shook her head. "He was a loner from Rampart Enclave. He found himself here in Crescent Crossing a few decades ago and quickly tired of the infighting. He brokered peace within the confines of this town's borders, and the rest is history."

I had to wonder if Ryder would have wanted any single enclave to have his level of oversight. No wonder he hadn't stepped down. "He's been winning this card game for decades?"

She nodded. "Every time a challenge was called, he'd organize the same card game, and he'd always win. Fate favored him, or so I thought." Sorrow softened her eyes, and I finally sensed more than just her distant mistrust. She'd genuinely cared for Ryder. "I'd sensed the strain in the air the moment I arrived that night. Although the meeting had been organized well in advance, Drake, as always, looked ready to challenge anyone. That fool Kai pretended at his usual naivete while surely scheming an angle, as was his nature. He's been caught cheating before, so I had my eyes on him. And your arrival, a fae of all things, set my teeth on edge. No disrespect intended."

Clearly, Harper was not a woman who pulled punches. At least I didn't have to wonder where I stood with her.

"None taken. Go on," I urged.

"Ryder seemed weary, as if the weight of responsibilities lay heavy on his shoulders," Harper continued evenly. "I remember he kept massaging his bum leg as if it was acting up again. Still, his keen eyes were alert as they took the measure of those gathered, missing nothing. When Ryder was called away by that phone call, tensions heightened even further. Drake radiated impatience and Kai made some flippant quip I had to ignore."

She paused and turned her gaze to the window, lost in thought. I sat quietly, giving her the time she needed.

"When you attempted conversation, we had no patience for niceties. Not under the circumstances. You were wide-eyed as you sat there, a mere passerby caught up in something beyond her comprehension."

Harper spared me a direct glance before continuing. "When Kai and Drake stepped away briefly, I wanted to speak frankly with you, but I realized anything I said might make you an even greater target to them, so I held my silence, watching you fidget with your wine glass until the men returned."

Harper faltered, and for an instant, her memories cracked her stoic facade. She drew an unsteady breath. "As you know already, soon after, Briar went to check on Ryder and we heard her scream. Then came the tragic discovery, which you well know the rest of. That's everything pertinent I can recall. Does that satisfy?"

"Forgive me, but it seems you're intentionally withholding your full perspective on events leading up to Ryder's demise. I want to understand what you're protecting. Or, more precisely, who?"

Harper met my probing look coolly. "You're imagining secrets where there are none. I've told you everything of value." She stood abruptly, ready to depart.

"Wait, I have one more question," I interjected, an idea striking me. "You stepped away briefly from the table that night. Where exactly did you go during that time?"

Harper hesitated, caught off guard by my query. "I went outside for a brief walk to clear my head."

I studied her closely. "Can you be more specific on where you went?"

Harper's jaw tightened almost imperceptibly. "If you must know, I went out to the inn's garden to commune with the moon for a bit. Does that satisfy your curiosity?"

Though her explanation seemed innocuous enough, something in her too-calm tone set my instincts tingling. I was convinced she was concealing something about those lost minutes. But pushing her further now would yield nothing.

"Yes, thank you for clarifying," I replied mildly, stifling my suspicions for now.

With a final terse nod, Harper spun on her heel and

exited, leaving me alone with only dead ends and a growing list of unanswered questions.

With aloof Harper having provided little new information, I awaited the arrival of the temperamental Drake with equal parts frustration and unease. Our last encounter still left my nerves jangled, though I could not deny an undercurrent of unwanted attraction simmered beneath within me despite his animosity.

To distract myself while waiting for his gruff knock, I turned again to perusing Ryder's meticulously organized shelves. I ran my hands along the finely engraved accent rail. "What am I missing?" I murmured.

Just then, a section of the paneled wall creaked ominously. I leaped back as a concealed compartment swung open right before my eyes. Inside lay a worn leather journal tucked behind a moonstone ring and a silver dagger. Hands trembling, I lifted the journal and opened it to a random page.

"Today I strengthened the enchantments sealing this space," I read aloud. "May it only reveal itself to my heir in their hour of need." My breath caught as I realized this was Ryder's secret cache, appearing to aid in my investigation.

I placed the moonstone ring on the middle of the desk. As I did, it fully hit me that fate had chosen me as Ryder's successor to safeguard all of this—the inn, the town, the enclaves. Me, a woman nearing her fae-borne midlife, who'd accomplished nothing noteworthy back in Denver or the fae territories despite my years and opportunities.

Meanwhile, the role of innkeeper here held such significance, serving as a pillar of this community for generations. It was a sacred duty entrusted to individuals of exceptional wisdom, fairness, and capability.

What had fate seen in me? I was utterly unqualified to mediate disputes of such consequence or unravel mysteries eclipsing my comprehension. Back home, I'd merely drifted along without direction or purpose for so long. Yet now the fate of this entire haven rested upon my woefully inadequate shoulders.

As self-doubt threatened to overwhelm me, I remembered Briar's steadfast faith in my yet-unknown strengths. Or perhaps her faith was in the workings of fate? I sensed the glimmers of a long-slumbering ambition awakening within me, realizing this unexpected challenge could help me find my true calling. Where once my empty life stretched endlessly ahead, now I found myself at the center of something far greater than myself.

I left the dagger in the compartment, noting that, as a weapon made of silver, it could be a potent defense against any wolf shifter. But I wasn't about to take up something I had no idea how to use besides point and poke.

I quickly looked through the journal but found the later entries blank. As I flipped through the most recent entries, cryptic notes about "gatherings in the high peaks," "an ill omen foretold," and "urgent safeguards needed under the full moon" stuck out.

Page after page contained Ryder's growing concerns about a clandestine threat convening beyond the town's borders that could irrevocably disrupt the town's delicate balance. He wrote of sleepless nights spent patrolling the surrounding woods, searching for any sign of trouble.

I leaned back heavily. As a fae lacking any magical abilities, I'd always resigned myself to living a mundane, ordinary life. Back in Denver, I'd steered clear of other fae, my routine holding no hint of enchantment or excitement.

Yet now, according to Briar, with the innkeeper mantle came access to arcane powers tied to this place and its ancient secrets. Me, plain old magic-less Lydia, potentially wielding forces beyond comprehension? It was almost laughable.

Still, I couldn't ignore the allure of this new mystical inheritance slumbering within me. Perhaps harnessing these gifts could help illuminate solutions to the gathering darkness Ryder sensed. More than that, awakening such extraordinary talents could inject a sense of meaning and purpose into the aimless rambling that had defined my prior existence. Where once my empty life had stretched bleakly ahead, now I found myself at the center of something extraordinary and consequential.

My hands shook as I re-read his speculative warning that the howling darkness sought to challenge everything and how hard and resolutely he'd worked to keep Crescent Crossing from descending into chaos. Had this unnamed danger silenced Ryder before he could unmask it?

Were my own days numbered if I continued Ryder's quest for the truth?

Just then, an additional detail caught my eye: the initials "CW" scrawled in the margins of the page listing his appointments for the night he was murdered. None of the card players or people I'd met so far had those initials.

I picked up the phone and called the front desk, where I knew Briar would answer. "Ryder was meeting with someone named CW the night he was killed. Does that ring any bells for you?" I asked her.

Briar hesitated a moment before answering. "CW? No one comes to mind. Ryder had acquaintances all over the enclaves, but I don't recall him ever mentioning someone with those initials."

I nodded, jotting the puzzling clue down in my notebook. "Thanks, gal." I hung up, adding this clue to my list of cryptic threads to investigate. But for now, I turned my focus back to deciphering the rest of Ryder's upsetting journal entries, hoping more answers waited within those pages.

I closed the journal and began pacing, unnerved. From Ryder's notes it seemed a secretive cabal was organizing, its motives unknown but an ominous threat to order here. What if they had spies already within the town, watching me?

"Get ahold of yourself, Lydia," I muttered under my breath. "You can't jump to conclusions. There has to be some reasonable explanation."

Yet the more I considered Ryder's obsessive scrawling about a gathering evil, the more I feared his murder was only the beginning. As the next full moon approached, would I meet the same grisly fate for daring to shine a light into the darkness?

Hearing heavy footsteps approach, I quickly replaced the journal, my pulse racing. Whatever sinister plans were unfolding in the mountain's shadows, I could not afford to show my creeping dread.

A brisk knock heralded the intimidating shifter. Without waiting for me to call out for him to enter, he strode into the room, scowling, the rich timbre of his voice cracking like a whip. "Let's get this over with."

I stood calmly as Drake entered, unwilling to reveal the uneasiness gripping my heart. But inwardly, my thoughts recoiled from the peril permeating this tranquil town I had so naively adopted as my own.

As Drake dropped unceremoniously onto the leather couch, the lingering scents of whiskey and pine washed over me. Clearly, he was here under duress and intended to reveal as little as possible.

I squared my shoulders, refusing to let him intimidate me. I told myself he was just a wolf taking up space and asserting dominance, but it was cold comfort. For all I knew, this was Ryder's killer, but I couldn't back down. "We'll conclude our business when I'm satisfied you've disclosed everything relevant."

Drake leaned back, regarding me with a simmering gaze. "And if I decide not to cooperate, sweetheart?"

I felt an unexpected thrill at the endearment. Our eyes met, and I could sense the lingering tension between us. "Please, refrain from calling me sweetheart. I assure you, I am quite capable of persuasion when necessary."

A ghost of a smile tugged at Drake's lips. "I'd pay good money to see you try persuading me to do anything, princess."

Heat flooded my cheeks at the suggestive note in his gravelly voice, even as irritation flared. I straightened, determined not to let this arrogant shifter fluster me. "Let's stay focused on the murder, shall we?"

Drake held my gaze, his eyes glinting with humor and a silent challenge. The tension between us would require delicate handling during the interrogation.

"You strike me as someone who values honesty, despite your gruff exterior. As the new town mediator, I'm simply requesting that you provide an accurate account of that night."

Drake considered me silently for a long moment before grunting in acquiescence. "Ask your questions then, innkeeper."

"Let's start with what you were doing when Ryder stepped outside. Did you follow him at any point?"

"Maybe I went to grab a smoke," Drake evaded.

I kept my tone conversational. "If you confronted Ryder outside, own up to it. It's important that we have all the facts."

Drake's jaw tightened. "You calling me a liar?"

"I'm just trying to understand what happened," I said evenly. "Please, tell me the truth."

Drake exhaled harshly, glancing away. "Yeah, alright. I wanted a private word about Flat Top territory negotiations. When I found him, he was still on his call. Happy now?"

I nodded. "What exactly did you say to him?"

"Just that Flat Top should get priority in the seasonal hunting ground rotations," Drake said gruffly. "Ryder refused, saying he'd talk later, after he was done with his call. So I left."

"And Ryder seemed fine when you last saw him?" I asked intently.

Drake met my gaze. "When I left him out there, he was alive and unharmed, still on his call. Alone. I walked away without laying a hand on him."

I searched his face but saw only sincerity in those piercing eyes. "Thank you for being so open and honest. I understand how tough this must be for you."

Drake stood abruptly, tension etched on his face. "I've said all I can. Watch your step, or you'll end up like Ryder."

I took a step back, pressing myself against the bookcase behind me. "Is that meant to be a threat?"

Drake closed the distance between us, his imposing figure looming close. When he spoke, his voice was rough with emotion. "This is hard-earned wisdom. Whoever killed Ryder is likely still in town. You seem determined to remain in his shoes as the mediator. It doesn't take a genius to realize you're putting yourself at risk."

He reached out as if to touch my face, then hesitated, clenching his fist and dropping it abruptly. I swayed toward him instinctively, my heart racing as the air pulsed with turbulent energy. For a moment, his eyes blazed with a soul-deep yearning before he tore his gaze away.

"Be careful, Lydia," Drake growled. "Or you'll share Ryder's fate." His jaw was taut with restraint.

Taken aback, I didn't know what to say to this mountain of a man. Overwhelmed by the unexpected fervor beneath our angry words, I instinctively placed my hand on my racing heart. Resisting Drake's pull would require all my willpower, or I risked losing myself in the inferno.

"Why are you here?" he demanded.

"Excuse me?" I stammered.

"You've been asking all of us questions, and turnabout is fair play. Why did you end up in Crescent Crossing on the day of Ryder's death?"

Drake was right. He had every reason to know what brought me to town. But I didn't want to disclose the details of my trauma to him. "I went through some difficult times back in Denver. My niece almost died. I watched a friend die. I narrowly avoided the same fate. I needed a break and had to get away from Denver. Hamish Bittersweet recommended this town. He sold it as a quiet little mountain village where no one would even notice me."

Drake blew out a long breath, a flicker of compassion in the creases around his eyes. "I guess that didn't work out for you. Hamish clearly hasn't been here recently," he muttered under his breath. "Look, you didn't ask for any of this. No one will blame you if you pass Ryder's mantle on to someone else."

I nodded. "Sure, but who would I trust? You?"

The hint of a smile pulled at the corner of his lip. "You've got to trust someone sometime."

I pursed my lips. It would take more than that to persuade me.

"Have it your way," he huffed.

As he turned to leave, I touched his arm lightly. "Drake, wait."

He looked down at my hand, and then back at me curiously.

"I know you cared for Ryder in your own way. We'll find out who did this, I promise."

Drake's expression softened a fraction. "Best of luck with that." Then he dipped his chin in gruff acknowledgment and took his leave.

I sank down on the couch, pondering the exchange with Drake. Though his account seemed forthright, I still sensed the cunning shifter harbored deeper insights he refused to share.

The pieces of this puzzle remained fragmented, obscuring the full picture. I needed to step back and examine what information had been gleaned before proceeding further.

As I sat reviewing my notes, the office door opened, and Hamish and Saige entered, both looking weary and frustrated.

"No luck gathering useful information around town, then?" I surmised.

Hamish shook his head, running a hand through his grizzled hair. "Everyone's keeping silent as the grave where Ryder's demise is concerned."

"We discovered there's unrest brewing among the enclaves," Saige added grimly. "It seems Ryder left you quite a mess to manage."

I gestured for them to sit, my pulse quickening. "Tell me what you found out. I need to understand what we're facing."

Hamish leaned forward, forearms on his knees. "The Elk clan is furious over the Flat Tops encroaching on their hunting territories. And the Bittersweets have been pushing controversial trades for their elixirs and potions."

"Meanwhile, the Flat Tops are paranoid about defending the mountain passes if conflict breaks out," Saige chimed in. "Ryder's compromises have satisfied no one lately."

I sat back heavily, disheartened. My role in maintaining equilibrium suddenly seemed impossible. The animosity between enclaves was too deep-seated.

Hamish gripped my shoulder. "Don't despair. With time and care, the balance can be restored. And you won't be alone in this."

Saige nodded. "Agreed. We can stay as long as you need."

Despite the monumental task ahead, my friends' steady faith kindled flickers of hope within me. United, perhaps we could do the impossible—bring lasting reconciliation to Crescent Crossing.

The next day, I decided to stay in the office, poring over Ryder's journals and notes, hoping to find more clues that could shed light on the tensions between the clans. Hamish and Saige had gone out to gather more information from the townspeople.

My peace was short-lived. Not even an hour into my research, the office door burst open without warning. I rose swiftly as an unfamiliar man strode in uninvited. His elegant dress and manner seemed oddly out of place here.

"Apologies for the abrupt entrance, but I come bearing troubling news that cannot wait," he announced without preamble. "It seems your resident charmer, Kai Wilder, has mysteriously vanished. I suspect his disappearance may prove inconvenient to your investigation."

I struggled to maintain composure in the face of his brazen entry and alarming announcement. "And who do I have the pleasure of addressing?" I inquired. "And how do you come by this information on Kai Wilder?"

The man smoothed his overcoat with an air of importance. "I'm Malachi Sterling. I serve as an instructor with the Bittersweet clan. And as for how I know about Kai's disappearance, he failed to show up for our scheduled meeting this morning. When I went to his residence to check on him, there was no sign of him or any indication of where he might have gone."

Though his words were polite, I detected a subtle disdain in Malachi's assessing gaze, making it clear he considered me unfit for my role. I drew myself up, refusing to be intimidated.

"How are you connected to Kai?"

Before Malachi could respond, Hamish strode back in, nostrils flaring. "What's this about Kai missing?"

Malachi repeated his account dispassionately while I struggled to process this new variable. "Has anyone else reported Kai missing or tried to locate him?" I asked, seeking more context.

"I've spoken with several of his associates, and no one has seen or heard from him since yesterday evening," Malachi replied. "It's highly unusual for him to miss appointments without any notice."

Had Kai simply fled to avoid being implicated in Ryder's murder? Or had some sinister fate befallen him too?

As Malachi concluded his report, I caught Hamish's eye, seeing my worry reflected there. After maintaining some semblance of order these past days, everything now felt like it had been cast into chaos again.

"Thank you for informing us," I told Malachi evenly. "Please relay any further updates you hear about Kai's status. In the meantime, we will continue pursuing all lines of investigation related to Ryder's murder."

With an insincere smile, Malachi took his leave. I sank into my chair, feeling the room tilt and swim around me. The combination of the high-stakes card game, Ryder's shocking demise, and Kai's sudden disappearance indicated the presence of malevolent forces conspiring around us. Where this maelstrom would lead, I dared not predict.

CHAPTER 7

Feeling the weight of recent events and the multiplying mysteries with each passing day, I headed out on a solitary walk. The hour was early, so the town was just beginning to stir, with only a few early risers going about their business. Still, I felt safe enough in the daylight and in public. Hamish and Saige had gone out to hunt and scout in the woods around the town, so I felt it fitting that I spend some time investigating on my own.

I turned onto the dirt path leading around the outskirts of town and followed it for a while. I was just about to turn back when I saw something that made me stop in my tracks. In the distance, a handful of wolves were crossing the road, yipping and playing with each other as they went. Even from here, I could tell they weren't ordinary wolves. I knew at once they must be shifters out taking a run together.

But what had I expected? The entire town was full of wolf shifters. Still, the sight filled me with an odd mixture of awe and longing; on one hand, it was magical to witness such wild beauty in motion, but it was bittersweet because I couldn't join them as they ran exuberantly through the woods. For a moment, I wanted nothing more than to shed my fae identity and join them in their carefree play.

But then reality set in again, and I shook off my reverie. A few moments later, the wolves had disappeared into the forest, and all that remained was silence, broken only by the distant call of a hawk high overhead. With one last glance over my shoulder toward where the wolves had been, I continued back into town with new determination burning inside me; seeing those shifters out there living wild and free had me determined to find a way back to my fire someday soon.

As I wandered back onto the dusty gravel streets of town, my mind was a whirlwind, trying to piece together the puzzle of Ryder's death. But something else caught my attention. Everywhere I looked, I saw raven images and symbols. They were etched into doorways, painted on murals, and even woven into the design of the town's flag that fluttered in the gentle breeze. The raven amulet Barnell had found near Ryder's body, which I now wore around my neck, seemed to pulse with a life of its own.

I paused in front of an intricate mural depicting a raven in flight against the backdrop of a crescent moon. The details were astonishing, from the glint in the raven's eye to the individual feathers that seemed to shimmer.

A shiver ran down my spine. Was the town's obsession with ravens merely a cultural quirk, or was there deeper significance? And more importantly, did it have any connection to the amulet and Ryder's death?

Lost in thought, I barely noticed a local passing by. The

elderly woman, with a shock of white hair and a hunched back, stopped to gaze at the mural alongside me.

"Beautiful, isn't it?" she remarked, her voice raspy with age. "The raven is a powerful symbol in Crescent Crossing. A protector and a harbinger."

I turned to the woman, curiosity piqued. "A harbinger of what?"

She simply smiled, her eyes twinkling with a mix of wisdom and mischief. "That, dear, is a story for another time." And with that, she continued on her way, leaving me with even more questions than before.

After my contemplative walk, my stomach rumbled, reminding me I had skipped breakfast. I headed to The Sugared Spruce, the town's renowned bakery. The tantalizing aroma of freshly baked bread and pastries wafted through the air as I approached, drawing me in.

Inside, the bakery buzzed with activity. Locals chatted animatedly, sipping on their morning coffee and enjoying an array of baked delights. I chose a corner table, ordering a warm croissant and a steaming cup of locally roasted coffee. As I waited, I couldn't help but overhear snippets of conversation from the neighboring table.

"...gatherings in the woods," one woman whispered, her eyes darting around nervously.

"I've heard the howls," another man chimed in, his voice low and filled with unease. "They're not like any I've heard before."

The group seemed engrossed in their discussion, trading tales of eerie occurrences and nocturnal meetings. I strained to catch more, my investigative instincts kicking in.

But as I leaned in slightly, my chair gave a telltale creak.

The gossiping townspeople turned their heads in unison, their eyes widening in surprise upon seeing me. The chatter ceased immediately, replaced by an awkward silence. The woman who had spoken of the strange gatherings cleared her throat, offering me a tight-lipped smile before quickly excusing herself. The others followed suit, leaving their half-finished pastries and coffee behind.

I took a sip of my coffee. The warmth did little to dispel the chill that had settled in the room. The townspeople were hiding something, at least from my pointy-tipped ears, and I was determined to find out what.

After my slightly unsettling experience at the bakery, I made a quick stop at the town's general store for some supplies. The wooden sign above the entrance read "Willem's Wares," and as I pushed open the door, a bell jingled overhead.

The store was a delightful mishmash of items, from canned goods to hand-knitted scarves. As I browsed the shelves, I couldn't help but overhear a conversation between two customers near the back of the store.

"I'm telling you, it's just like the old days," a gruff male voice said, his tone low and urgent. "The signs are every-where, if you know where to look."

His companion, a woman with a worried expression, shook her head. "I don't want to believe it, but you're right. A raven's shadow never fades, and it seems to be growing darker by the day."

The mention of the exiled shifter catchphrase caught my attention, and I moved closer, pretending to examine a display of locally made jams.

"Excuse me," I said, turning to face the pair. "I couldn't

help but overhear your conversation. What did you mean by 'a raven's shadow never fades'?"

The man and woman exchanged a startled glance, their faces paling slightly. "I'm sorry, I don't know what you're talking about," the man said, his voice suddenly guarded.

The woman nodded, her eyes darting nervously around the store. "We were just discussing the weather, that's all. If you'll excuse us, we really must be going."

Without another word, the pair hurried past me and out of the store, leaving me standing there with a growing sense of unease. It was clear that they knew, but they were too afraid to speak openly about it.

As I made my way to the counter with my purchases, I couldn't shake the feeling that the town was keeping secrets from me. Secrets that could hold the key to unraveling the mystery surrounding Ryder's death and potentially much more.

Behind the counter, a portly man looked up from the ledger he was scribbling in. He adjusted his spectacles and came around to greet me with an extended hand.

"You must be the newcomer I've heard so much about! I'm Willem, owner of this fine establishment," he introduced himself jovially.

I shook his hand. "Nice to meet you, Willem. I'm Lydia. I just arrived in Crescent Crossing recently."

"Welcome to our little corner of the world, Lydia," Willem said warmly. "I hope you find what you're looking for here." He gave me a friendly pat on the shoulder before returning to his place behind the counter, resuming his work on the ledger. "My goodness, I never thought I'd see a fae wandering into my shop!" he exclaimed. "But here you are. The new innkeeper, if rumor proves true?"

I nodded. "I've taken over running the Howl Away Inn for the time being."

"Well, ain't that something?" Willem chuckled in amazement. "You're always welcome here. Now, what can I get for you today?"

"I don't mean to pry, but I was wondering if you knew anything about Ryder. Or might you have any idea why someone would harm him?"

Willem's pen froze mid-sentence, and he looked up, his eyes widening slightly. For a moment, he seemed at a loss for words. "Everyone knew Ryder. Oh, such a tragedy," he began, his voice shaky. "I can't imagine who'd want to hurt him."

I leaned in, sensing there was more to the story. "I've heard whispers around town about strange gatherings and other odd happenings. Do you know anything about that?"

Willem's gaze darted around nervously, and he swallowed hard. "Look, Lydia, there are things in this town that are best left alone. People are scared, and they have reason to be." He seemed to choose his words carefully, as if afraid of saying too much.

Before I could press further, Willem abruptly excused himself. "I just remembered something I need to check in the backroom," he said, almost too hastily. And with that, he disappeared behind a curtain, leaving me alone in the store.

I waited for a few minutes, but it became clear that Willem had no intention of returning. With a sigh, I placed money on the counter to cover my scant purchases. As I exited the store, I couldn't shake off the feeling I was diving deeper into a mystery the townspeople were desperate to keep hidden.

I returned to the Howl Away Inn, the weight of the morning's whisperings pressing heavily upon me. Yet as I wandered the grounds before retreating to my office, subtle anomalies leaped out at me. The bench beneath the oak tree had been moved closer to the trickling fountain, just as I'd wished for more shade there. And a painting of a copse of ash trees, their limbs reaching towards the heavens, now hung in the upstairs hallway—remarkably similar to the forests I'd grown up around and where I felt most at home.

Venturing into the library, I trailed my fingers along the leather-bound spines, only to find new titles on healing crystals, flower essences, and nude forest bathing—all curiously aligned with my interests. This transformative energy pulsed from the walls like a heartbeat.

As I retreated to my bedroom, I shook my head in bewilderment. The sunflower-patterned wallpaper, floral bedspread, and crystal lamps were distinctly different from just this morning. The inn continued to unveil its sentience in small yet impactful ways, reshaping its spaces to mirror my essence.

Though the magic permeating every fiber of the building unsettled me, I also felt a growing sense of kinship and belonging within these living walls. Our fates were intertwined now. Whatever the coming days led, the Howl Away Inn would be by my side.

The familiar surroundings of my office beckoned, a sanctuary where I hoped to find solace, gather my thoughts, and piece together the rapidly forming puzzle. However, as I opened the door, a chilling sense of dread washed over me. I distinctly remembered locking the room, but now it lay in utter disarray. Drawers were yanked open, papers littered the floor, and Ryder's meticulously organized files were a chaotic mess. Someone had been desperately searching for something.

I quickly scanned the room, my heart racing. My thoughts immediately went to the silver dagger and Ryder's journal. With trembling fingers, I slid open the hidden compartment, sighing in relief upon finding both items untouched.

As I absorbed the tumultuous aftermath, shards from a shattered whiskey bottle sparkled menacingly on the floor, a stark testament to the intruder's frantic search. The stench of Kai's cologne lingered in the air, but I knew better than to jump to conclusions based on that alone.

Overwhelmed yet determined, I began tidying the mess, hoping to find clues about the intruder's identity and motives. As I worked, my fingers brushed against the moonstone ring I'd discovered in Ryder's stash. An electrifying energy surged through me, causing the room to blur and shift, hinting at deeper mysteries yet to be unraveled.

Suddenly, I was no longer in my office but standing in the same space, witnessing a scene from the past. The inn's walls looked newer, and the furniture was slightly different. I realized I was seeing an echo of a past event, a memory imprinted on the very fabric of the room.

In this vision, I saw Ryder looking anxious, pacing back and forth. He was deep in conversation with a shadowy figure whose face I couldn't quite make out. Their voices were muffled, but the tension between them was palpable. Suddenly, the scene shifted violently, and I caught a brief, horrifying glimpse of Ryder's murder outside the inn, bathed in moonlight. The vision was fleeting, and before I could discern more details, it faded, returning me to the present.

Gasping for breath, I pulled my hand away from the ring, my heart racing. The weight of what I had just witnessed pressed down on me. The ring had revealed fragments of the past, moments forever etched in time. It was both a gift and a curse, providing me with a clue but also immersing me in the raw emotion of that fateful night.

I realized the ring was more than just a piece of jewelry; it was a key to unlocking the mysteries of the Howl Away Inn. As I grappled with the emerging magical abilities gifted to me by the inn, I knew I had a powerful tool at my disposal. But the responsibility weighed heavily on me, and I was determined to use this newfound gift wisely.

Shaken by the vision, I took a moment to compose myself before continuing to tidy the office. Once the room was back in order, I made a mental note to discuss the break-in and the ring's revelations with Hamish and Saige as soon as possible.

The day's events had left me feeling burdened, yet there was no time for rest. Briar's briefings and the notes Ryder left behind made it clear: the escalating conflict between the Elk and Flat Top enclaves required my immediate attention. As the newly appointed mediator of Crescent Crossing, I had arranged for a crucial meeting in the inn's grand hall today, with the goal of negotiating peace between these rival groups. Although I would have preferred Briar's presence by my side, she had recommended against it, opting instead to equip me with detailed insights into the representatives of both factions beforehand.

Nalani Silverpine, the Elk's esteemed representative, sat

poised and regal on one side of the long wooden table. Her emerald eyes, though calm, held a fire that spoke of her dedication to her people. Opposite her, Drake Frost of the Flat Tops, with his towering presence and gray eyes, exuded an aura of cold authority. The air was thick with tension, with each side's distrust palpable.

Taking my place at the head of the table, I tried to project confidence, even as doubt gnawed at my insides. "Thank you both for coming," I began, my voice unwavering. "I must admit, I'm not fully versed in the deep-rooted history between your enclaves. If you could enlighten me, perhaps we can find a way to coexist."

Nalani, her voice melodic yet firm, responded first. "Our disputes, Lydia, are as old as the mountains themselves. They revolve around territory and water rights. The landmarks that define our boundaries have been passed down through spoken word, and over time, interpretations have diverged."

Drake's gruff voice cut in, each word deliberate. "The Flat Tops have always held to our version of these histories. The landmarks speak to us in ways the Elk can't understand. But they've always seen it differently."

Nalani's eyes flashed with irritation. "It's not about seeing it differently, Drake. It's about honoring the true essence of the stories. Your enclave has twisted them to fit your own narrative."

Drake's jaw tightened. "You accuse us of twisting tales? The Elk have conveniently forgotten key elements that favor our rights."

I raised a hand, trying to interject some calm into the escalating argument. "Both of you have valid points, and I respect the depth of your histories. But what if we find a middle ground? A compromise that seems fair to both sides and then move forward?"

Both Nalani and Drake looked at me, their expressions a mix of shock and disbelief. Nalani's voice was incredulous. "You suggest we just... forget? Disregard what our ancestors fought for?"

I took a deep breath, choosing my next words carefully. "I'm not asking you to forget your histories or the sacrifices of your ancestors. What I'm proposing is that we find a way to honor the past while creating a future that works for both enclaves."

Drake shook his head, his eyes narrowing. "Easier said than done, Innkeeper. The Flat Tops have always held our ground, and we're not about to give it up now."

Nalani's lips tightened into a thin line. "The Elk won't be bullied into submission. We have our own claims, and we won't back down."

The tension in the room was palpable, with both sides digging in their heels. I realized that finding a compromise would require more than just a single meeting. It would be a delicate process of building trust and finding common ground.

"I understand that this is a complex issue, and there's no easy solution," I acknowledged. "But as the new mediator, I'm committed to working with both enclaves to find a way forward. It may take time, but I believe we can find a path to peace if we're willing to listen to each other and be open to new possibilities."

Despite my impassioned plea, it was clear that neither was ready to commit. The meeting concluded without a resolution, leaving me grappling with the enormity of the task ahead.

As the representatives filed out, I felt the weight of my responsibilities pressing down on me. The challenges of my new role were becoming evident, and I realized that navigating the complex politics of Crescent Crossing would require more than just diplomacy.

After the tension-filled meeting, I needed a breather. I wandered over to the inn's cozy lounge, hoping to find a secluded corner to reflect. But as I entered, the familiar chattering of Barnell, the teenage bellhop, reached my ears.

"Lydia!" he exclaimed, waving me over with his usual exuberance. He was seated at a table, a jigsaw puzzle spread out before him. "Care to help me with this before the dinner rush hits? It's a tricky one."

I couldn't help but smile. Barnell's cheerful demeanor was a welcome contrast to the day's ominous events. "Alright," I said, taking a seat opposite him. "But only if you promise not to cheat."

Barnell feigned shock. "Me? Cheat? Never!" He winked, his fiery red hair bouncing as he laughed. "Besides, how can you cheat at puzzles?"

As we pieced the puzzle together, Barnell regaled me with tales of his latest misadventures around Crescent Crossing. From accidentally dyeing the water in the town fountain blue to his ongoing quest to perfect the art of pancake flipping, his stories were filled with humor and youthful enthusiasm.

I found myself laughing along, the weight of my worries momentarily lifted. The puzzle, an intricate depiction of Crescent Crossing landscape, slowly came together, mirroring my journey of piecing together the town's mysteries.

As we placed the last piece, Barnell looked up at me, his eyes sincere. "You know, despite all the weirdness going on, I'm glad you're here," he said. "Crescent Crossing needs someone like you. Someone with fresh eyes."

His words touched me, and I couldn't help but smile. "Thanks, Barnell. That means a lot."

The lighthearted interlude with Barnell served as a reminder that, amid the challenges and uncertainties, there were moments of joy and genuine connection to be found.

As evening settled over Crescent Crossing, the soft glow of lanterns illuminated the inn's dining room. I had arranged a private dinner with Hamish, Saige, and Briar, hoping to discuss my growing concerns about the townspeople and the day's unsettling events.

The wooden table was set with an array of dishes, with the aroma of roasted meats and fresh herbs filling the air. As we ate, I recounted my experiences, from the raven symbols I'd noticed around town to the whispers I'd overheard at The Sugared Spruce.

Hamish listened intently, his brow furrowed in thought. "It's clear that something's amiss," he said, taking a sip of his wine. "The townspeople are on edge, and it's not just because of Ryder's murder."

Saige nodded in agreement, her green eyes sharp. "There's a climate of fear that's taken hold. It's as if they're all hiding something."

As the conversation deepened, I realized I felt more energized and driven than I had in years. Managing the inn had awakened a sense of purpose within me. The thought of returning to my mundane former life felt impossible now.

Briar, ever the diplomat, chimed in, "Maybe they're just wary of outsiders, especially with the recent events."

I leaned forward, speaking in a whisper. "I believe someone is trying to intimidate me, perhaps to deter my investigation. My office was searched, and I know I left the door locked."

Hamish's protective instincts flared. "Don't go anywhere on your own. We'll make sure you're always accompanied," he declared. "We won't let anything happen to you, Lydia."

Saige added, "We should also monitor the townspeople and try to gather more information. There's more to this than meets the eye."

Briar agreed, "We're in this together. We'll get to the bottom of it."

The dinner concluded with a renewed sense of purpose. As we parted ways for the night, I felt grateful for the allies I had found in Hamish, Saige, and Briar. Together, we would face the challenges ahead and unravel the mysteries of Crescent Crossing.

After dinner, I retreated to my room, hoping for a moment of solitude to process the day's events. The soft glow of the bedside lamp cast a warm light across the room, creating a comforting ambiance. I began to unwind, changing into my nightgown and letting my golden hair cascade freely down my back.

As I approached my bed, a glint caught my eye. Laid out on my pillow was a single, glossy raven feather. Its dark sheen seemed to absorb the room's light, making it appear even more ominous. A chill ran down my spine. This was no random occurrence; it was a deliberate message.

I picked up the feather. Its sleek texture was cold to the touch. Memories of the raven symbols I'd seen around town and the amulet I now wore flooded my mind. Someone was watching me, trying to intimidate me, and this was their latest ploy.

My heart raced. I felt exposed. The inn, which had become my sanctuary, now felt like a place of potential danger. I quickly scanned the room, half-expecting to find another clue or threat, but nothing else seemed amiss.

Taking a deep breath, I placed the feather on my bedside table. I wouldn't let this act of intimidation deter me. If anything, it only strengthened my resolve to uncover the truth behind Ryder's murder and the mysteries of Crescent Crossing.

Climbing into bed, I tried to push the unsettling thoughts from my mind. But even after I closed my eyes, I tossed and turned. The image of the raven feather lingered, a haunting reminder of the unseen forces at play.

Unable to find sleep after the discovery of the raven feather, I stepped out onto my room's balcony for some fresh air. The night had deepened, the moon casting a silvery glow over Crescent Crossing. The cool mountain breeze gently tousled my hair, and the distant sounds of nocturnal creatures created a serene backdrop.

Leaning against the railing, I took a moment to appreciate the beauty of the night. The waning gibbous moon hung high in the sky, its light reflecting off the babbling brook that ran alongside the inn. But as my gaze wandered further into the distance, I noticed something unusual.

From my vantage point, I could see groups of wolves moving stealthily through the forest's edge. Their silhouettes, illuminated by the moonlight, seemed to converge from different directions, forming larger packs. The sight was both mesmerizing and eerie.

A sense of unease settled over me. Why were they gathering in such numbers? Was this typical behavior, or was this related to the Elk vs. Flat Top territory dispute I had tried to mediate earlier? Or was there another, more sinister reason for their assembly?

I strained my ears, trying to pick up any sounds or conversations, but the distance was too great. The wolves moved with purpose, their actions coordinated and deliberate.

Retreating from the balcony, I felt a renewed sense of urgency. The gathering of the wolf shifters was a clear sign tensions were escalating. The equilibrium of Crescent Crossing was under threat, and I found myself at the heart of it all.

Determined to uncover the truth and restore balance, I knew I had to explore the resources at my disposal. Taking a leap of faith, I slid Ryder's moonstone ring onto my finger as I returned to my bed.

CHAPTER 8

The soft, silvery glow of the moonlight bathed my room, casting ethereal shadows on the walls. As sleep slowly claimed me, the moonstone ring on my finger seemed to radiate with energy. Its glow intensified until it enveloped my senses completely. When at last I drifted off, realities blurred, and the ring pulled me into its vivid dreamscape.

I arrived atop a craggy outcrop, the icy mountain wind whipping around me. Far below, shadowy figures moved about furtively, their hushed voices rising faintly. I strained to make out their whispers, but the dream winds swept all but the intonation away. Anger. Frustration. Pain. Who were these shrouded souls gathered under the watching stars?

I peered closer, searching for answers. At the assembly's heart sat a weathered stone etched with a raven in flight, wings outstretched. As I beheld the raven's dark form, a single glossy feather broke free, drifting down until it came to rest upon the stone.

I reached for the feather reflexively, seeking understanding. But as my fingers grazed the inky plume, a brilliant flash blinded me. I shielded my eyes against the searing light.

When at last I could see clearly again, the figures had vanished. Only the stone remained, now pulsing rhythmically like a heartbeat. Before my eyes, the carved raven seemed to take flight, soaring skyward on an unseen wind. Its obsidian eyes found mine, piercing my soul with wisdom that unsettled and eluded me.

I awoke with a start, my heart racing wildly. The disorienting remnants of the vivid dream still clung to me like cobwebs. I knew with startling certainty that this vision held the key to unlocking Crescent Crossing's shadowy secrets, if only I could decipher its coded warnings.

I felt an unexplainable draw to the place where Ryder had tragically died. Maybe, with the power of the moonstone, I could gain some clarity and some vision to solve the enigma.

Unable to resist the pull any longer, I got out of bed, slipped on my shoes, and wrapped a shawl around me before quietly making my way through the inn's shadowy corridors. With each step, I felt the Howl Away Inn's energy swirling around me, beckoning me onward through the darkness. I let my connection to this sentient sanctuary guide my path to the place where Ryder had drawn his final breaths. I remembered Hamish telling me to go nowhere alone, but I didn't want to wake them up after the day we'd all had. Besides, the night was calm, with stars twinkling above, and I couldn't imagine I was in danger in the silent night.

Soon I stood, bathed in moonlight, in the spot where he'd taken his final breath. Kneeling down, I sensed the inn's spirit enveloping me in comfort and encouragement. "Guide me to the truth," I whispered, placing my palm on the cool earth.

As I lingered there, memories of Ryder and his shocking demise flooded through me. The silence of the night was abruptly broken by a foreboding rustling sound coming from behind the building. The sound of twigs snapping, leaves pounding against something hard, and wood creaking made my blood run cold.

The residual energy from my dream sharpened my senses, making every sound and every whisper of the wind more pronounced. The trees swayed back and forth in the pitch-black darkness as though they were sentient and trying to warn me of what was lurking beyond the bend. The rustling grew louder and more deliberate, and an icy dread crept up my spine, sending terror rippling through my body like shockwaves. I could hear my heart racing in my chest thunderously as I considered what kind of beast or creature might emerge from that dark space.

With stealthy grace, I edged closer to the mysterious sounds, my heart a symphony of rapid beats. Relying on my fae-born night vision, I attempted to unveil the creature lurking in the darkness. As I cautiously rounded the corner, my efforts to remain unseen were thwarted by the piercing gaze of luminescent eyes. There, a few feet from me, stood a wolf, its red-brown fur raised. The eerie glow behind its eyes cast light on the muddy streaks adorning its coat, and its mouth was rimmed with ash, giving it a fearsome appearance. This was no mere wolf, but a wolf shifter, perfectly attuned to the nocturnal world in a way that my fae heritage could not match. It had been waiting for me, its presence a stark reminder that some creatures are masters of the night, far beyond my own capabilities.

My heart slammed against my ribs as a tidal wave of

panic threatened to consume me. I forced myself to take slow steps back from the menacing creature, fighting every instinct that urged me to turn and flee blindly into the dark forest. I knew such a reaction would only spur the beast to give chase and rip me apart from behind in a matter of seconds.

So I willed my quaking muscles to move gradually away, maintaining trembling eye contact with the wolf. Those glowing orbs stared through to my frantic core, sensing my terror. In my ears, my own shuddering breaths and the thunder of my heartbeat drowned out all other sounds. The pungent scent of damp fur flooded my senses.

When the wolf bunched its haunches, preparing to strike, my field of vision was constricted as though I were looking through a long tunnel. Operating solely on adrenaline now, I tried, in vain, to dodge left as the creature lunged. But its reflexes were lightning-quick. I gasped at the searing pain as its claws shredded through the tender skin of my upper arm; the force knocking me off balance.

Dizziness overwhelmed me, a sickening sensation that threatened to plunge me into darkness as hot blood seeped through my torn sleeve. The beast's claws had left deep, agonizing wounds, and pain radiated from them in waves. I blinked, fighting against the blur of agony and disorientation. Vulnerable and expecting the wolf's lethal blow, a raw, desperate energy surged within me.

In that moment of sheer instinct, a power I hadn't known I possessed awakened. It started as a spark deep within, building with an intensity that felt as though it could either save or consume me. This energy coalesced in my core, rushing through my veins like wildfire, seeking an escape. As it reached my trembling hand, the sensation was both terrifying and exhilarating, a testament to a force I was only beginning to understand.

Then, with a brilliance that pierced the night, golden light burst forth from my palm. It was as if the sun had been captured within my skin, blazing outwards in a radiant beam that momentarily stunned the wolf shifter. My forearm, marked by the triskele tattoo, radiated with a white-hot glow, a beacon in the shadowed forest. Memories of Briar's words echoed in my mind, a reminder of the mystical gifts the inn bestowed upon its caretaker. In that moment, the power within me had found its purpose, casting a light strong enough to challenge the darkness before me.

Could it be that my intense fear and pressing need had awakened some dormant magic tied to my new role as mediator? Ryder's mantle had passed to me more than just the inn, but also the supernatural powers linked to it. This eruption of fiery magic was the first sign that forces beyond my comprehension had awakened within me. For better or worse, my life would never be the same.

My fleeting moment of relief evaporated, giving way once more to a suffocating sense of dread. The shifter's brief disorientation vanished, replaced by a bloodlust so intense it erased any semblance of reason. As it prepared to launch itself at me once more, I braced myself, fearing these thunderous heartbeats might herald my end.

The night was charged with palpable tension, a silent witness to the impending clash. Then, as if summoned by the very essence of the night itself, a colossal black wolf with white-tipped ears burst from the shadows, hurling itself at my assailant. The ensuing battle was a spectacle of primal ferocity and raw power. The two wolves clashed with a violence that was both horrifying and mesmerizing. Their forms intertwined in a chaotic dance of snarling jaws, flashing teeth, and razor-sharp claws, each strike and parry a testament to their wild nature. The earth beneath them shuddered, absorbing the impact of their fierce duel, while their roars reverberated through the forest, shattering the silence.

The black wolf, its fur as dark as the void from which it had emerged, seemed to dominate the skirmish. However, in a desperate bid for survival, the rogue shifter found an opening. With a swift, agile maneuver that spoke of its wild desperation, it slipped from the grasp of its darker counterpart. The rogue wolf, seizing this momentary advantage, darted into the night, its retreat a blur of shadow and speed. The black wolf halted at the edge of the clearing, its menacing growls fading into the night as it watched the rogue disappear, leaving an uneasy peace in the wake of the chaos.

The black wolf with the white-tipped ears turned its gaze to me, and in its eyes, I recognized a familiar intensity. It was Drake. He shifted back to his human form, rushing to my side, his face etched with concern.

"Are you alright?" he asked, his voice filled with urgency as he examined the gash on my arm. "I would have followed him, but I could smell your blood."

I tried to find my voice, but all I could focus on was the fact that he was fully clothed. "How... How are you dressed after just shifting?"

A hint of amusement danced in his eyes as he applied pressure to my wound, and the corner of his mouth lifted in a half-smile. "Would you have preferred me naked?"

I felt my cheeks warm up. "That's not what I meant. It's just... your wolf's form is so massive."

His gaze softened. "I'm sure there are more important questions to consider right now than shifter mysteries," he murmured.

Swallowing hard, I tried to regain my composure. "Like why that wolf was after me?"

He sighed, running a hand through his hair, making it even more tousled. "There are those who don't want you to uncover the truth about Ryder. They'll go to great lengths to ensure you remain in the dark."

The gravity of his words pulled me back to the present danger, but the lingering electricity between us was undeniable. "Did you recognize him?"

He shook his head. "No, I didn't recognize his scent, and with the dirt and ash, I couldn't recognize his markings, either. You might think of this as a small community, but there are enough wolves that come in and out of this town to keep it confusing. I think the only one who knew all of us was Ryder."

The night's chill seemed to seep into my bones as I stood there, still shaking from the wolf's vicious attack. Drake's steady presence was comforting yet also confusing, given our brief and volatile history. The same formidable shifter who had once threatened me had now risked himself to save my life without hesitation.

Feelings of shock and vulnerability threatened to overwhelm me. The attack had dredged up traumatic memories I thought I'd left safely behind in Denver. I squeezed my eyes shut, willing my racing heart to slow.

Drake's kind touch on my shoulders grounded me. "Just breathe, Lydia. You're safe with me now." His soft eyes shimmered with genuine concern.

I focused on inhaling slowly, the sweet mountain air finally cutting through the panic fogging my mind. As my trembling gradually subsided, I lifted my gaze to meet Drake's. In those gray depths, I now saw only sincerity and care reflected back at me.

"Thank you for saving me," I managed hoarsely. "I don't understand why you did it, but I'm grateful."

Drake shook his head, his brow furrowed. "I haven't made this easy on you. But regardless of our disagreements, I'd never stand by and let you get hurt." He paused, considering his words. "Maybe it's time we put the past to rest and try to move forward."

I bit my lip, hesitating. Could I trust this unpredictable man? Yet when I searched my feelings, I realized that, despite our rocky history, some deeper connection had taken root between us.

"I think that's a good idea," I said finally. "A fresh start."

Drake gently helped me to my feet, his strong arm supporting me as we made our way back to the inn. The adrenaline from the attack was fading, and I could feel the pain from my wounds intensifying with each step.

As we reached the porch, Drake eased me down onto a bench. "Let me take a look at that arm," he said, his voice filled with concern. He carefully rolled up my sleeve, revealing the deep gashes left by the wolf's claws. The sight of the wounds made my stomach churn, and I had to look away.

"We need to stop the bleeding," Drake said, his tone urgent. He quickly tore a strip of fabric from his shirt and wrapped it tightly around my arm, applying pressure to the wounds. "This will have to do for now, but we need to get you inside and properly clean and bandage these cuts."

I nodded, gritting my teeth against the pain as Drake helped me to my feet once more. We made our way into the inn, the warmth of the fireplace a welcome respite from the chilly night air.

Drake guided me to the plush couch, easing me down gently. "Stay here," he instructed. "I'll be right back with the first aid kit."

As I sat there, the reality of what had just happened began to sink in. The trauma of nearly being torn apart by teeth and claws reopened old wounds I thought had already started to heal. I could almost feel the ghostly echoes of blows landing on my body and hear chilling laughter ringing in my ears.

Would the demons of my past ever stop pursuing me?

Drake returned quickly, a well-stocked first aid kit in hand. He sat down beside me, the weight of his presence steadying me as I spiraled into dark memories. Ever so slowly, my trembling breaths evened out. The familiar surroundings of the inn came back into focus, reminding me I was safe now.

I turned to Drake, conflicting emotions welling up inside me. "You didn't have to save me, but you did," I breathed. "I don't know how to repay that debt."

Drake shook his head firmly. "You owe me nothing. You're the innkeeper now. You serve the town and clans, and we're all indebted to you for it." He took another look at the deep scratches on my arm.

As he carefully began cleaning my arm, his touch was surprisingly gentle, contrasting with the brusque exterior he often displayed. I studied his face, noting the intensity in his gaze—the very feature I'd recognized from his wolf form.

My curiosity grew as he tended to my wounds. "How did you know where the first aid gear was?"

He paused for a moment before replying with a sly smile.

"Let's just say the occasional slash and fang isn't unusual in this shifter town," he said wryly. "We sometimes have to work out our issues with our claws and fists."

I couldn't help but smile at his joke, despite the gravity of the situation we were still in. I felt myself being drawn closer to Drake, almost as if his presence was pulling me in like the tide. But I shook off my daze and leaned back from him, deciding now wasn't the time for such thoughts.

I thought back to the woman who had first arrived in Crescent Crossing just a short week ago—adrift, haunted by trauma, devoid of any spark or purpose. She bore little resemblance to the woman I felt myself becoming in this place—compassionate, quick-thinking, and empowered.

Somehow, the unexpected challenge of investigating Ryder's murder and protecting this haven had reignited a sense of vitality and meaning when I'd needed it most. At a midlife crossroads back in Denver, I'd lost my way. But here, I'd found my calling.

Once, I would have quailed at the thought of mediating dangerous disputes or confronting those who threatened this community. But cradled within the sheltering mountains and buoyed by steadfast allies, I'd tapped into wells of courage and resilience I'd never known existed.

This ordeal had dredged up traumatic memories from my past, yet instead of consuming me, the pain had honed my empathy and strengthened my spirit. Out of the ashes, the true Lydia had emerged—one bold enough to face evil head-on, yet wise enough to do so with compassion.

As Drake dabbed at my skin with a cotton swab soaked in antiseptic, he remarked, "That light from your hand during the fight—it seems you've got some shifter magic in you after all." I shook my head, still in disbelief, but he continued in a gentle tone. "The magic chooses its vessel. Fate must have seen something special in you that night to select you as our innkeeper." Meeting my gaze, his eyes were filled with understanding and empathy. "You don't have to face this journey alone, Lydia."

When he finished wrapping up my wounds with bandages, Drake smiled at me. "I think you'll live," he said softly, his voice filled with kindness. "But if you ever need more protection from shifters like the one tonight, don't hesitate to call on me."

I had no idea what to make of this man who could be so surly one moment yet so gentle the next. But I couldn't deny that I felt oddly safe in his presence.

"Thank you," I whispered gratefully.

For a moment, we sat in pensive silence, the crackling fireplace the only sound. I sensed Drake's piercing gaze resting heavily on me. As I looked into his eyes, I saw a churning ocean of emotions swirling within. It made me stop and think.

"What brought you to the inn just in time to save me from that attack?" I asked at last, my voice still shaky from the night's harrowing events.

Drake sighed heavily, raking a hand through his dark, tousled hair. "I suspect the same reason you were out in the moonlight. I was looking for clues. Look, I know I've given you every reason to doubt me, but believe me, I'd never intentionally wish you harm, Lydia. Questioning your right to be here doesn't mean I'd stand by and watch you be torn apart."

His candid words took me by surprise. Before I could stop myself, I found myself opening up to him about my troubled past—how the traumas I'd suffered there had driven me from Denver, seeking solace, only to stumble into deeper troubles plaguing this supposedly tranquil town.

As I shared memories of the vicious cruelty I had endured, Drake listened with rapt focus, his steely gaze never straying from my face. In those fierce gray eyes, I glimpsed a growing flicker of empathy piercing through his usual gruff demeanor.

When at last I fell silent, Drake drew a deep, bracing breath, as if steeling himself to unburden a long-hidden truth. "I know all too well how pain can haunt you. I lost my mate, my Thalia, years ago because of tragic circumstances beyond my control." His voice grew thick with anguish. "It changed me and turned my heart to stone. My bitterness and mistrust of outsiders like yourself was born of that grief. But I see now that directing my anger at you was unfair. And for that, you have my solemn apology."

Drake's heartfelt confession stunned me. The formidable shifter I had judged as a potential enemy now sat before me, vulnerable and remorseful. At that instant, the frigid barriers separating us started to melt away, giving way to the initial delicate threads of comprehension, compassion, and reliance that united us.

I bit my lip, hesitating, before voicing my deepest fear. "After what happened in Denver, I don't know if I'm strong enough to face the threats lurking here too." My voice trembled with shame at this admission.

Drake grasped my hand, his rough palm pressing against my own. "You're far stronger than you know. And you won't have to find that strength alone." His unwavering faith kindled my flickering courage once more.

We sat in silence then, hands loosely entwined, drawing solace from one another. A bridge between us had been forged from trauma's ashes. The warmth of the fire seemed to amplify the weight of our shared confessions, drawing us into a cocoon of intimacy. As the moment hung in the air between us, the space between us on the couch seemed to shrink.

There was an undeniable tension, a magnetic pull, that neither of us seemed willing to acknowledge fully. Yet this primal attraction was both unexpected and inconvenient. Instead of acting on it, we both seemed to retreat, burying our feelings beneath layers of mistrust and past pain.

When our eyes met, an unspoken connection seemed to pass between us. I drew in a sharp breath, my pulse quickening. But the gravity of recent events swiftly doused the flicker of attraction, leaving us both looking away awkwardly.

Just then, the sound of rapid footsteps coming down the stairs broke our connection, and we reflexively pulled away from each other. Hamish burst onto the scene, sniffing the air and quickly assessing the situation. "I smelled blood and magic," he gruffly explained, his eyes darting between us. "It seems I missed something."

I recounted the wolf's attack and the unexpected surge of magic from my hand. Hamish listened with a grim expression, then turned to Drake. "I'm glad you were here when this happened. Is this one of the inn's powers Lydia can learn to harness?"

Drake nodded, his gaze unwavering. "I saw Ryder do it before."

"How do we know we can trust you?" Hamish asked Drake. "Last I checked, you were a murder suspect."

"If he'd wanted me dead, he wouldn't have saved me from that rogue wolf," I said. "I'm pretty sure we can trust him." Feeling overwhelmed, I sank back onto the plush couch and put my head in my hands. "There's something else," I said finally, my voice quavering. "I had this vivid dream tonight that showed me clues about what really happened to Ryder."

Drake's eyes filled with concern as he sat down beside me. "Tell us everything," he urged, his gravelly voice gentle.

After haltingly recounting every fragment of the dream I could recall, I sank back against the plush cushions.

Drake grasped my hand bracingly. "We'll figure this out, Lydia. But for now, you should rest."

I started to protest, but Hamish cut in. "Drake's right. We can pick this up in the morning. I'll gather Saige and Briar first thing tomorrow so we can all examine your vision thoroughly."

Despite my burning urgency to decipher the clues, I could not deny the bone-deep exhaustion seeping through every fiber of my being. I nodded wearily and let Hamish guide me upstairs, his sturdy presence steadying me. He left me to sleep after checking my room and finding it free from threats.

Yet sleep evaded me, my mind racing to analyze each haunting detail. I tossed and turned restlessly beneath the silken sheets until the first pale rays of dawn crept across my room. Rising hastily, I knew that further rest would have to wait. The mysteries lurking within the dream's shadows called to me.

I hurried downstairs to find Hamish, Saige, and Briar already gathered around the table in my office expectantly. Freshly brewed coffee steamed in mugs before them. Drake stood leaning against the stone fireplace, arms crossed, brow furrowed in thought.

I joined them at the table, my nerves thrumming with anticipation. "Let's reexamine the vision," I began without preamble. "The raven imagery seemed significant. Could it relate to local lore?"

"Possibly," Saige replied. "Ravens have long been seen as harbingers in these parts."

After haltingly recounting every fragment of the dream I could recall, I leaped up, rushing to grab pencil and paper from my desk.

"I need to draw the specific raven symbol I saw—the one that then appeared in my room," I announced.

Ignoring Saige's skeptical frown, I carefully sketched the raven form from my memory—wings outstretched in flight, eyes glinting knowingly.

When finished, I presented the rendering to my companions. "Does this symbol carry any special weight in regional history?"

Hamish scratched his stubbled chin. "It does look familiar..."

"I recall it being associated with periods of instability in the past," Saige offered reluctantly. "But nothing specific."

I sat back, considering thoughtfully. Rediscovering this enigmatic sign was a promising step.

"Briar, can you check the town archives for any old texts referencing raven symbols?"

Briar nodded briskly, her curiosity clearly piqued. "Of course. I'll check after the breakfast rush. It's a weekday, so Barnell can handle the lighter lunch crowd."

"I'll join you," suggested Saige.

The rest of us focused our attention on the books in Ryder's office. By joining forces, we hoped to illuminate the raven's secrets and restore stability. This was our purpose, and we would see it done. I repeated those resolute words like a mantra in my mind. But even as we all voiced our staunch determination, an icy doubt needled at my spine.

The clues hinted at an organized faction operating in the shadows, cunning enough to outwit even Ryder. I realized we might be heading into dangerous territory against an unseen enemy. Yet standing idle while tensions escalated was unacceptable.

CHAPTER 9

After our lunch break, Barnell again entertained me with hilarious anecdotes of his recent adventures. Though still shaken from the wolf attack and subsequent magical outburst the previous night, I genuinely chuckled as Barnell enthusiastically recounted his latest baking mishap.

"So I'm helping out old Willem in the shop yesterday, right, making a big batch of maple candies," Barnell began, his freckled face lighting up eagerly. "I grab the little jar of what I think is sugar, dump a huge scoop into the mix, then keep on stirring away, oblivious as can be."

He paused for dramatic effect, leaning in conspiratorially. "Then Willem wanders over, scoops one of the cooled candies out of the tray and pops it straight into his mouth without even looking first. And suddenly..." Barnell trailed off, waving his fork emphatically as his eyes went wide.

"His big bushy mustache stood straight on end, I tell ya! His eyes just about popped outta his head from the saltiness," Barnell exclaimed, barely able to get the words out between fits of laughter.

"The look on his face was truly something to behold! I swear that mustache of his looked like it might take flight right off his lip!" He shook his head, his shoulders still shaking with mirth at the memory.

His youthful enthusiasm and dramatic retelling of events was infectious, and I couldn't help laughing along. The gloom of recent troubling events temporarily lifted by his breezy joy. Barnell just had a knack for finding humor and adventure in the everyday mundane.

As he launched into another colorful yarn involving a mishap with the laundry that turned most of the inn's linens pink, I noticed his shirt had what looked like a hastily mended tear along the sleeve.

"Barnell, what happened to your sleeve?" I asked. "It looks like you snagged it on a branch or something."

The boy's freckled face reddened slightly, and he dropped his gaze. "Oh, that's nothing! Just got a little carried away exploring the other day." He paused, as if considering something. "Actually, while I was hiking up near Raven's Roost, I noticed the trail showed signs of a lot of use lately. It's for sure seen more traffic than just the occasional hiker."

I lifted a brow, intrigued by this observation. I knew from the maps in Ryder's office that Raven's Roost was an isolated cliff area northeast of town where few ventured. Could this location be where the nighttime groups of wolves were assembling? "Interesting. I may need to check out this trail myself soon."

Barnell nodded eagerly, always excited to play the role of a helpful guide. "I'd be happy to show you the way! We could pack an afternoon snack and make a real adventure of it."

I smiled at his enthusiasm, touched by his offer. "That sounds perfect."

Barnell's innocent observation had presented a promising new lead to investigate. Perhaps the once-quiet cliff area could shed light on who had gathered in my dream and what their connection might be to the disturbing events plaguing Crescent Crossing.

As I sat sipping my afternoon tea, I found my thoughts drifting back to the traumatic events in Denver that had driven me to seek refuge in Crescent Crossing. Though I tried to avoid dwelling on those painful memories, echoes of the cruelty I had endured still haunted me.

I thought back to how I had willingly put myself at risk in order to help Becka uncover the secrets of the fae intrigue in the city. My desire to protect her and help her companions had made me a target for those who wished to control her.

In the end, I had narrowly escaped with my life, while others had not been so fortunate. The damage inflicted upon me had run deeper than the physical wounds and forced my flight from my home and the life I'd built.

Now here I was again, caught up in supernatural mysteries and putting myself in harm's way in my role as innkeeper and mediator. If I kept up with my mission to mediate between three clashing enclaves, there was a chance I'd face more attacks like the one from last night. It seemed danger and intrigue followed me, no matter how far I traveled to outrun it.

Part of me wondered if it was too late to walk away, let someone else take up the mantle and handle the brewing unrest between the enclaves. Just focus on healing and leave these troubles firmly behind me.

Yet, even as that thought crossed my mind, I knew in my heart that it was futile. Like it or not, fate had entwined my destiny with that of the Howl Away Inn and Crescent Crossing.

No, I had been given this unexpected chance to start over and use my pain and experiences to help others. I could not turn my back on that purpose, however daunting the road ahead appeared. Just as I'd steeled my resolve, the inn's front door swung open, accompanied by a burst of cool mountain air. None other than the roguishly charming Kai sauntered in, raking a hand through his artfully tousled blond hair.

"Ah, Lydia, I was hoping to find you here," he remarked breezily, as if he hadn't vanished without a trace for several days after being questioned about Ryder's murder.

I crossed my arms, irritation flaring. "And just where have you been, Kai? Your sudden disappearance seemed poorly timed, given the circumstances."

Kai waved a hand dismissively. "No need to get worked up. I simply took an impromptu camping trip up in the high peaks to clear my head after that dreadful business with Ryder. You know how a run under the moonlight with the wind in your fur can make everything seem better."

His guileless explanation rang hollow. I would never run as a wolf under the moon and stars or know what it might feel like to have fur. I didn't miss the subtle dig at my fae heritage and how I wasn't, and would never be, a shifter. I studied him intently, searching for any revealing reaction.

"Hmm, interesting that you took a little vacation right when tensions in town are nearing a boiling point," I replied evenly. "One could see how that might be misconstrued."

Kai pursed his lips, looking vaguely annoyed at my persistence. "I can see you're determined to doubt my intentions. But I've told you all I know about what happened that awful night already." He paused, regarding me with a pitying look. "Are you getting enough sleep? You look exhausted. This mediator business seems overwhelming for you. If you find it's becoming too much, you could always step aside and let someone better qualified take over." He flashed his most charming grin. "Why, I'd even volunteer myself if you wished to return home to the big city."

I bristled at his condescending words. "If I didn't know better, Kai, I'd think you were trying to undermine me," I bit back icily.

Kai held up his hands in a pacifying gesture, but his eyes glinted slyly. "Just trying to help, that's all. But suit yourself—clearly you have everything under control."

With an exaggerated bow, he sauntered right back out the door, leaving me fuming in his wake. Whatever Kai was hiding, I was more determined than ever to uncover the truth. I would not cave to his manipulations or be driven off. Not when so much depended on me now.

Still irritated after my unsettling encounter with Kai, I stepped into the entryway of the inn, where I knew they kept an assortment of local hiking maps for guests to use. I flipped through them until I found one showing the trails around Raven's Roost Peak that Barnell had mentioned after lunch. Tracing my finger along the looped route to the secluded cliff area, I again wondered what I might find there.

I was folding up the map to tuck into my bag when heavy footsteps entered the lobby. I turned to see Drake approaching, his gray eyes scanning the room before settling on me.

"Saw your buddy Kai leaving," Drake remarked without

preamble, jerking his chin toward the door. "Didn't seem too happy breezing past me outside."

I crossed my arms defensively. "Yes, well, Kai was just suggesting—again—that I'm in over my head and should let someone else take over around here."

Drake nodded thoughtfully, scratching his stubbled jaw. "Can't blame him for being rattled with a fae as our mediator. Big change for folks. Takes time to adjust."

I bristled slightly. "So I should just step aside and let tensions boil over?"

"Easy now," Drake said placatingly. "Just saying you don't have the experience here Kai does. Or some others."

His words felt like wavering faith after our recent connection. "Didn't you promise to help me?" I asked.

Drake sighed wearily. "I did. But after the attack..." His eyes flashed with concern. "You're a bigger target if you stay now."

I looked away, a pang of hurt piercing me at his change of heart. Perhaps I'd imagined the spark of something deeper growing between us. Clearly, Drake agreed with Kai that I was out of my depth. Their lack of faith, especially Drake's, cut deeply and filled me with doubts all over again.

After my discouraging exchange with Drake, I decided some fresh air would clear my head. I walked out the door and headed into the lively streets of Crescent Crossing, basking in the warm sunlight of the sunny morning.

As I strolled down the road, centered only on the crunch of gravel beneath my boots, a familiar gravelly voice called my name. I turned to see Drake approaching, his hands tucked casually in his pockets.

"Didn't mean to upset you," Drake said, falling into step beside me. "Just speaking without thinking."

I hesitated, warring with anger and hurt. Yet the sincerity in his eyes gave me pause. "It's fine," I replied tensely.

We walked on in uneasy silence before Drake spoke again, his tone gentler. "I know fate chose you to lead for a reason. And I've seen how hard you're trying. I didn't mean to imply otherwise."

I didn't want to answer that directly, and I was still irritated after Kai's suspicious visit, so I took the opportunity to redirect the conversation. "I wonder where Kai really disappeared to on those days he vanished," I mused aloud. "His camping story is questionable."

"Kai does construction around here sometimes," Drake offered with a shrug. "I'd asked around and heard he was helping shore up a washed-out road for the Flat Tops."

I paused, bothered because Drake seemed so quick to provide Kai with an alibi. "Well, I wish he had just said that rather than conjuring up some story of running in the moonlight," I replied.

"Running in the moonlight is special," Drake started, but when he saw my expression, he held up his hands. "Sorry. Kai loves playing the mystery man. Could be all there is to it."

I exhaled heavily, trying to temper my frustration.

Sensing the lingering tension, Drake changed tacks. "Look, I just meant fate clearly brought you here for a reason. But there is no shame in walking away if it gets to be too much."

I crossed my arms. "Walk away and put who in charge instead? You?"

Drake's expression remained neutral, but I saw a glint of

interest in the notion. "I know the area and people pretty well," he replied casually.

I bristled at the subtle implication that he was better qualified as the mediator, although, as a local and wolf shifter, he certainly would be. Drake likely hoped I would step aside, but I was determined to prove I could handle this.

"Hmph," I deflected diplomatically.

"About earlier, I wasn't implying anything," he began gruffly. "Just thinking aloud."

Unsure how to respond, I just nodded. But when he glanced my way, his eyes were unexpectedly vulnerable.

"Truth is, the thought of you getting hurt scares me," he admitted hoarsely. "I just want you to be cautious."

I drew a sharp breath as he reached out to brush loose hair from my face. Our eyes locked, and the world receded. But doubt made me pull back abruptly.

Regret flashed across Drake's face. "Guess I'm not thinking straight today," he muttered, raking a hand through his hair. "You know where to find me if you need me."

Before I could respond, he was walking away stiffly. I watched him go, heart and head at war. Our paths kept converging, yet past hurts erected barriers. For now, I could only move ahead cautiously, one step at a time.

After my tense conversation with Drake, I continued strolling through the streets of Crescent Crossing to clear my head. The cool mountain air helped settle my rattled nerves as I wandered aimlessly for a time, lost in brooding thoughts.

I was winding my way along the rustic shops when hurried footsteps approached from behind. I turned to see Saige catching up with me, her face creased with concern.

"Lydia! There you are," she began without preamble.

"What are you doing out here alone? It's not safe, especially with the full moon nearing."

I sighed, raking a hand through my windswept hair. "I just needed some space to think things through, and I didn't figure I was in any danger during the day on a public street."

Saige fell into step beside me, her expression frank. "I know tensions are high, but you must keep a level head. Hamish was right that you need to have someone with you."

"Easier said than done to keep myself level lately," I admitted ruefully. "Drake was walking with me, but he runs so hot and cold. One minute I feel we're communicating fine, the next he's undermining me."

Saige thoughtfully hummed as we ambled along the quaint cobblestone street, with an old bakery to our left and a flower shop to our right. "He is mercurial. But remember, his volatility likely stems from past pain."

I chewed my lip. "I suppose you're right. But his wavering faith cuts deeply when I'm already doubting myself."

"Understandable," Saige replied. "But you cannot let others shake your resolve. This is your destiny now, Lydia. Only you can decide your path."

Her blunt words resonated within me, rekindling my inner spark. She was right—I controlled my fate here. Drake's doubts were his burden to carry, not mine.

Up ahead, the graffiti wall's eerie raven silhouette appeared, its eyes seeming to follow us as we drew closer. I felt a shiver of apprehension, my dream coming back in flashes.

Noticing my sudden tension, Saige gripped my arm bracingly. "Your instincts are leading you. Don't ignore them, even if you don't understand yet. When the time comes, you'll know how to act."

I met her steady green gaze, drawing courage from her faith. Dark dreams and whispered warnings would not make me falter or flee.

As we wandered the town, I stopped in some shops and chatted with locals, hoping to better understand their perspectives and continue building connections.

But the townspeople regarded me with wariness, their responses clipped and guarded. At The Sugared Spruce bakery, whispers ceased abruptly when I entered, replaced by taut silence. The shopkeeper avoided my gaze, quickly handing me my scone order with a terse, "Have a nice day."

At the general store, Willem's Wares, I found Willem restocking the shelves. "Lydia! Good to see you again," he greeted me warmly.

Saige trailed silently beside me down the aisles as I gathered supplies.

"How's business been?" I asked, picking up a basket.

"Oh, fine, fine," Willem replied airily as he arranged cans on a shelf. "Steady as she goes."

I glanced around as I picked up a bar of honeysuckle-scented soap from the shelf. The store was busier than on my last visit. I noticed a few patrons whispering furtively in the corners, eyeing Saige and I with thinly veiled suspicion.

"This is my friend Saige, visiting from out of town," I introduced.

"A pleasure, miss," Willem tipped his cap. He studied Saige curiously. "Which enclave do you hail from, if you don't mind me asking?"

"The northern Sawatch pack," Saige answered.

"I see, I see. Don't see many Sawatch folk through these parts," Willem said.

"It's my first time passing this way," Saige added.

I continued browsing the shelves, selecting a few essential items I needed. A nice wooden-handled brush, some candles, and a jar of locally sourced honey found their way into my basket. Saige picked up a few snacks, her keen eyes taking in the store's wares.

"And how is your family doing?" I continued, keeping my tone light despite the tense atmosphere.

"Quite well, thank you. My son came through town yesterday with his pups," Willem said, smiling fondly. "My wife was beside herself with joy. Getting so big now, those little rascals. Handful for their poor parents, though."

I chuckled along with Willem, but my laugh sounded strained and hollow even to my ears. The other customers had fallen into loaded silence, watching our exchange.

An awkward silence fell. Sensing the tension, Willem quickly finished bagging my items with a fleeting smile. "Well, nice chatting, ladies. You both take care now."

I could tell Willem felt just as uncomfortable with the way the patrons were scrutinizing us. His demeanor was still friendly, but more reserved than our last encounter. I got the sense he had more to say out of earshot of the cliquish townspeople. Still, his affable welcome was a lone bright spot during my disheartening efforts to connect around town.

My continued efforts to diplomatically engage were met only with cool indifference and suspicion, no matter how I softened my approach. After the third shopkeeper practically shoved me out the door, I finally admitted defeat.

Deciding to return to the inn, dejection consumed my

entire being. I had hoped to earn the town's trust as their new mediator. But their persistent rejection left me questioning if I could ever belong here. Perhaps I was foolish to believe an outsider could ever gain acceptance in this insular community, especially with my fae heritage.

The townspeople's indifference compounded the lingering self-doubts seeded by Drake's lack of faith in me. I worried if even those closest to me secretly wished I would just walk away, sparing them the burden of my stumbling leadership attempts.

But giving in to despair served no one. I had to believe that with time and perseverance, the town would come to accept me. And I must find the wisdom and courage within myself to rise to this duty, regardless of others' lack of confidence.

After the disheartening failed attempts at connecting around town, I meandered through the rustic streets, deep in thought, with Saige walking silently at my side. I was so lost in brooding that I nearly collided with someone rounding a corner. I looked up to see Harper regarding me sternly, arms crossed.

"Just the woman I hoped to find," she remarked without preamble. "We need to talk."

I tensed, steeling myself for yet another confrontation about my capability to mediate disputes as an outsider. "What can I do for you, Harper?"

She tilted her head, considering me. "Walk with me. You and your... guard?"

I glanced at Saige, who had been supporting me with her silent presence. "Yes, Saige is here with me."

Harper arched a brow, her eyes glancing at the bandage on my arm. "What happened to your arm?"

If Harper was in league with my attacker last night, then she would well know what had happened, but I didn't have any evidence that she was. Perhaps she was asking to throw off suspicion? Or perhaps she asked because she was a normal person who cared about the wellbeing of others as a matter of course. I didn't know her well enough to tell.

"Just a scrape," I replied.

Harper shook her head. "You say it's just a scrape, but now you have this one by your side." She looked at Saige. "Haven't I heard you worked security for the fae?"

Saige gave a curt nod. "I did."

"House Rowan, right?"

Saige gave another nod.

"At least you're used to the role, then," Harper added before turning back to me. "I admire your determination to make this work, despite the complications." Harper's eyes flashed knowingly. "But perseverance alone won't mend the deep rifts between our kind. This requires finesse and discretion."

I bristled at the subtle criticism. "If you have guidance to offer, I'm listening. If it's just more criticism, you can make an appointment for some time next year."

Harper's stern expression softened almost imperceptibly. "You mistake my intent. I meant only to say that change comes slowly in these parts. Pushing too hard or too fast could backfire." She arched a brow. "But perhaps your outsider status gives you clarity we lack."

I absorbed her pragmatic words as we continued down the street. She wasn't wrong in her blunt assessment.

When I remained silent, Harper continued with uncharacteristic hesitance, "I know the Bittersweets have seemed wary of your appointment. But fear drives prejudice. What's needed is a bold gesture of trust from their new mediator."

Harper's enigmatic gaze held my attention, as I was intrigued by the unique perspective it provided into the mindset of their secluded clan. "What sort of gesture did you have in mind?"

"Come this way," Harper replied. "This is a lovely trail."

She led us along a winding path into a tranquil park. A small lake glittered ahead, surrounded by whispering aspens. We ambled along the shoreline as Harper explained.

"You could establish a mediator's council with representatives from each enclave," she suggested. "I won't suggest potential representatives from the other enclaves but appointing me as your first advisor would signal good faith to the Bittersweets."

The idea of a mediator's council was brilliant, and it instantly deepened my respect for Harper. Adding Harper to the council could help balance the innate distrust between enclaves. And it showed my willingness to collaborate, but making Harper the first member could also show a preference for Bittersweet. But that might be worth it if it won Harper over too.

"It's a bold idea, and I think it's just what I need," I mused aloud. "Bringing your experience into a formal advisory role feels right."

Harper nodded, a hint of a smile touching her lips. "Now you're thinking like a mediator. With time and discretion, fences can be mended."

I returned her smile, a flicker of optimism stirring

within me. This council could be the key to earning the Bittersweets' trust. And prove my desire to unite, not divide.

"So, will you be on my advisory council?" I asked Harper.

She inclined her head. "I accept your invitation."

"Good. Can you meet later today, say at seven p.m., at the inn?"

"I'll be there."

After our lakeside discussion, Harper excused herself. Saige and I lingered by the shimmering water a while longer, both lost in contemplative silence.

My mind turned to who else I might appoint to the council Harper had proposed. I needed advisors who could provide wise counsel while representing their enclave's interests fairly.

"Saige, who do you think would make a good addition from the Elk clan?" I asked. "And don't say Kai."

Saige pondered the question. "If she's willing, Nalani has a balanced perspective. The pack respects her greatly because she is known for her integrity."

I nodded thoughtfully. Nalani's steady wisdom could help temper disputes and clashing personalities.

"For the Flat Tops, maybe their healer, Aja?" Saige suggested. "She's level-headed and cares deeply about the welfare of all shifters, regardless of their lineage."

"Excellent choices," I agreed. I hesitated before adding, "Drake could give the Flat Tops too loud a voice."

Saige pressed her lips together but didn't argue. We both knew Drake's volatile temperament posed risks. But his presence might ease tensions.

Sensing my ambivalence, Saige said gently, "It seems you

two are developing a complicated dynamic, but don't ignore what your heart says just because it's difficult."

I smiled wryly. "You always give blunt, but accurate, advice." Sobering, I added, "I just can't afford to repeat past mistakes when so much is at stake."

Saige nodded, her green eyes sympathetic. "Be cautious, but don't let fear rob you of new happiness either. You've endured enough loneliness."

I blinked back sudden tears at her understanding. With Saige's counsel, perhaps I could follow my heart without losing myself.

As the afternoon sun beat down on the serene lake, I felt a sense of hope for my future. The beauty of the scene was breathtaking, and I felt a sense of peace as I breathed in the crisp mountain air. The sun glinted off the water's surface, and I spotted shimmering trout jumping in the lake. A bald eagle soared above a snowcapped mountain peak, its wings sweeping majestically as it surveyed the valley below. The trees rustled with a gentle breeze, and the meadow grass swayed in unison. In the distance, a herd of elk grazed peacefully on the mountainside.

The creatures here were finding joy in this moment, and it made me think perhaps I could too. I allowed myself to feel a glimmer of hope for what might come next, knowing that no matter how much my life changed, I'd always have these moments to carry with me.

CHAPTER 10

As Saige and I made our way back to the Howl Away Inn after our brief respite at the park, a flicker of movement near the inn's side entrance caught my eye. I quickly grabbed Saige's arm, pulling her into the shadow of a strand of aspen trees before the figure emerging could spot us.

Peering between the clustered trunks, I stifled a gasp as I recognized the man furtively slipping out the side door—none other than Malachi Sterling. My pulse quickened as I noticed he clutched a medium-sized box close to his side, his hooded gaze darting around before he slunk off toward the woods bordering the inn's grounds.

"What business could he possibly have here?" I whispered to Saige. Her sharp green eyes narrowed as we watched Malachi disappear into the tree line, his hasty exit through the side door clearly suspicious to her as well.

"Whatever it is, he clearly didn't want to be seen," Saige murmured back. "But we need answers." She made to follow, but I grasped her shoulder, holding her back.

"Not yet," I cautioned, thinking fast. "I know who might know more."

I quickly led Saige inside to the front desk, where Briar was wiping down the counter. At my greeting, she glanced up, her eyes widening when she noticed my breathless state.

"What's happened?" she asked in alarm. "You look as if you've seen a ghost!"

"Not quite, but close," I managed wryly before asking in a low voice, "Does Malachi Sterling often have packages delivered here to the inn?"

Briar's brow creased in surprise at the question. "Yes, occasionally. He just picked up one, actually, which is a little weird since he picked up one the other day too. We receive mail for travelers just passing through town who may need to pick up a letter or small parcel during their stay. Why do you ask?"

I quickly explained spotting Malachi leaving the inn in a suspicious rush moments earlier, box in hand, before heading off into the forest.

Briar nodded thoughtfully. "He does come across as someone who prefers solitude, and he has a reputation for..." she lowered her voice to a barely audible whisper, "...always being busy, but it usually just entrails getting up into everyone else's business."

I shared a pointed look with Saige, my suspicions deepening. Whatever Malachi had collected from the inn, he clearly aimed to keep it secret. I was now certain the man knew far more than he let on about the strange happenings plaguing Crescent Crossing. I would have to be cautious in my interactions with him.

I retreated to my office at the inn, my mind racing. Saige

asked me to promise that I would bring Hamish along if I left the inn, and then she left to uncover Malachi's plans. His furtive behavior certainly seemed to confirm he was hiding something sinister beneath his innocuous facade. But what exactly? And to what end? Hopefully, Saige could find out.

I sank into the worn leather chair behind the heavy oak desk, gazing out the window overlooking the pine grove. The peacefully swaying boughs stood in stark contrast to the chaos churning within me.

Taking a deep breath, I reached for the telephone and dialed the number listed for the town healer. After two rings, a serene female voice answered.

"Crescent Crossing Clinic, this is Aja Larkspur speaking."

"Hello, Aja, my name is Lydia Ash. I'm the new owner of the Howl Away Inn. I apologize for the abrupt call, but I need to speak with you privately this evening around seven, if you have time. It's rather urgent."

"Of course, Lydia. I am always glad to help however I can. I will come to the inn as you request."

I exhaled in relief at her ready agreement. "Wonderful, thank you, Aja. I look forward to making your acquaintance."

After confirming the time, I bid her a pleasant afternoon and hung up the phone, feeling optimistic that the healer's wisdom could prove invaluable in the challenges ahead.

I dialed Nalani next. After two rings, her melodic voice answered.

"Greetings, this is Nalani."

"Hello, Nalani, it's Lydia Ash. I apologize for the unexpected call, but I need to meet with you privately this evening at seven. It's rather urgent."

"Of course, Lydia. The Silver Pine always answers the call of a friend in need. I will come to the inn as you request."

I exhaled in relief at her ready agreement and made a mental note to ask Briar what the Silver Pine business was about. There were so many shifter traditions and so little time to become an expert. "Thank you, Nalani. I look forward to our discussion."

I bid her a pleasant afternoon and hung up the phone.

I paused for a moment, considering. Harper, Aja, and Nalani had agreed to meet tonight. Now, if I could just convince them to commit to working with me, I knew I'd have the right team to tackle whatever mysteries presented themselves.

Drake and Kai, as the chosen representatives of both of their enclaves, likely would have been the more natural choices for me. I felt a pang of guilt at not involving either of them in my advisory circle. But I didn't trust Kai, and while Drake was certainly capable enough, his presence would complicate matters far more than necessary.

No doubt they would be slighted by my exclusion of them. But what else could I do? My priority was safety first, and with two powerful alpha males like Drake and Kai together in a room full of secrets, it was almost certain that something explosive would occur. It just wasn't worth the risk at this stage in our investigation.

Still, I couldn't help but feel slightly guilty about excluding them, even if it was for the greater good.

My gaze drifted again to the serene Ponderosa pine grove outside my window, where a pair of squirrels frolicked playfully up and down the tree trunks. If only restoring balance among the divided enclaves could be so simple. But I had to believe tonight's meeting could set us on the path toward reconciliation and trust. Aja and Nalani were influential voices. With care, we could find common ground. I had to cling to that fragile hope.

Glancing at the clock, I saw it was just past two. That left me several hours to dig deeper into the mysteries surrounding Ryder's demise before my guests arrived.

A few hours before my important evening meeting, I paid a visit to Crescent Crossing's records hall. I hoped to uncover historical clues about the raven symbol that had appeared in my dream vision. Hamish, seeing my determination, offered to accompany me.

The records hall was housed in an imposing stone building at the town's center. Inside, rows of meticulously organized filing cabinets held everything from property records to town council minutes from over a century ago.

Our entrance caught the attention of the elderly clerk, Walter, who looked up from his newspaper in surprise.

"You must be the new innkeeper," he said, peering at me over his spectacles, "and her companion. Whispers about you have been making their rounds."

I smiled slightly. "I'm sure my arrival was unexpected. I'm Lydia, and this is Hamish."

Walter chuckled. "What brings you both to our records hall?"

I described my interest in the town's raven iconography. Walter's brows rose in curiosity.

"The raven," he mused, "is central to our local legends. Let me show you our section on regional folk tales."

He led us to the shelves holding leather-bound volumes. Selecting an aged tome titled Myths and Legends of the

Crescent Range, he said, "This might shed light on the raven's importance."

I carried the book to a sunlit table. Donning archival gloves, I searched its pages. A chapter caught my attention. It discussed Ravenfeather, a legendary seer.

Ravenfeather was said to be a mystical figure the early shifter clans revered for her foresight. She provided guidance and her visions influenced tribal decisions. Her arrival ushered in a new era for local shifter culture, where the enclaves were governed more democratically while also maintaining the authority of the alphas.

I was engrossed by an illustration of Ravenfeather—an ethereal figure with raven wings, holding a staff inscribed with runes.

Hamish leaned in closer, peering over my shoulder at the book's illustration. "It's fascinating how Ravenfeather's emissaries were depicted as these ravens," he mused aloud.

I nodded in agreement. "Yes, and look here." I pointed to the text. "It says their appearances were considered omens. Either a sign of good fortune or a warning of danger and upheaval."

Hamish raised an eyebrow. "And the tribes interpreted the ravens' patterns and numbers to glean deeper meanings, it seems. It's remarkable how highly they regarded these symbols."

Though Ravenfeather's prominence waned as the tribes modernized, the symbolic reverence for ravens persisted.

My heart raced. The stylized image in my dream must have ties to this lore. But its message was elusive, especially when I tried to apply it to Ryder's murder.

I returned the book, thanking Walter. It was already

afternoon, and I still wanted time to prepare for the night's meeting. The hall had offered insights, yet the dream's message remained veiled.

Departing with Hamish, I felt the weight of looming uncertainties. Tonight's gathering with allies like Aja, Nalani, and Harper was crucial.

When we returned to the inn, Hamish walked me to my office.

"I'm going to take some time to go through Ryder's records," I told him. "Let's meet up about six with Saige and Briar and go through what we've found so far before the meeting."

"I'll leave you to it," he replied.

I closed the heavy wooden door and flipped the iron latch, ensuring I would not be disturbed. There was much yet to be done, and precious little time before dusk fell for me to research undisturbed.

I crossed the room to Ryder's secret compartment and checked to ensure the hidden cache of artifacts remained undisturbed. If Malachi had been searching for answers among Ryder's possessions earlier, the secrets here remained safely concealed. For now. Finding nothing amiss, I took another look at the tomes Ryder had hidden in this secret cubby. While sorting through the stash of artifacts Ryder had concealed, one book caught my eye—a dusty, aged tome with cracking leather binding titled Enchantments and Charms of the Innkeeper.

Intrigued, I carefully lifted the book from its shelf and carried it to the desk. I gently turned the fragile yellowed pages, my eyes widening at what I found.

Page after page contained intricate illustrations, symbols,

and descriptions of magical practices specific to shifters: elemental conjuring spells, scrying rituals, and telepathic charms, among other esoteric arts.

According to the introductory passages, these arcane skills had been developed over generations by the most talented wolf-shifter mystics who possessed innate supernatural talents and then gifted them to the innkeeper. These exceptional individuals were few and far between, but each saw empowering the innkeeper as a necessary step in protecting the town of Crescent Crossing and enabling a lasting peace.

I sat back heavily, struck by implications. As a non-shifter, such magical capabilities were utterly beyond my reach. Yet Briar and others had hinted at latent powers tied now to my role as the Howl Away Inn's caretaker.

If only I had a teacher. But no, all I had were dusty old pages.

My fingers absently traced the inscrutable triskele tattoo on my arm, signifying my inheritance of the mantle and all it encompassed. Though I remained skeptical about wielding such unfathomable magic myself, evidence of its existence now laid undeniably before me.

If I could somehow tap into even an echo of the potent gifts detailed in these pages, might it aid in protecting this haven from gathering darkness? A chill shuddered through me at the thought.

I pored over the spell book. Though apprehensive, I felt compelled to at least attempt some of the magical practices it described, if only to understand more of my emerging talents.

I started small, trying to conjure a flicker of flame in my palm, which the book claimed even novice practitioners could manage. My first few attempts failed utterly, with not even a wisp of smoke rising from my fingertips. But I persisted, carefully pronouncing the incantation and envisioning a spark catching and spreading.

Riveted, I watched a tiny orange beam of light shoot from my palm and hit the floor. After nearly an hour of concentration, the ball of flame was only the size of a dime. It flickered like a candle on its last leg, casting trembling shadows on the office walls. My breaths came in shallow bursts as I struggled to withstand the heat. Slowly, the fire grew larger and brighter, radiating a comforting warmth. The glow intensified in response to my elation.

But the rigorous practice left me drained, both physically and mentally. Part of me was worried I'd opened a door that could not be shut. Yet, clearly, fate had gifted these talents for some purpose. I hoped my strengthening abilities might illuminate solutions, not invite new peril. But only time would reveal which path my steps along this winding road led down.

My gaze fell upon the carved wooden raven pendant Barnell had discovered outside near where Ryder's body was found. An idea struck me.

The spell book described using objects linked to an individual to establish a psychic connection through scrying. Though I was hesitant, I attempted it, focusing my energy on the wooden pendant.

Taking a deep, bracing breath, I held the carved raven talisman in my palm and whispered the scrying incantation, concentrating on its creator. At first, only darkness swirled within the pendant's smooth wooden surface. But gradually, indistinct visions coalesced.

I glimpsed shadowy figures moving furtively through the

moonlit forest depths, their faces obscured. A palpable sense of menace radiated from them, along with the unsettling feeling they still lurked nearby.

The vision swallowed me whole, plunging me into the heart of the visceral memory. Fear crashed over me in relentless waves as I once more faced the rogue wolf, its hackles raised and fangs bared in a vicious snarl. The savage growls reverberated through my bones, deafening against the oppressive silence of the dense forest.

Moonlight glinted off the wolf's red-brown fur as it crouched, coiled, and was ready to strike. The stench of its fetid breath assaulted my nostrils, hot and rank with the promise of blood. My pulse thundered in my ears, a desperate staccato rhythm.

In a blur of motion, the wolf lunged, a mass of rippling muscle and slashing claws. But before it could reach me, a streak of black crashed into its flank, sending them both tumbling to the loam in a writhing tangle of fur and fury. Drake had arrived to intervene, just as he had that terrifying night.

The rogue wolf twisted and fought against him, its form shimmering and contorting grotesquely as it struggled. For one heart-stopping moment, it shifted into its semi-human form, caught between existences. I stared into its contorted visage, a mix of man and beast, and my blood turned to ice in my veins. The face glaring back at me, lip curled in a feral sneer, was part wolf, part human.

The human part looked like Kai Wilder, and yet that wasn't quite right. Perhaps it was the shapeshifting making the image muddled and unclear?

Revulsion and fear surged through me, burning like acrid

bile in the back of my throat. Kai, who had seemed so charming and guileless, had been the one to terrorize me that night, to attack with such ruthless savagery and malevolent intent. The man behind the monster was no longer a mystery.

As suddenly as it had swept me up, the vision released me, abandoning me to swirling shadow. I surfaced with a shuddering gasp, my heart like a caged bird fluttering madly behind my ribcage. The scrying pendant felt searing against my palm, a tangible reminder that the dark truth could no longer be denied.

Unease rippled through me as I considered the implications of this newly uncovered evidence. Kai's deception ran deeper than I had realized. But I could not confront him until I understood the full extent of his role in the ominous happenings plaguing Crescent Crossing. For now, I needed to proceed with the utmost care around the cunning shifter.

The scrying had provided insight, yet it also vividly reminded me that magic always carried unanticipated risks. I would need to rein in my curiosity and use it only when necessary until I better understood my burgeoning talents. With such power came grave accountability. But I could not turn away from my duty to illuminate the shadows threatening this haven.

After a sharp rap at the door, I jumped up to see who'd arrived. Hamish, Saige, and Briar stood ready for our pre-meeting discussion, and I ushered them quickly inside. But before I could greet them, Hamish stooped with a frown, retrieving a folded sheet of paper from the floor.

"It looks like this was slipped under your door," he said grimly. "Have a look."

I unfolded the paper, reading the jagged scrawl with a sense of foreboding.

Leave at once, or what happened to Ryder will befall you too. Heed this single warning: depart Crescent Crossing before the full moon rises.

I paled, my pulse quickening as I processed the sinister threat.

"What does it say?" Saige asked sharply, noting my distress.

I handed her the note with a trembling hand. "A warning to leave Crescent Crossing before the full moon, or I'll meet Ryder's fate."

Saige's eyes flashed as she read it, then she passed it to Briar, whose brow creased in concern.

"The author is surely tangled up in the strange happenings here," Briar said. "But who?"

My first instinct was Malachi, given his odd behavior that day and how he'd snuck away from the inn earlier. I couldn't discount Kai either, considering he was near the inn that morning and he'd been featured as the suspect in my vision. After my revelation while scrying with the necklace, I'd gone from thinking of him as a potential threat to a definite one. His earlier betrayal had cut deep, as I now knew he was the wolf who had attacked me in the woods.

I sank into my chair with a weary sigh. In this den of deception, I could no longer distinguish friend from foe. Doubts sowed by the note had cracked the firm foundations I thought I'd built. Suspicion reigned supreme: who could I trust in this not-so-sleepy town? With a few exceptions, my trust only extended as far as those standing in front of me.

"Who can I truly trust beyond you three? Well, and Barnell. He's a fountain of pure innocence."

"We are with you, Lydia," Hamish said firmly. Saige nodded in agreement.

"You can rely on all of us," Briar added.

After a moment, I drew a resolute breath, meeting each of their gazes. "The time for doubt and fear is over," I said firmly. "Tonight marks a new chapter for Crescent Crossing. One where hope can take wing, free of the shadows that have too long gripped this divided town."

Briar gripped my shoulder. "Ryder would be proud. Oh, while you were at the records hall, I did some digging into my family's old journals and texts," Briar said. "I found several references to raven and wing symbols that seemed important during an uprising a few generations ago. Some of the shifter clans had wanted to break away entirely from the enclaves back then."

I nodded, intrigued by this complementary information. "That aligns with the old myths about Ravenfeather that I uncovered. The raven must symbolize that past resistance movement you mentioned."

"Exactly," Briar agreed. "My ancestors wrote about how the raven became a sign of defiance and a call for dramatic change. But the rebellion was ultimately quashed by the enclave elders."

"Still, it's fascinating those old divisions echo in the present day rifts," I mused. "Ravenfeather was all about adding democratic elements to managing packs, in addition to the alpha rule. I wonder if these raven-related symbols are from people looking for a change in the order of things?"

"It would explain why Ryder was targeted," Hamish added.

Saige spoke up next. "While you two did your research, I tracked Malachi deep into the forest until he reached a remote area where I lost him. No buildings or structures that I know of out that way. It felt like a strange place for him to just disappear."

"Some shifters maintain hidden warrens in remote areas to spend extended time in their primal forms," Briar offered. "Malachi could have access to one of those to slip away unnoticed for periods of time."

"Clever," I said. "So he clearly doesn't want to be followed. He could hide something big that far off the beaten path. Should we consider searching for his warren?"

Hamish looked concerned. "With the threats made against your life, Lydia, we need to know who might be coming for you. But spreading ourselves too thin could be dangerous."

A grave nod was my response. "You're right. We need to stay focused. The truth is here in Crescent Crossing, I'm certain of it."

"Where do we focus our efforts, then?" Saige asked.

I considered for a moment. "Let's pursue the raven lead; dig deeper into what happened during that uprising generations ago. There must be more documented if we know where to look."

The path ahead remained uncertain, but with loyalty like ours, we would navigate it together. Each clue brought us one step closer to illuminating the shadows that gripped this troubled town.

I cleared my throat to get everyone's attention. "I found

an educational tome in Ryder's things and spent some time today practicing. Now I have a breakthrough to share. Watch closely..."

Taking a deep breath, I focused intently and conjured a tiny flicker of flame in my palm, no bigger than a marble.

Saige gasped. "Amazing! I didn't know you could do that."

Briar leaned in, scrutinizing the fire. "Incredible. I've never seen a non-shifter wield our elemental magic before. I wonder if you can because of your fae heritage?"

"I wasn't blessed with fae powers, but I agree, Briar. My lineage, combined with the innkeeper's gift, might be why I can use it."

Hamish looked impressed but also concerned. "Still, a marble-sized fireball won't stop a determined killer. How quickly can you develop your skills?"

"I'm not sure, but I'll practice and put the time in," I replied. "You're right that my talents are limited for now. I'm still just scratching the surface of what Ryder could no doubt do with the innkeeper's arcane gifts."

"Did you learn anything else?" Briar asked.

"I was able to scry with the raven medallion necklace," I replied. I described my vision when scrying with the raven pendant, including witnessing Kai's savage attack.

"So Kai is definitely not to be trusted," I concluded. "Yet it doesn't confirm he killed Ryder. I'm unsure if he meant to kill me that night or just scare me off."

Briar nodded thoughtfully. "And we still suspect Malachi is up to something sinister as well."

"Yes, every instinct tells me one of them is responsible for

Ryder's death," I agreed. "We just need to uncover the proof."

"Harper approached me earlier today suggesting I make a gesture to the enclaves by including them in my mediator role as a circle of trusted advisors in order to get the alphas and their packs to support me, since I'm an outsider," I explained. "I've already invited Harper, Aja, and Nalani to join us tonight for the first meeting."

Saige tilted her head. "Won't Kai and Drake feel slighted you included Harper but not them? All three of them were appointed by their alphas to potentially replace Ryder."

"Likely so," I admitted with a sigh. "But I'd rather not mix too much fire and gasoline together in a small room right now. I definitely can't trust Kai, and things with Drake are just too... volatile."

Hamish raised an eyebrow. "Fair point. Though we can't fully exclude Harper as a suspect, either. Inviting her here is a bit like letting the proverbial wolf in with the sheep."

"Well, that's a truly terrible metaphor in shifter territory, especially made by a shifter," Briar said wryly.

We all chuckled, breaking the tension. Glancing at the clock, I saw it was five minutes to seven.

"Oh well, for better or worse, it's time," I said resolutely. "Let's go welcome our guests and hope this council illuminates more than it ignites."

With hope in our hearts but caution in our steps, we set out to convene and see what wisdom or new mysteries the evening held.

CHAPTER 11

J took a deep breath to steady my nerves before opening the door to the private meeting room. Harper, Aja, and Nalani were already seated around the circular oak table, murmuring quietly among themselves. At my entrance, they looked up expectantly.

The room was awash in the warm glow of flickering candles, their dancing light casting elongated shadows across the walls. The air was heavy with the mingled scents of aged parchment, leather-bound books, and the faint aroma of Harper's signature jasmine perfume. A fire crackled invitingly in the hearth, dispelling the chill that had seeped into my bones during the walk from my office.

"Thank you all for coming," I began, hoping my voice sounded more assured than I felt. This first official gathering of my fledgling council marked a pivotal moment, either lighting the path to reconciliation or inviting disaster through missteps.

Before I could continue, the door burst open again, sending a gust of cold air swirling through the room and making the candles sputter. Drake stormed in, his footsteps echoing heavily on the worn wooden floorboards. His eyes flashed in the dancing firelight as he fixed me with an accusing glare. "So this is where you've been hiding," he bit out, his deep voice cutting through the stunned silence. "Making decisions without input from the enclaves you're meddling with."

I held up a hand placatingly, the flickering shadows playing across my face. "Drake, now isn't the time. I'll explain later."

But he cut me off, his fist slamming into the table with a resounding thud that made the candles jump in their holders. "Explain how you were too cowardly to include me? How you don't trust the Flat Tops enough?" His words hung in the air, sharp and bitter.

"If you'd stop and look around the table, you'd notice the Flat Tops are represented. It's you I chose not to include, which is my right as the innkeeper. Is it not?" My voice was calm and measured, but inside my heart raced at his raw fury.

That shut him up, but I could swear I heard his molars grinding in the tense stillness.

Hamish's eyes narrowed as he marched into the room, his lips a thin line. He seized Drake's arm with a steel grip and spoke in a grave tone. "That's quite enough," Hamish uttered. Then, without waiting for a reply, he tugged Drake towards the door, continuing to address him in a stern voice. "Come on, let's take a walk and discuss."

Drake gave me a long, hard look before nodding in agreement to Hamish's suggestion. With a final scowl at me, Drake allowed himself to be led away, leaving the clear implication that he was not done with this conversation.

The door clicked shut, and a heavy silence filled the room.

I cleared my throat awkwardly. "My apologies. Please know I intend no disrespect."

Harper waved a hand dismissively. "We know well Drake's temper. There is no need to justify yourself."

The others murmured their agreement, nodding slowly as they exchanged glances. Harper leaned back in her chair, a satisfied smile playing on her lips, while Aja and Nalani sat up straighter, their eyes bright with anticipation.

I exhaled in relief, feeling the tension drain from my shoulders as I realized I had their support. "Thank you," I said sincerely, meeting each of their gazes in turn. "I know this council will play a crucial role in providing guidance on issues affecting all enclaves. Together, we can work towards a future of unity and understanding."

Aja clapped her hands together, her bangles jingling musically. "Absolutely! I'm eager to get started," she declared, her enthusiasm infectious.

Nalani nodded, her expression thoughtful. "I agree. We should establish a clear timeline for addressing the various petitions and concerns from each enclave," she suggested, tapping a slender finger against her chin. "That way, we can ensure everyone feels heard and respected."

Harper leaned forward, her eyes sparkling with determination. "I have some ideas on that front," she said, reaching into her satchel and pulling out a stack of neatly organized papers. She spread them out on the table, revealing a detailed list of Bittersweet grievances and proposals.

The advisors readily embraced their roles, launching into an animated discussion as they pored over Harper's documents. They gestured energetically, their voices rising and falling as they debated the merits of each point. Nalani frowned, shaking her head as she argued for a more balanced approach, while Aja nodded vigorously, her long hair bouncing with each emphatic movement.

I sat back, watching the scene unfold with a growing sense of pride and relief. The council was already working together seamlessly, their diverse perspectives and experiences combining to create a truly formidable force. With their help, I knew we could tackle even the most daunting challenges facing Crescent Crossing.

I held up my hands in a placating gesture. "Let's not jump ahead of ourselves," I said. "We need to set the groundwork first, ensuring each enclave has an equal voice in this process."

Aja frowned thoughtfully as she considered my words. "I believe we should also consider how to handle circumstances that arise where all enclaves cannot agree on a course of action," she said slowly.

The others nodded in agreement and began debating the best way to resolve such disputes while still maintaining fairness and respect between the enclaves. Eventually, we tentatively settled on allowing me, the innkeeper, to cast the deciding vote in cases where the enclaves failed to agree, subject to review by future councils if deemed necessary. With a shared sense of accomplishment, we turned toward more immediate matters, such as organizing information gathering sessions with each enclave and coordinating feedback from those consultations into a comprehensive report for continued discussions at subsequent meetings. As we adjourned for the evening, I was cautiously optimistic about the council's prospects for achieving consensus on crucial issues. Even the aloof Harper seemed pleased.

Aja's serene voice rang out. "Well done, Lydia. Ryder would have balked at such a structure, but I prefer this methodical approach."

Buoyed by their unanimous support, I brought the productive first meeting to a close. With steadfast allies lighting my way, I felt ready to navigate any turbulence ahead.

As I showed the advisors out, I caught sight of Drake lingering in the lobby, arms crossed and expression stormy. My shoulders tensed, preparing for another confrontation.

Sure enough, once the others had left, Drake strode over. "We need to talk. Now." Without waiting for a response, he grasped my elbow and led me firmly outside to the inn's moonlit garden. I was surprised by his assertiveness, but oddly, not that much bothered—as if I had expected it—and allowed him to take control.

When we were alone, Drake wheeled around, eyes blazing. "I can't believe you're shutting me out. Don't you get how much the Flat Tops stand to lose if you favor the other enclaves?" He paced agitatedly.

I raised my hands placatingly. "Drake, that's not my intention at all. I included the Flat Tops. I'm just trying to be fair while limiting tensions."

"Fair?" Drake spat. "Is it fair to exclude me while Harper whispers poison in your ear?" He stepped closer, using his formidable height to loom over me.

I stood my ground. "I understand your frustration. But this council is meant to give equal voice to all sides." I kept my tone calm and even. "Your perspective would absolutely be valued if you could only keep your head."

Drake searched my face, as if gauging my sincerity. For a moment, his eyes softened. But just as quickly, his temper flared again.

"You need someone to challenge you, not just pat your back." He raked a hand through his hair in frustration. "But maybe you want spineless pawns instead of honesty."

With that, he turned on his heel and stalked off into the night, leaving me shaken in his wake. I wrapped my arms around myself against the sudden chill. Drake's mercurial moods left me perpetually off balance, never knowing which version of him I would face next. With a weary sigh, I headed back inside, my emotions churning.

Lost in brooding thoughts after my confrontation with Drake, I didn't notice the stealthy figure slipping out of the shadows as I re-entered the inn.

Suddenly, a hand clamped over my mouth from behind, and I was spun around and shoved roughly against the stone wall of the courtyard. The rough edges of the weathered stones dug into my back, scraping my skin through the thin fabric of my blouse. Heart pounding wildly, I stared up into the cold, golden eyes of Malachi, mere inches from my face.

"We meet again, little fae," he sneered, his hot breath ghosting across my cheek. The scent of stale tobacco and whiskey assaulted my nostrils, making my stomach churn. "Not so brave without your guard dogs now, are you?" His grip on my jaw tightened, his fingers biting into my flesh.

I struggled in vain to break free, but Malachi had me pinned, his body pressing against mine in a suffocating embrace. Up close, I noticed a strange, almost feral gleam in his eyes that sent a chill down my spine, like a rabbit caught in the predatory gaze of a wolf.

"Why are you still here, pretending to be the innkeeper? This isn't your place," he hissed, his voice low and menacing. "You should walk away before someone gets hurt."

As Malachi issued his sinister threat, he leaned in even closer, his lips grazing the shell of my ear. Revulsion rose in my throat like bile, and a scream built in my chest, but it remained trapped behind his clammy palm.

In that moment of desperation, something stirred deep within me—a primal, pulsing energy that seared through my veins like liquid fire. The blood surged through my body, electric and alive, until it reached my hands, where it pooled and coalesced into a tangible force. My skin tingled and burned as if I had plunged my fists into the heart of a star, and an otherworldly glow emanated from my fingers, painting the darkness in shades of shimmering gold.

Malachi's eyes widened in sudden shock and fear as he felt the power radiating from me, his grip loosening just a fraction. Seizing my chance, I unleashed the pent-up energy in a blinding flash of light and searing heat. An invisible force slammed into Malachi like a battering ram, ripping him away from me and sending him flying backward through the air. He hit the ground with a heavy thud, his body crumpling into a groaning heap on the cobblestones.

Stunned, I stared down at my hands, now returning to their normal, unremarkable state. Residual sparks of energy danced across my skin, leaving behind a faint, tingling sensation. I realized with a mix of awe and trepidation that my awakening magic had acted instinctively to protect me, responding to my desperate need. But questions would have to wait. I turned and fled further inside the inn, my heart thundering against my ribs as I called out frantically for Hamish and Saige.

Moments later, I stood trembling as I described the disturbing encounter to my allies. Their expressions hardened with concern and outrage. Without a thought, Hamish dashed out of the door in search of Malachi, but he returned a few moments later. The scoundrel had already disappeared without a trace.

"Attacking you outright proves Malachi must be tied to the conspiracy behind Ryder's death," Hamish growled. "He's growing desperate. We must be getting close to the truth."

Saige nodded grimly. "This changes things. We need to be more vigilant than ever." She turned to me. "But don't let him intimidate you. Finding justice for Ryder is worth the risk."

Their support steadied my shaken nerves. I lifted my chin, my resolve renewed. "You're right. We're seeing this through, no matter what Malachi or anyone tries to do to stop us."

Moments after my disturbing encounter with Malachi, the sound of rapid footsteps and a door slamming shut echoed down the hallway. Drake burst into view, his face etched with concern. I waved off Hamish and Saige, knowing Drake might set my teeth on edge, but he wouldn't harm me.

"I came back to talk things out after I had a few minutes to cooling off." His gaze scanned me swiftly, seeming to pick up on my emotional distress. "Are you alright? You seem out of sorts."

"I'm okay," I replied, still on edge from the confrontation. "Malachi ambushed me outside, but I got away."

Drake's expression darkened, fury rippling across his chiseled features. "If I ever get my hands on him..." He clenched his fists, his jaw tight. After a long breath, he met my eyes, his own clouded with turmoil. "I'm sorry. I shouldn't have left you alone out there."

I wrapped my arms around myself, still shaken. "You couldn't have known Malachi would be waiting." An uneasy silence fell between us. I could sense Drake's inner conflict, but neither of us seemed to know what to say.

Finally, Drake raked a hand through his hair. "I'm glad you're not hurt." He hesitated, emotions warring on his face. Yet again I felt our bond had deepened but remained undefined.

On impulse, I reached out, brushing his arm. A jolt passed between us, and I glimpsed echoes of his churning feelings—fear for me, fury at Malachi. And beneath it was a tentative longing that mirrored my own conflicted heart.

I drew back abruptly, my pulse racing. Drake stared at me, a realization dawning about my emerging gift. "Your magic. Did you sense something about me?"

I gave a jerky nod, my cheeks flushing. An awkward silence fell. We both seemed unsure of how to navigate this new dynamic developing between us. The implications hung unspoken in the air.

Desperate to break the tension, I cleared my throat. "It's getting late. I should try to rest."

Drake nodded, looking vaguely relieved. "Of course. Good idea." He moved toward the door, then hesitated. "Let me know if you need anything." His tone was gruff, but his eyes were unexpectedly vulnerable.

I managed a timid smile in return. "I will. Thank you, Drake."

After he left, I held a hand to my chest, my emotions churning. Denying the deepening connection between us grew harder each day. But with so much uncertainty ahead, I couldn't let my heart lead us astray.

The next morning, I gathered Hamish, Saige, and Briar in my office to discuss last night's events. Settling into the plush leather armchairs, I quickly recounted the ominous encounter with Malachi for Briar and told them all of my unsettling new ability to sense emotions.

"Somehow, I picked up Drake's feelings last night," I explained. "I know it's hard to believe, but when I touched Drake's arm, it just kicked in. I sensed genuine sincerity," I told the others. "Despite his temper, I'm sure he wasn't involved in killing Ryder."

Hamish furrowed his brow. "Are you certain you read him accurately? Drake can be cunning when he wants to be."

"I agree we can't fully lower our guard with him yet," said Saige bluntly. "Past grudges run deep for some."

I bit my lip. "You both make fair points. This magic is still new to me. I could have misinterpreted things." I sighed. "But my instincts say Drake was being genuine last night."

Briar spoke up gently. "Only you can decide who is trustworthy, Lydia. Remember, the act of being dishonest has a ripple effect. Follow those, and you'll find the truth."

I nodded slowly, absorbing her guidance. Drake still had impulsive tendencies, but my heart said he was not a cold-blooded killer. I would proceed cautiously, while following my intuition, as Briar advised.

"For now, let's just keep a close eye on Drake and the others," I decided. "If anyone seems poised to escalate tensions between the enclaves, that could reveal darker motives."

My friends murmured in agreement.

"It's useful information your newfound empathy provided," Hamish said. "But we'd be wise not to rely wholly on this new power yet."

"Agreed, it needs more understanding," said Saige. "But it's encouraging that your innkeeper's magic grows stronger daily."

I nodded. "Any insights you have on safely developing these skills would be invaluable."

"We'll scour the archives for any relevant texts," Briar promised. "There must be records of past innkeepers' experiences to guide you."

I smiled gratefully. "In the meantime, we need to keep watching Malachi and Kai closely. I'm convinced one of them holds the missing pieces in all this. Malachi's brazen attack on me last night shows he's becoming more desperate," I said gravely. "He must be afraid we're close to exposing the truth."

Saige nodded. "Desperate men make mistakes. He implicated himself with that reckless move."

"Perhaps," mused Hamish. "Or it could be deliberate misdirection while the actual killer lies low." He leaned forward intently. "We must examine every angle before accusing Malachi outright."

I raked a hand through my hair in frustration. "You're

right. We can't rush to judgment. But either way, Malachi is tangled up in this somehow."

Hamish nodded. "Aye, we'll monitor them both closely and see what cracks form in their facades." He gave my shoulder a reassuring squeeze, his calloused hand warm and comforting through the fabric of my shirt. "Patience and care are key."

As our discussion wound down, I reflected on how far we'd already come in unraveling the mysteries surrounding Ryder's demise. Only a week ago, I'd been plunged unwillingly into the dangerous secrets threatening Crescent Crossing. Now, we had promising leads and my own mystical abilities were awakening.

I rose from my chair and paced to the window, gazing out at the misty mountains beyond. The morning sun was just beginning to peek over the horizon, painting the sky in a breathtaking array of pinks and golds. Yet even as I marveled at the beauty, a sense of unease coiled in my gut. Glaring gaps remained in the puzzle. We still lacked the incriminating evidence needed to expose the killer, and mastering my unfurling powers would require deeper study than we currently possessed.

Turning back to face my companions, I shook my head ruefully, my fingers absently tracing the triskele tattoo on my forearm. "We've made progress, but this feels far from over." I met each of my friends' gazes, searching their faces for any hint of hesitation or doubt. "I don't know what lies ahead, but I need to know you all remain committed to seeing this through."

Hamish stood abruptly, his chair scraping against the

hardwood floor. "Always," he stated, his voice ringing with conviction. "We're here for you."

Saige and Briar echoed his unwavering sentiment, rising to their feet as well. Saige's green eyes flashed with conviction, while Briar's gentle smile held a steely resolve.

I exhaled slowly, feeling the tension ease from my shoulders as I basked in their steadfast support. "Then let's keep digging," I said, my voice growing stronger. "There are answers here somewhere."

We retired to my office and gathered around the ancient oak table, our heads bent together as we pored over the various maps, documents, and arcane tomes spread before us. The musty scent of old parchment and leather filled the air, mingling with the earthy aroma of the tea Briar had brewed. The occasional rustle of paper was the only sound as we worked, each of us focused on our appointed tasks.

As we sifted through the documents, Briar suddenly let out a gasp. "Lydia, look at this!" She pointed to an entry in the shipping logs, her finger trembling slightly.

I leaned in, my eyes widening as I read the entry. It was for a package addressed to "C. Wilder," and the signature on the delivery confirmation was none other than Malachi's.

"The sender's address includes the phrase 'A raven's shadow never fades.' It's the same catchphrase we've been hearing around town," Briar added.

Hamish frowned, his brow furrowing. "This can't be a coincidence."

I nodded, my mind reeling with the implications. "We need to confront Malachi about this. He's been hiding something from us all along."

Step by step, the flickering light of truth would guide us through the darkness. Straight to the heart of Crescent Crossing's secrets.

CHAPTER 12

The veil between dreams and reality blurred as I drifted into restless slumber. Silver moonlight filtered through my window, the brilliant light splashing in contrast across the dark floorboards. As exhaustion claimed me, the moonlight seemed to shine even brighter, resonating with the subtle energy humming in my veins.

Gradually, vivid visions swirled through my mind's eye. I glimpsed shadowy figures moving through a mist-veiled forest of ash trees beneath the watching stars. Their hushed voices carried on the wind though their words remained obscure. A palpable unease emanated from the gathering, as if portending dangers untold.

I drifted closer, straining to decipher their obscured faces, but all remained shrouded in secrecy. Only their raven feathers stood out starkly against the inky night, glinting in the moonlight. The mysterious figures seemed to be engaged in some sort of ritual, their movements deliberate and purposeful. The air crackled with an ancient, arcane energy that set my nerves on edge.

The perspective shifted, drawing me between mossy ash trees to view a woman's slender form silhouetted against the glowing crescent moon. As she half turned, long blonde tresses cascaded down her back in gentle waves. Pointed ears marked her unmistakably as fae, yet her lineage remained unclear. Her eyes glowed with an otherworldly intensity, as if she could see into the afterlife itself.

Before I could discern the details of her shadowed face, the vision fractured abruptly, leaving only swirling darkness tinged with unease. The woman's image lingered in my mind, a haunting reminder of the secrets yet to be unveiled. I couldn't shake the feeling that she held the key to unraveling the mysteries that plagued Crescent Crossing and the strange events surrounding Ryder's death.

I awoke with a sharp gasp, my heart racing. As the haunting dream fragments quickly faded, I knew with unsettling certainty that a dire warning had surfaced from my subconscious. But deciphering the coded imagery would require a deeper understanding of the forces at play.

Over steaming mugs of tea in the cozy lounge, I recounted the dream as best I could recall to Saige, Hamish, and Briar. Their expressions turned grave as I described the details.

"More raven symbolism, and even more pronounced," mused Saige with a furrowed brow.

"Aye, clearly an omen, but of what?" Hamish stroked his grizzled beard pensively.

I frowned, grasping at the elusive threads. "If only I could have seen that fae woman's face or heard what was said."

Briar leaned forward intently, her emerald eyes sharp. "This woman was alone among raven-adorned shifters beneath the moonlight and ash trees. She must be connected to the old Ravenfeather legends."

I nodded slowly. "The parallels can't be a coincidence. But what was she meant to convey? Or what was my mind trying to tell me about her?"

We sat in brooding silence until Hamish finally spoke. "Have you gleaned anything more from the archives or Ryder's records about this Ravenfeather?"

"I've barely scratched the surface," I admitted. "Any insights you can add from the historical texts would help immensely."

"We'll keep digging," Briar promised. "There must be more clues in Crescent Crossing's complex past about the significance of these raven signs and visions."

I mustered a wan smile, uplifted by their unwavering support.

I bid my friends a pleasant morning before retreating to my room to prepare myself for the day ahead, my thoughts churning with questions from last night's vivid dream. Yet as I sat at the polished vanity brushing out my hair, my mind wandered back to the intense confrontation with Drake.

Our dynamic ran hot and cold, vacillating between charged chemistry and icy distrust. Try as I might to keep my heart guarded, his surprising tenderness and protectiveness sometimes kindled flickers of desire that felt at odds with my role as innkeeper and investigator for Ryder's murder.

With a resigned sigh, I set down my hairbrush. Before seeking answers in mystical dreams or historical archives, I first had to unravel my own conflicted emotions swirling within. I refused to repeat past mistakes and lose myself again.

A knock at my door jolted me from brooding thoughts. I opened it to find Saige standing there, her sharp green eyes filled with understanding.

"A walk and talk?" Saige suggested gently.

I readily agreed, grateful for her perceptiveness. We stepped outside into the crisp morning air, wandering the grounds in peaceful silence at first as I gathered my turbulent thoughts.

Finally, I spoke hesitantly. "I'm so conflicted when it comes to Drake. One moment he's gentle and protective, the next he's accusing me of failing as a mediator." I shook my head, frustration welling up. "His unpredictable moods leave me perpetually unbalanced."

Saige listened thoughtfully as we meandered beneath the sprawling pines. "You two do have a complicated dynamic," she acknowledged. "His volatility likely stems from deep wounds and distrust."

I sighed heavily. "You're probably right. But how do I stay impartial as the mediator when he stirs up such powerful feelings in me?"

Saige deliberated before responding. "The heart wants what it wants, despite our best intentions. Yet yours has been too often bruised in the past."

She gently grasped my hand. "Keep listening to your instincts where Drake is concerned. Don't ignore them just because it's difficult. And know that some walls between souls are meant to crumble, but only when the time is right."

I absorbed her wisdom as we walked on in pensive silence, blinking back sudden tears.

After looping back around, we paused beneath the broad oak outside the inn. I turned and embraced Saige fiercely.

"Thank you," I whispered. "I'm so grateful to have you here to help me find clarity."

Saige returned my embrace with equal warmth. "Anytime. That's what friends are for."

With my turbulent emotions somewhat settled for now thanks to Saige's steadfast support, I felt ready to face the challenges of the day ahead.

"Let's take a walk through the town and see if we can learn anything," I said.

As Saige and I navigated the crowded streets of Crescent Crossing, I noticed Malachi approaching with a calculated ease. His voice was low and tinged with concern as he drew near. "Lydia, I couldn't help but overhear some townsfolk discussing your investigation into Ryder's death. Could you share any findings with me?"

Keeping my guard up, I responded cautiously, "The investigation is ongoing, Malachi. I'm afraid there's not much I can share at this point.

His brow furrowed in apparent frustration. "Surely, you must have discovered something by now. Ryder's death has deeply affected our community. Perhaps you could use some help? A raven's shadow never fades, and I fear the consequences if the killer isn't found soon."

The mention of the phrase caught my attention, further igniting my suspicion. "That's an interesting phrase you used —'a raven's shadow never fades.' I've been hearing that a lot lately," I remarked, watching his reaction closely.

Malachi's demeanor shifted subtly, a flicker of surprise in his eyes before he regained composure. "It's just something shifters say during trying times. But if there's any way I can assist your efforts, please let me know. I have resources that might be useful."

Seizing the opportunity to confront him, I pressed on. "Speaking of resources, you've been receiving an awful lot of packages at the inn recently. One of which was marked with that same curious phrase—'a raven's shadow never fades.'"

Caught off guard, Malachi's facade of calm faltered. "Lydia, as I said, it's a phrase shifters use in difficult times, nothing more. I'm not sure what you're implying."

I leaned in, my voice firm. "Don't lie to me, Malachi."

He stepped back, his expression hardening. "You have no idea what you're playing at here. The winds of change are blowing, and you can't stop them."

With those cryptic words, Malachi turned and walked away, leaving me more determined than ever to uncover the truth. I watched his retreating figure until it disappeared into the crowd, a sense of foreboding settling in my stomach.

Saige and I returned to the inn, and I made my way to the study, hoping to have a few moments of quiet reflection. But when I entered, Hamish and Briar were already there waiting for me.

"Lydia, we found some troubling texts you should see," Hamish rumbled in his low baritone, his expression grave.

He led me to the ancient oak desk where he and Briar had arrayed several old leather-bound journals engraved with the innkeeper's mark.

"These are the personal accounts of some of your predecessors here," Briar explained. "They describe unexpected consequences when accessing their mystical abilities tied to the inn."

I scanned the fragile pages with growing unease. One

former innkeeper, a woman named Amara, wrote extensively about the toll her mystical practices had taken over the years:

"After long sessions peering through the obsidian scrying stone, an aching fatigue permeates my very bones, leaving me bedridden for days, unable to summon the strength to move or speak. The visions granted often bring more perturbation than clarity. I fear extended use of such seeing stones extracts a heavy physical and spiritual price."

Another passage described disturbing side effects experienced by an innkeeper named Damien:

"Since dabbling in runic spells of concealment and disguise, my dreams have become increasingly tormented. No longer do I experience tranquil rest. I am currently plagued by intense nightmares, where I find myself lost in shapeless voids and pursued by nameless, malevolent entities. Their ghostly hands grasp at me as I run endlessly through shadows without refuge."

Entry after entry outlined the inexplicable conditions those tapping into the inn's arcane powers had endured: aggressive insomnia, periods of memory loss, and schizophrenia-like symptoms. I sat back heavily, now significantly more wary of embracing gifts I barely comprehended. Should I recklessly sprint along this magical path, completely oblivious to the consequences, all because of my curiosity?

As I was lost in my thoughts, Hamish's weathered hand on my shoulder brought me back to reality. "You won't have to walk this path alone," he assured me gruffly. "We'll help you find balance and control."

I exhaled shakily, nodding. If I proceeded with care, guided by trusted allies, perhaps I could wield the magic responsibly when needed. But first, I had much to learn about its demands and limits. The texts had illuminated a fraught road ahead.

"I know you're eager to experiment with your new abilities, but based on these, you must proceed cautiously with developing your talents," Saige cautioned. "The magic can overtake those unprepared for its demands."

I nodded slowly, knowing wisdom lay in their warning. The flickering magic humming through my veins seemed more volatile the more I embraced it. I would need to temper my curiosity moving forward and lean on my allies' guidance.

As I processed the sobering truths revealed in the journals, a subtle pull guided my gaze to a shelf holding more of Ryder's old records. Among the orderly tomes, one leather folio engraved with a raven insignia seemed to call out to me. My heart quickened instinctively at the sight of it, though I couldn't say why.

It was as if the awakening magic in my blood recognized significance in this unassuming text that my conscious mind had yet to grasp. Curiosity compelled me to retrieve the folio and gently lift the cover. The mystical energy thrumming within me resonated with what lay inside.

On the aged pages, I found meticulous sketches of the exact raven symbol that had haunted my dreams, alongside transcribed oral histories from the era of Ravenfeather. This was no mere coincidence. The magic flowing through my veins had called out across the centuries to these kindred pages, holding the key to unlocking my troubling visions' meaning. Overwhelmed by the profound potential of my emerging abilities, I knew there were countless other enigmas yet to be discovered through our mysterious bond. What had once seemed volatile and unknowable now felt filled with promise and insight.

"This manuscript is all about Ravenfeather's era," I told the others excitedly. "It could hold the key to deciphering the meaning of my visions."

Briar's eyes lit up. "Of course you went straight for it. What a thrilling discovery!" We spent some time turning through the pages together.

"There are several references to other books in here," I pointed out. "Like these two: The Silver Path of the Night and The Shifting Moon."

"Those are both in the archives," Briar replied. "Saige and I can start cross-referencing them right away, if that's alright with you." I agreed, and Briar carefully gathered up the folio and left with Saige.

New secrets awaited revelation in those timeworn pages. Despite the warnings of previous innkeepers, I had to trust that the flickering magic within me would illuminate our path forward when the time was right.

As I settled in at the polished oak desk to review notes from recent developments on Ryder's murder, the office door suddenly banged open without warning, making me jump. I looked up to see none other than Kai standing there, an almost feral gleam in his icy blue eyes. His clothing was torn and dirty, and his hair was tangled, almost as if he'd been roaming wild in the woods.

"Kai, so nice to see you again. You're looking well today," I managed, keeping my voice steady with effort. Behind him, I noticed Hamish rising swiftly to his feet, his body tensed and wary.

Kai's lip curled derisively. "No thanks to you, innkeeper,"

he spat, slamming the door and striding farther into the office. "Word is, you've been conspiring against me in my absence."

I forced myself to breathe evenly and lifted my chin. "There is no truth to any conspiracies, I assure you. I suggest you sit and catch your breath. I've been meaning to follow up with you about Ryder's murder, but you've been conspicuously absent. Is now a good time to talk?"

With visible effort, Kai contained himself, perching stiffly on the corner chair. His hands, I noticed, shook ever so slightly. Just what had happened to him out there?

"Tell us where you've been and what you've heard," urged Hamish in a calm but firm tone from his post by the door.

Kai's stare bored into me, a strange fervor animating his gaunt features. When he spoke, he didn't answer my question, seemingly caught up in his own internal universe. "You play at authority, but you are blind to the vipers slithering around you." He leaned forward intently. "Drake plots to turn the enclaves against your wishes. And Harper whispers poison, seeking only to elevate the Bittersweets."

I absorbed this dire pronouncement, keeping my expression neutral. "Bold accusations. On what evidence?"

Kai slammed his fist down. "Must I spell it out? They mean to use you for their own ends!" He stood abruptly, raking a hand through his tangled hair. "Trust none of them. Do not let down your guard!"

I exchanged a quick glance with Hamish, silently communicating the need to keep Kai from leaving before we could properly question him. Hamish nodded almost imperceptibly, positioning himself between Kai and the door.

"Kai, wait," I said, rising from my chair. "We need to

discuss this further. If there's a genuine threat, we must address it."

Kai's eyes darted between Hamish and me, a flicker of panic crossing his face. "No, no more talk. You'll see the truth soon enough." He made a sudden, desperate lunge for the door, but Hamish intercepted him, grasping his arm firmly.

"Easy now, Kai," Hamish rumbled. "We just want to understand."

Kai wrenched his arm free with surprising strength, his eyes wild. "No! I've said too much already. They'll come for me!"

In a flurry of movement, Kai shoved Hamish aside and wrenched open the door. Before either of us could react, he bolted out of the office and down the hallway, his footsteps echoing in his wake.

Hamish and I gave chase, but as we reached the inn's front entrance, we saw Kai's figure disappearing into the woods, swallowed up by the shadows. We stood there for a moment, catching our breath and exchanging worried glances, before retreating to my office.

I sank into my chair, my mind reeling from Kai's cryptic warnings. Part of me wanted to dismiss his words as the ravings of a madman, but another part couldn't shake the nagging feeling that there might be some truth hidden beneath the surface.

"What do you think?" I asked Hamish, my voice barely above a whisper. "Could Drake and Harper really be plotting against me?"

Hamish frowned, his brow furrowed in thought. "I don't know," he admitted. "Kai's behavior was erratic, to say the least. But we can't afford to ignore his warnings entirely."

I nodded, my fingers absently tracing the triskele tattoo on my forearm. The mark of the innkeeper, a symbol of the heavy responsibility I bore. "We need to keep a close eye on everyone," I said finally. "Trust no one fully."

"You can trust Saige and I, and Briar and Barnell are with you too. I'm sure of it." Hamish placed a comforting hand on my shoulder. "We'll sort this out, Lydia."

I managed a thin smile, grateful for his unwavering support.

Hamish glanced at the clock on the wall. "It's about lunchtime. I'm going to grab a bite to eat. Would you like me to bring you back anything?"

I shook my head, my gaze already drifting back to the scattered papers on my desk. "No, thanks. I'm not really hungry."

Hamish frowned, concern etched in his weathered features. "You need to keep your strength up, Lydia. Skipping meals won't do you any good."

I waved a hand dismissively. "I'll be fine. I just want to keep digging through these records. There has to be something here that I'm missing."

Hamish sighed, recognizing the stubborn set of my jaw. "All right. But promise me you won't leave the inn without someone you trust. Kai's warning may have been cryptic, but we can't afford to take any chances."

I nodded, meeting his gaze. "I promise. Now go get some food. I'll be here when you get back."

Hamish hesitated for a moment, as if he wanted to say more. But then he simply nodded and turned to leave, his footsteps heavy on the worn wooden floorboards.

As the door clicked shut behind him, I let out a breath I

hadn't realized I'd been holding. The silence of the empty office closed in on me, only interrupted by the ticking of the clock and the faint sound of birdsong coming from beyond the window.

But as I turned back to the scattered papers on my desk, I couldn't shake the feeling of unease that had settled in the pit of my stomach.

My gaze fell upon a leather-bound journal of Ryder's, its cover worn and faded with age. With a heavy sigh, I reached for the journal and flipped through its pages. As I scanned the cramped, spidery handwriting, a particular passage caught my eye.

"The visions come more frequently now, each one more vivid and disturbing than the last. I fear I am losing my grip on reality, unable to distinguish between the waking world and the realm of dreams. The power that flows through my veins is both a blessing and a curse, a heavy burden that I must bear alone. Who else could understand the toll it takes on my mind, body, and spirit?"

I felt a chill run down my spine as I read the words, a sense of recognition washing over me. The previous innkeeper's experiences mirrored my own so closely that it was almost eerie. The weight of my newfound abilities, the isolation that came with my role, and the constant sense of unease and paranoia.

And I'd only been here a week.

Late into the afternoon, I pored through the tomes on magic Saige and Briar had discovered, my nerves still unsettled after the morning's disturbing encounter with Kai. A knock at my door made me jump. I cautiously cracked it open to see Drake looming there, his expression unreadable.

I opened the door wide, motioning for him to enter, but he just stood there. Wordlessly, he pressed something into my palm—a silver dagger in a beaded leather sheath.

"For protection when you're alone," he asserted gruffly.

His calloused fingers grazed my wrist as I automatically curled my hand around the dagger's grip. The contact sent a spark through me. Drake's piercing eyes locked with mine, our faces just inches apart.

"Promise you'll keep this close." The intensity of his tone caught me off guard. I could only nod mutely.

Seemingly satisfied, Drake stepped back and raked a hand through his hair. But despite the distance between us again, that magnetic pull still lingered in the air. Instead of saying anything else, Drake nodded and strode off down the hall, ending our conversation.

I drew a shaky breath once I'd closed the door. Drake's gift moved me, reflecting his protective instincts. Yet it complicated matters further between us. My heart and head remained at war, uncertain which path led to wisdom or folly.

With his capricious temper and our clashing roles, I knew entanglement with Drake spelled only heartache. But each charged encounter etched him deeper beneath my skin. Denying that truth grew harder each day, no matter how I tried to steel my resolve against him.

I turned the silver dagger Drake gifted me over in my hands, conflicted emotions welling up. On one hand, his concerned gesture awoke an undeniable longing. On the other hand, it could be seen as an attempt to sway me to show favoritism toward Flat Tops.

Yet when our gazes had locked, I'd glimpsed past the

gruff exterior to the sincerity in Drake's eyes. He cared deeply, but he couldn't bring himself to fully show it. No doubt, his past losses still haunted him. But perhaps certain fires burned too hotly to be contained.

With a resigned sigh, I reluctantly set down the dagger on my desk. Wisdom demanded caution with regard to our connection for now. But my doubts about which path to take only multiplied with each passing day.

There was another knock on my door. "Come in," I called out.

Harper entered, her brisk steps bringing her quickly to my desk. She didn't take a seat, so I understood her visit would be brief. "Congratulations! The initial council meeting was a success. So much so, I'm requesting another meeting for us to dive deeper into the water rights issues."

I supposed I should rejoice in Harper's acknowledgment as the compliment it was. "Of course, I will see if we can get one setup for next week?"

"That would be advisable." Harper's eyes roamed over my desk, covered with papers. Her lips pressed into a thin line as she picked up the dagger, her gaze shooting back to mine.

"I know Flat Top artistry when I see it. Drake's transparent attempts to gain your favor for his enclave are beneath you both," she said bluntly.

My cheeks flushed under her piercing stare. I opened my mouth to explain it wasn't like that, but Harper continued on critically.

"I know Drake can be protective in his way, but you walk a finer line than he does. As our mediator, you must avoid even the appearance of bias." Her tone allowed no debate as she handed the dagger to me.

Chastened, I turned the dagger over in my hands. As much as it pained me, Harper's guidance was sound. Although I appreciated Drake's gesture, I recognized that keeping such a gift would create more complications than it solved.

When I further considered other potential unnecessary yet interesting entanglements with Drake, my heart stuttered. Why it hadn't occurred to me before now, I didn't know. Perhaps that's why Drake had been keeping his distance? To honor my role as mediator between the enclaves?

"You're right," I said finally, meeting Harper's gaze. "I will return his gift."

Satisfied, Harper gave a curt nod. "A wise decision. I'll leave you to it." With that, she briskly departed.

Alone again, I sighed heavily before slipping the dagger into my pocket. Wisdom demanded keeping Drake at a careful distance. Yet even the thought of parting with his gift left an unexpected ache in my chest. But what other choice did I have?

I spotted Drake and Willem standing in the courtyard outside the inn, their conversation quiet but animated. As I drew closer, Drake's eyes swept up to meet mine, his expression softening as he smiled at me.

Wordlessly, I held out the sheathed dagger, aware of Harper observing discretely from the porch. Drake's bewildered expression darkened as he took it from me.

"I cannot, in good faith, keep this gift," I began carefully. "I know your intent was good. But as mediator..."

Understanding dawned in Drake's expression, followed

swiftly by outrage. "Did someone convince you I'm manipulating you somehow by giving you protection?" He shook his head in disgust, his gaze landing on Harper. He let out a low growl. "I know it must have been her. That woman could sniff out ill intent in raindrops."

I shifted uneasily. "Drake, please try to understand."

But he cut me off, his eyes blazing. "Oh, I understand perfectly well." He turned on his heel, frustration etched in every line of his body. Then he stormed off without another word, leaving me alone with my regrets.

I stood there, watching his retreating figure until he disappeared from view, a heavy weight settling in my chest. The hurt and anger in his eyes had been unmistakable, and it pained me to know that I caused it. I understood his frustration and his feeling of being misunderstood and misjudged. But I also knew that, as the innkeeper and mediator, I had to maintain a delicate balance. Even the slightest hint of favoritism could upset the fragile peace between the enclaves.

Still, a part of me longed to run after him, to explain that it wasn't about a lack of trust or a belief in his ulterior motives. It was about the greater good, about putting the needs of Crescent Crossing above my own desires. But the words stuck in my throat, and I remained rooted to the spot, watching as the distance between us grew.

With a heavy sigh, I turned back towards the inn, my heart torn between duty and longing. I knew that the path I had chosen was a solitary one, fraught with tough decisions and personal sacrifices. But as much as it hurt, I had to believe that it was the right one.

CHAPTER 13

As I continued sifting through the relative chaos of Ryder's messy office, my eyes fell on a stack of old records and files I hadn't thoroughly examined yet. My heart raced as I hoped these documents could hold the key to uncovering the truth about the growing unrest in Crescent Crossing. But as I dug deeper, my mind became clouded with doubts and fears. What if I found something that incriminated someone I'd grown to like in this tiny town? I couldn't bear the thought of having to choose between loyalty to my new friends and the truth. With a heavy heart, I persisted in my search, hoping I hadn't misplaced my trust.

As I sifted through property deeds, council notes, and maps, a name stood out: Cade Wilder.

Another Wilder. That couldn't be a coincidence.

Skimming the document, I learned Cade had been exiled from the Elk clan nearly ten years ago, accused of a series of severe transgressions, though never formally charged. The primary accusations included burning a sacred grove near the Bittersweet Spring, thus violating the sacred bounds of Bittersweet territory and damaging a sacred site. More disturbingly, he was also accused of threatening to harm the Ryder. His actions had sown deep discord, leading to his banishment. Cade had vanished shortly after, leaving a shadow over the Elk clan.

But what stunned me even more was the attached note in the document, revealing a startling fact: Cade Wilder had an identical twin brother, Kai Wilder. This revelation added an extra layer of complexity to the already tangled web of events unfolding in our midst.

As I absorbed this shocking information, my gaze fell upon the raven amulet that Barnell had found near Ryder's body. Its intricate design seemed to call out to me, demanding attention. With trembling fingers, I picked it up, tracing the delicate lines of the raven's wings.

Suddenly, a series of fragmented images flashed through my mind, like a dream that was just out of reach. I saw hooded figures gathered around a fire, their faces obscured by shadows. The raven symbol was prominently displayed on their cloaks, seeming to dance in the flickering light. Whispers of ancient words filled the air, but I couldn't quite make out their meaning.

As quickly as the vision had come, it faded, leaving me gasping for breath. I looked down at the amulet in my hand, realizing that it held a far greater significance than I had initially believed. The raven was not just a mere decoration; it was the mark of a secret society, one that had been linked to past uprisings and rebellions.

With a renewed sense of urgency, I delved deeper into the documents, searching for any mention of the raven symbol or the mysterious group it represented. Scattered throughout the pages were references to a faction known as the "Ravenshadow," a cabal of exiled shifters who had sought to overthrow the established order in Crescent Crossing.

I sat back heavily, my pulse racing as I confirmed the shared birthdate. The sly, seductive Kai I knew had a destructive and unstable twin. This revelation shed new light on Kai's potential motives and connections to the mysterious happenings plaguing the town.

I had to talk to Kai about Cade and his exile. But I couldn't sit around and hope he'd return; I had to go find him.

I hurried downstairs, nearly colliding with Briar in my haste. "Do you know where Kai lives?" I asked urgently. "It's imperative I speak with him right away."

Briar's brow furrowed. "I'm afraid I don't have that information. But perhaps Nalani Silverpine would know, being a member of Kai's clan."

A surge of hope filled me. As the town doctor and a skilled herbalist, Nalani had extensive connections across the enclaves. Surely she could direct me to Kai.

I quickly located Hamish and Saige, briefing them on the shocking revelation about Kai's criminal twin. Their expressions hardened with concern.

"We're coming with you," Hamish asserted, his protective instincts flaring. "Kai has much to answer for."

Soon we stood before Nalani's clinic, a charming log cabin emitting the earthy scent of drying herbs. The healer listened intently as I explained the urgency of finding Kai quickly.

"I understand your need to speak with him," Nalani acknowledged. "However, I must consider my ethical duties to guard my patients' and my enclave's privacy."

Sensing her hesitation, Saige interjected pointedly. "Surely ethics allow exceptions when public safety is at stake? Or within the scope of a murder investigation?"

Nalani's piercing green eyes assessed each of us before she nodded reluctantly. "Considering recent troubling events, I will provide his location just this once. But for my patient and pack, discretion is imperative. Don't go assuming I'll help without proper cause in the future."

After securing Kai's address, Hamish drove us out, slowly following the winding dirt road leading deep into the wilderness. The damp forest air pricked at my skin as we drew closer to his secluded cabin deep in the trees. I fortified myself, hoping to coax the sly shifter into revealing the truth.

As we approached Kai's cabin, the dense evergreen forest seemed to part, revealing a rustic, two-story structure nestled in a small clearing. The cabin's weathered, honey-colored logs blended seamlessly with the surrounding woods, as if they had sprouted from the earth itself. A wide, wrap-around porch hugged the front of the cabin, its rough-hewn planks creaking beneath our feet as we climbed the steps.

The cabin's windows were shuttered, and tendrils of smoke curled lazily from the stone chimney, hinting at the warmth and light within. A sleek, black car was parked haphazardly near the front door, its polished surface at odds with the rugged, natural beauty of the surrounding landscape.

The air was heavy with the scent of pine and damp earth, and the only sounds were the whisper of the wind through the trees and the distant call of a hawk. It was a place of solitude and peace, far removed from the prying eyes of Crescent Crossing.

I steeled my nerves as we approached the front door. It burst open before we reached it. A disheveled Kai stood in the entryway, his cheeks creased with concern and his usual poise visibly shaken.

"You finally managed to track me down. To what do I owe the pleasure?" His tone held a bitter edge as he regarded the three of us warily.

I crossed my arms and declared, "Why don't we start with you explaining why you failed to mention your twin brother Cade, exiled from Elk lands over serious crimes?" Kai stumbled, his face becoming ashen. He quickly ushered us inside the rustic cabin and refused to glance in my direction again. I could feel the dread dripping off him at the mere mention of his twin brother's name.

He started speaking quickly as he walked back and forth across the threadbare rug in front of the fireplace. "Listen, I don't want you to believe anything my brother said. Cade is dangerous and untrustworthy. I tried to give him another chance, but..." Kai's voice trailed off, and guilt was clear in his expression.

"So you brought your criminal twin back to town, hid him from the authorities, and are shocked that it did not work out as planned?" I asked. His dismay was clear on his face.

Kai held up his hands placatingly. "It's not that simple. Cade just showed up. He's still my family. How could I turn him away?" He turned to stare into the flickering fire, his shoulders slumping. "When Cade showed up a few weeks ago, half-starved and ranting, what was I supposed to do?" Kai continued quietly. "We were inseparable as pups. I couldn't abandon him, no matter what he'd become. He's not well." He finally faced me, turmoil etched on his features. "I had no idea he was so far gone." Kai gripped the mantle, knuckles white. "I was a fool for trusting him. And now my poor judgment has put you directly in harm's way."

Saige, Hamish, and I exchanged a glance. "I'm gathering that," I answered.

As Kai delivered his story about his twin's arrival, I thoughtfully watched him. He was very different from the agitated man who had barged into my office, spouting wild theories and cautioning me.

The stark contrast sparked a startling realization: that disheveled figure had not been Kai at all, but his exiled twin, Cade, masquerading as his brother. Likely, Cade intended to misdirect suspicion and undermine my efforts as the new mediator.

"That wasn't you in my office yesterday, was it?" I interjected, already knowing the truth. "That was your brother posing as you to throw me off."

Kai froze mid-sentence, paling slightly as understanding dawned. "You're absolutely right," he confirmed grimly. "I never went to the inn yesterday. That was undoubtedly Cade stirring up chaos and trying to implicate me."

He dropped his face in his hands. "I'm such a damned fool. I knew he was unstable, yet still, I trusted he would cause no further harm here. Now my poor judgment has brought turmoil to Crescent Crossing. Can you ever forgive me?"

I said nothing, letting the heavy silence emphasize the gravity of his mistakes. Kai had placed everyone at risk by keeping silent. But blinding remorse still gripped Kai, leaving the full truth out of reach. I needed to tread carefully.

I moved closer to Kai, choosing my next words carefully.

"I think it's time you tell me everything about why Cade was exiled. Don't spare any details."

Kai nodded resignedly. "I suppose, as Ryder's replacement, you have a right to know." He leaned forward, grief etched on his face.

"Ten years ago, Cade committed grave offenses against the clan. He burned a sacred grove near the Bittersweet Spring, violating the revered territory of their pack. Then he threatened the innkeeper, Ryder, a figure whose neutrality and kindness had long held our community together. The evidence was circumstantial, but the acts were too heinous to ignore. Our alpha had no choice but to banish him permanently."

He raked a hand through his blond hair. "We were young shifters, almost still pups, all cocky and wild. I thought Cade was just challenging norms and being reckless in his own way. I never imagined..." His voice broke.

"After his banishment, Cade cut all ties with me and the rest of the Elk clan. He blamed us for not standing up to Ryder and our alpha on his behalf. After that, Cade disappeared into the wilderness, living more as a feral wolf than a man. I had always hoped that solitude might bring him peace, even redemption. Not all wolves are destined for a pack." Kai shook his head bitterly. "But in my heart, I feared that such isolation might only deepen his resentment and mental turmoil."

Kai lifted his eyes to meet my gaze. "When he showed up again out of the blue, half-starved and crazed, I felt compelled to take him in, for old time's sake. But the brother I once knew seems long gone, leaving only darkness in his wake."

Kai fell silent, guilt and grief etched on his face. After a long pause, I gently prompted him. "What happened when Cade first returned to Crescent Crossing?"

He sighed heavily, sinking back against the leather couch. "A few weeks ago, he showed up at my door in the dead of night, haggard and raving. I could scarcely believe it was him after so many years apart."

Kai's eyes took on a faraway look as he delved into the painful memories. "Cade begged me to take him in, insisting he had nowhere else to turn. He seemed so broken and desperate. I hadn't the heart to turn my twin away, no matter his past sins or instability."

He dropped his gaze, ashamed. "Cade claimed he only wished to make amends and start fresh, so I agreed to shelter him here temporarily while he got back on his feet. But deep down, I knew it was a risk."

Kai turned to stare into the fire, turmoil in his eyes. "I thought with time and guidance, his bitterness might heal. Now I see that was terribly naïve. The darkness has consumed him entirely."

He looked up at me, anguish etched on his face. "I wanted to believe redemption was possible for my brother. But in my blindness, I've welcomed chaos into this valley."

Kai hung his head in shame. But I knew the forces Kai had helped unleash were not so easily contained again.

I leaned forward, keeping my voice low but firm. "Kai, you know I must ask—where was Cade the night Ryder was murdered?"

Kai flinched as if struck. "Surely you don't think he was involved in that horror?" He searched my face desperately. "Ryder was a hardass, but it was the alpha who exiled Cade, not the innkeeper. Cade was a troublemaker. Unstable. Restless. But he'd never commit such evil, no matter how much bitterness festered in him over the years."

I pressed further, unrelenting. "The raven calling card left at the scene points to those exiled for past crimes. And Cade had motive to get revenge against Ryder."

Kai shook his head vehemently. "You're mistaken. My brother has been unwell, but he remains incapable of such depravity."

His denial rang hollow.

"Exactly what level of depravity is Cade capable of?" I asked Kai bluntly. "What further evil is he prepared to unleash?"

The piercing truth left Kai speechless, his eyes locked on mine without any response. I knew Cade was ensnared in the spreading darkness. But familial bonds blinded Kai to the threat his twin posed.

I stood to take my leave, resolve renewed. Cade's wicked influence corrupted this valley. But Kai's loyalty left him unable to accept the horrible truth. I would need to confront Cade myself before further innocent blood was spilled.

As we made to depart, I turned back once more to Kai, who sat slumped on his couch, anguish carved into his features.

"I know how difficult this is to accept, but you must open your eyes to the truth about Cade before it's too late." I kept my tone gentle but firm.

Kai just shook his head wordlessly, the light of revelation still too piercing for him to withstand. Blinding remorse and the shattered remains of fraternal loyalty obscured his vision.

I realized with a shiver that Kai would not help me halt

his brother's ruinous plans. Only my allies and I could do that now.

I braced myself and left Kai to his struggles with the shadow closing in around him. Hopefully, the light would reach his heart eventually. But Crescent Crossing needed urgent attention now, not a wait for Kai's salvation.

As we descended the cabin steps, I turned to Hamish and Saige, resolve etched on my face. "Kai refuses to believe his twin's corruption, so investigating Cade falls to us alone."

Saige's expression hardened. "We can handle it. Cade clearly hopes to hide behind his brother's silence."

"We'll drag this scoundrel into the light," Hamish growled. "Just point the way."

With their steadfast backing, my anxieties faded away. As we walked back toward the car, Kai called out urgently for us to wait. I turned to see him standing on the porch, anguish carved into his features.

"There is one more thing you should know," he began haltingly. "Cade had a close friend once, before everything fell apart. Malachi Sterling. They were nearly inseparable back then."

This startling revelation stunned me. Malachi seemed solely driven by his own selfish agenda. Yet perhaps his steadfast loyalty to his old friend Cade better explained the man's cryptic motivations.

I stepped closer, scrutinizing Kai's face. "Tell me everything about their history together," I demanded.

Kai nodded wearily, his eyes distant as he delved into the memories. "Cade, Malachi, and I grew up together since our parents all worked in town. We were close as littermates, despite coming from different packs. We were always getting into mischief, exploring the woods and pushing the boundaries of our abilities. Malachi and Cade had a special bond though. They understood each other in a way I never could."

He paused, a sad smile tugging at his lips. "Malachi was the one who could calm Cade's restless spirit, and Cade was the only one who could draw Malachi out of his shell. They balanced each other, I suppose."

Kai's expression darkened as he continued. "As we grew older, Cade became more reckless, more defiant of authority. Malachi tried to rein him in, but he was also fiercely loyal. When Cade was accused of those terrible crimes, Malachi was the only one who stood by him, even when the evidence seemed damning."

He sighed heavily, his shoulders slumping. "After Cade's exile, Malachi was never the same. He withdrew from the pack and became bitter. I think a part of him died that day, along with his faith in the justice of our laws and traditions."

I absorbed this quietly, suspicions swirling. Had Malachi been aiding Cade all this time out of a misplaced sense of loyalty and shared anger? If so, he likely knew far more about Ryder's murder than he'd revealed.

I looked at Kai and saw the burden of the past reflected in his haunted expression. "I appreciate what you've told me. You've taken the first step in regaining my trust."

As we left Kai to wrestle alone with past demons, new possibilities took shape around Malachi's potential motivations. With this fresh perspective, perhaps even that enigmatic man's facade would finally crack.

I mulled over the implications of Cade and Malachi's connection as we made our way back to the car. If they had been working together, it could explain Malachi's evasive behavior and his attempts to undermine my authority as the new innkeeper. But why? What did they hope to achieve by sowing chaos and discord in Crescent Crossing?

Suddenly, a thought struck me like a bolt of lightning. The mysterious "CW" that Ryder had scheduled to meet with on the night of his murder—could it have been Cade Wilder? The pieces fell into place in my mind. If Cade had returned to Crescent Crossing, seeking revenge for his exile, Ryder would have been a prime target.

I felt a chill run down my spine as I considered the possibility. Had Ryder discovered Cade's presence in the valley and confronted him, only to pay the ultimate price? And was Malachi somehow involved in the murder, either as an accomplice or as a witness?

The gravity of these possibilities weighed heavily on me. I knew I had to tread carefully, gathering more evidence before confronting either Cade or Malachi directly. But I also knew that time was running out. With each passing day, chaos threatened to consume Crescent Crossing, and I was the only one who could stop it.

I turned to Hamish and Saige, my voice low and urgent. "We need to find out everything we can about Cade's whereabouts on the night of Ryder's murder. And we need to keep a close eye on Malachi. I have a feeling he knows more than he's letting on."

They nodded grimly, their expressions mirroring my determination. Together, we would unravel the tangled web of secrets and lies that had ensnared Crescent Crossing. And we would bring those responsible for Ryder's death to justice, no matter the cost.

CHAPTER 14

The setting sun cast long shadows across the rustic exterior of the Howl Away Inn as Hamish, Saige, and I made our way up the winding path. Despite the tranquil surroundings, an uneasy silence hung over our small group. My nerves felt frayed after the tense conversation with Kai and the chilling revelations about his exiled twin brother, Cade. Hamish and Saige flanked me protectively, their expressions grim.

I hesitated at the carved oak door, steeling myself before entering the inn's cozy lounge. Drake and Briar looked up sharply from their muted discussion by the hearth as we approached. Taking in my disheveled appearance, Briar set down her coffee cup, concern creasing her brow.

"You found Kai, then?" she asked. "You look dreadful, like you're in shock."

I sank onto the plush leather couch, running a hand through my windswept hair. "We found him alright. And the ghost of the past he's been hiding—his twin brother Cade."

Drake straightened, his piercing eyes narrowing. "Cade Wilder? The one exiled over a decade ago?"

I nodded wearily. "The same. Only now he's back and Kai's been sheltering him in secret."

Drake swore under his breath, rising to pace before the fire. "Kai betrayed us all by allowing that criminal back here. We should banish him too." His hands clenched into fists.

Briar paled, pressing a hand over her mouth. "Wait, do you think Cade could be responsible for Ryder?" She could barely choke out the question.

"It's possible," Saige said, exchanging a look with Hamish. "Either way, he poses a threat that must be addressed."

I leaned forward intently. "Which is why we need to organize search parties to comb the town and wilderness for any sign of him." I stood up with a firm resolve. "Let's gather the others, then. We can find Cade and figure out what he's been doing with his free time, besides harassing me." Picking up the phone, I dialed Harper, Aja, and Nalani's numbers. "Come quickly," I urged them when they answered. "We need to meet at once."

Squaring my shoulders, I strode toward the meeting room.

Yet even as flickers of hope stirred, an icy dread lingered that finding Cade could prove far more perilous than any of us expected. The thought of what he might be capable of after years of being removed from civilization sent a shiver down my spine. But we had to try. For Ryder's sake and for the town's safety, we would do whatever it took to find Cade.

I didn't have long to wait before my council arrived. Accompanied by Drake, whom I had asked to join us as we would need his assistance in searching for Cade, I surveyed the circle of uneasy faces gathered around the oak table. Harper, Nalani, and Aja watched me intently, clearly unsettled by the gravity of my mood. Drake took a position alone in the corner, with his arms tightly crossed and a stormy expression on his face. I took a deep breath before speaking.

"I'm afraid troubling revelations have come to light," I began gravely, meeting each of their gazes. "Kai Wilder has been secretly sheltering a significant threat in our midst—his twin brother Cade."

Shock and dismay rippled palpably through the room. Harper's eyes widened, her hand flying to her mouth in a gesture of disbelief. Nalani and Aja exchanged alarmed glances, their brows furrowed with concern. Aja leaned forward, her hands clasped tightly in front of her, while Nalani sat back in her chair, her usually serene expression replaced by one of apprehension.

Drake's reaction was the most intense. His hands clenched into fists, his knuckles whitening as he gritted his teeth. I could practically feel the protective instincts radiating off him in waves.

Keeping my tone even, I continued, "As some of you may recall, Cade was exiled over a decade ago for alleged crimes against the Bittersweet clan and threatening the prior innkeeper. Despite his exile, he has mysteriously resurfaced here in Crescent Crossing. Needless to say, the timing of Cade's return does not bode well," I added grimly. "Given the heinous acts resulting in his banishment, I believe he poses a real danger that we cannot ignore."

"And Kai knowingly brought this dangerous criminal into our midst, hiding him even after Ryder's vicious murder," Drake bit out through gritted teeth, his simmering rage clear. "There must be consequences for such a betrayal."

I lifted a hand placatingly. "While Kai's deception is deeply troubling, family loyalty likely swayed his poor judgment. Regardless, finding Cade must be our top priority because we don't know what he's capable of." I met Drake's turbulent gaze steadily. "We will address Kai's role once the immediate threat is contained."

Drake's jaw tightened, but he gave a curt nod of acceptance. The rest of the council also appeared to be resigned to pragmatic caution for now.

"We need to organize search parties immediately to scour the town and surrounding wilderness for any trace of Cade," I declared urgently. "I'll need all of your help to recruit skilled volunteers we can trust to assist in this exhaustive hunt."

Harper's response rang with conviction. "The Bittersweets have never turned away from a challenge, and this threat is too great to ignore. I will speak with our alpha at once to secure every available resource until the fugitive is found."

Aja's expression was somber yet resolute. "The Flat Tops stand united with you in hunting down this threat by any means necessary," she vowed solemnly.

"Absolutely," Nalani replied, her melodic voice resonating with gentle strength. "I'll share maps and alert our remote allies. And I can speak to the Elk alpha to alert our long-range patrols in the back country."

Fragile hope flickered in my chest at their unified support. With our combined efforts, we had a chance of locating Cade before he could slip away or inflict more harm under the cover of darkness.

As the council members dispersed, Drake caught my arm, pulling me aside with an urgency that set my nerves on edge. I glimpsed Hamish shadowing us protectively as Drake led me out of earshot down an empty corridor.

Drake's expression was uncharacteristically grave as he turned to face me. "We need to talk privately," he said, his tone somber.

Unease crept over me as I considered his notoriously mercurial temper. "What's on your mind?" I asked warily.

He raked a hand through his dark, tousled hair, pacing restlessly in the narrow passage. "I have serious concerns that your proposed strategy of coordinated search parties is too passive and inefficient to succeed against someone like Cade."

Drake's frustration was palpable as he continued. "Cade is a ghost. Only a master at evading trackers could survive alone in the unforgiving wilderness for years. Those volunteers you want to recruit won't stand a chance at finding him."

Drake's direct rejection of the planned search effort caught me off guard. Keeping my tone carefully neutral, I asked, "Then I assume you have an alternative strategy in mind?"

Drake's intense gray gaze fixed on me, his voice dropping lower but ringing with conviction. "To catch a cunning monster like Cade, we need to be more ruthless ourselves. Use you as bait to draw him out when he can't resist the temptation."

Before I could react to this alarming proposal, Hamish

intervened protectively, his expression thunderous. "That's far too dangerous. I absolutely refuse to place you at such risk," he argued.

I hesitated, seeing potential merits but also major risks in Drake's radical plan. "You raise a fair point that we're facing real challenges tracking an experienced fugitive in the wilderness," I acknowledged. "But we need time to evaluate all options, not just rush into provocation without considering the consequences."

Drake appeared satisfied by my willingness to at least entertain his daring proposal, but Hamish remained visibly troubled and disheartened by the concept.

I attempted to reassure them both as diplomatically as I could. "For now, let's keep this discussion private while we carefully weigh all the risks and scenarios," I suggested delicately. I then retreated to my office, my thoughts roiling with the complexity of our situation.

Alone again in the stillness of my office, I sank into the worn leather chair behind the heavy oak desk, the weight of recent events bearing down. In that private space, away from prying eyes, I finally let the armor of composure fall away.

How did we end up in this dangerous situation, where even my former allies are suggesting levels of manipulation and danger that I find difficult to comprehend? My thoughts turned to Ryder and his tremendous burden of maintaining stability amid simmering chaos. What had guided him during crises that threatened to eclipse reason? If only he'd left a map to managing peace in this mountain shifter town hidden in this office.

Yet even in this dark hour, I knew with bone-deep certainty that one truth remained fixed: the lives of innocents depended on my ability to hold chaos at bay. Although Drake's plan made me feel uneasy, displaying any division or uncertainty at this point could have disastrous outcomes. Regardless of the heavy risks on my mind, my utmost concern was to protect the people of Crescent Crossing.

I drew a long, shuddering breath, steadying myself. For better or worse, my course was plain. Seeking refuge in principles would not save lives. I faced challenging decisions and had to have faith in my decision-making abilities to navigate the dangerous path ahead.

When I heard a cautious knock at my door, I composed myself and responded, "Come in."

Drake opened the door yet lingered in the doorway, his gray eyes inscrutable. "Good. I'd hoped I'd find you alone. Have you given more thought to my suggestion?" His casual tone barely concealed the tension thrumming beneath.

I rose to face him, my turmoil carefully veiled. "I have. And I don't think it's a good idea."

Drake searched my face, a hint of shock cracking his stoic facade. He stepped closer. "You won't even consider it?"

I hesitated. "I understand the motivation behind your plan, but I can't ignore the risks involved. If we did this, I don't see how we could keep the situation under control."

Drake nodded, his expression serious. "Don't you trust me? I give you my word that I won't let any harm come to you."

I felt a flicker of warmth at his fierce protectiveness, even as a part of me bristled at the idea of being seen as vulnerable. "I appreciate that, Drake. But I need to know that you'll follow my lead on this, and I can't act without my friends. Promise me you won't do anything rash."

Drake held my gaze, his eyes intense. "You have my word."

I let out a slow breath. "Okay. Thank you."

Drake grasped my hands, his own calloused and feverishly warm. "We'll catch Cade," he vowed solemnly. "One way or another. You have my word."

Despite my lingering doubts, I managed a taut smile in return. My choice had been made the moment I shut Drake down.

Drake gripped my shoulders and then left, leaving me with my turbulent thoughts.

Later that evening, unable to sleep, I retreated to the sheltering boughs of the old oak tree in the inn's garden, seeking solace to gather my churning thoughts. The baying of distant wolves echoed up from the shadowed valley, underscoring the unease permeating the darkened hollows and wooded ridges surrounding Crescent Crossing.

Footsteps on the gravel path heralded Saige's approach. Though I kept my gaze fixed on the moonlit mountains, the familiar presence of my staunch friend beside me brought some small comfort amid the unrelenting chaos.

We remained in calm silence for a while until the mounting heaviness on my heart urged me to share the worries that were tormenting my restless mind.

"Cade's return has stirred up a dark history," I confessed softly. "I fear what will happen next if we can't catch him." I turned to Saige, turmoil in my eyes. "What if my best efforts cannot prevent more bloodshed?"

Saige considered my words before responding gently. "Your compassion has unified us so far. Do not abandon hope when it is most needed." She gave my hand a bracing squeeze. "Through every trial and doubt, your determination to protect this haven has never faltered."

I searched Saige's steadfast gaze, drawing courage from her unwavering faith in me. She was right—no matter how bleak the road ahead appeared, giving in to despair served no one.

I managed a small, grateful smile. "Thank you for reminding me what truly matters."

Saige returned my smile warmly. "Anytime. That's what friends are for."

With Saige's wisdom resonating within me, the jagged edges of my frayed nerves were soothed. Her support reignited the flame of hope within me, a flame that no darkness could ever put out. With my determination restored, I was now prepared to face whatever puzzle awaited me, ready to unravel its secrets.

CHAPTER 15

Unease plagued me as I lay awake in the wee hours of the morning, listening to the mournful sighs of the wind outside my window. Days had passed since our confrontation with Kai and the revelation of his twin brother Cade's return, yet my mind still echoed with the ominous implications of this discovery.

Restless, I ventured into the garden, seeking solace beneath the star-strewn sky. As I approached the inn's boundary, a glint of something caught my eye. Bending down, I retrieved a small wooden disc, no larger than my palm. Brushing away the dirt, I revealed an intricate etching of two ravens flanking a crescent moon.

A shiver ran through me as I traced the unfamiliar symbol with my fingertip. Instinct told me this was no mere trinket but a sign of something more sinister at play.

Just as I slipped the disc into my pocket, a flicker of movement at the tree line caught my attention. Unease slithered down my spine as I squinted into the darkness, but despite my fae night vision, I couldn't track the movement.

Heart pounding, I spun towards the inn, only to find Drake's imposing form blocking my path. His eyes, usually sharp and assessing, now glinted with an uncharacteristic hardness.

"We need to talk," he said, his tone brooking no argument as he grasped my arm and guided me back inside to the fire lit lounge.

"What were you thinking, going out there alone?" Drake demanded, his gravelly voice laced with a mix of concern and frustration.

I bristled at his accusatory tone, pulling my arm from his grasp. "I couldn't sleep, so I went for some fresh air. But that's not the point. Look what I found." I withdrew the wooden disc from my pocket, holding it up for him to see.

Drake's brow furrowed as he examined the etching. "The symbol is used by those who have been exiled as shifters or are outcasts from packs. Did you see who left it?"

I shook my head, a chill running through me as I remembered the phantom figure vanishing into the shadows. "For a moment, I was sure someone was out there watching me. But I didn't see anyone."

Handing the disc back to me, Drake's jaw clenched, a muscle ticking in his cheek. He stalked to the window, scanning the darkness beyond. "And your first instinct was to confront them? Alone?" His tone was sharp, disapproval clear in the set of his shoulders.

"I didn't go chasing after them," I countered, lifting my chin. "Like I said, I was just restless."

Drake turned to face me, his expression a mix of determination and something harder to define. "There's no sign of anyone now, but we can't let our guard down. I'll post extra sentries tonight, and tomorrow we'll dig deeper into this disc's origin. It might be the lead we need to draw Cade out of hiding."

I nodded, trying to ignore the lingering unease from my brush with the unseen observer. Drake must have sensed my disquiet because he took a step closer, something flickering in his eyes before he caught himself.

"Get some rest," he said gruffly. "No point in running yourself ragged."

Before I could respond, he turned on his heel and strode away, tension coiled in every line of his body. I watched him go, the weight of the disc heavy in my pocket and a tangle of emotions twisting in my chest.

As Drake's retreating footsteps faded, I was left with a strange ache in my chest. The distance between us seemed to grow with each terse exchange, a chasm that I feared might never be bridged. The path forward was shrouded in uncertainty, with only the faintest glimmer of hope to guide us.

Seeking solace from the tumultuous thoughts swirling in my mind, I retreated to my office despite the early hour. I placed the wooden disc on my desk and contemplated what it might mean. Sometime later, I was startled awake when I heard a knock at the door.

Briar entered, a thick, leather-bound tome tucked under her arm. "Morning," she greeted, a smile on her face. "I found this book on local symbols in the lounge and thought it should be returned to your office." Her eyes fell on the disc, and her expression shifted. "Where did you get that?" she asked, her tone sharp.

I recounted the events of the previous night, from my restless venture into the garden to the discovery of the disc. As I spoke, Briar crossed the room in a few quick strides, setting the book down and flipping it open to a section on exile marks. She pointed to an illustration that matched the symbol on the disc perfectly.

"It's a Marauder's mark," she said grimly. "A sign used by shifters cast out from their packs, usually for violent or treacherous acts. They carve these symbols into cursed objects when seeking revenge against those who banished them."

A chill ran through me as I looked down at the disc, my fingers trembling slightly as I turned it over in my hands. The implications of Briar's revelation settled heavily in my gut.

"These marks have appeared throughout history, often preceding brutal attacks by exiled shifters against their former packs and the communities that drove them out," Briar continued, her voice somber. "If this disc is here, it could mean Cade isn't acting alone. He may have allied himself with other outcasts, and they could be planning something far more sinister than mere threats and sowing discord."

I thought back to the shadowy figure I thought I'd seen lurking at the edge of the woods, and a sense of foreboding washed over me. If Briar was right, the appearance of this disc could be the portent of a coming storm, one that threatened to engulf Crescent Crossing in violence. It was a possibility I couldn't ignore, and one that I knew would require swift and decisive action to prevent.

"I hope it's just Cade trying to rattle us," I said, my voice grim.

Before Briar could respond, a sharp knock at the door drew our attention. Drake stood in the doorway, his face impassive as he scanned the room. Hamish stood behind him, his body poised and alert for any potential threats.

"Drake mentioned you found something important," Hamish said, his eyes falling on the disc in my hands.

I handed over the wooden disc and the open book, watching as Hamish's face darkened while he read the passage on exiled shifter marks. "This confirms my suspicions," he muttered. "Cade is definitely not acting alone. We need to fortify the inn's defenses immediately."

As Drake launched into a description of the additional security measures he planned to implement, I felt a flicker of impatience. "Shouldn't we be doing more to protect the entire town? As the innkeeper, I have a responsibility to ensure the safety of everyone in Crescent Crossing."

Drake's fist slammed down on my desk, his eyes flashing with frustration. "You can't expect to influence the town if you haven't earned their respect first. Right now, they see you as an outsider, a fae who doesn't belong."

He leaned in closer, his voice low and intense. "You need to focus on demonstrating your strength here, at the inn. Show them you can secure this place against any threat. Only then will they start to take you seriously as a leader."

His words stung, prodding at the insecurities that lingered in the back of my mind. I knew my primary duty was to safeguard the inn, but a part of me still yearned for acceptance from the town's residents.

Perhaps sensing my inner turmoil, Drake's expression softened slightly. "I know it's difficult being thrust into this position as an outsider. But you can't let the shifters see any weakness. Stand your ground, and they'll come to respect your authority."

I looked away, acknowledging the truth in his words even as they chafed. The responsibility of my new position weighed heavily on me, and I understood that there would be no easy resolution in gaining the trust I required to effectively lead.

Determined to take action, I called for an emergency meeting with Aja, Nalani, and Harper for the second time in as many days. The atmosphere in the room grew somber as I passed around the disc and the book, the implications of the exiled shifters' symbol clear to all.

Aja examined the wooden disc closely, her brow furrowed in concentration. After a moment, she pulled out her phone and began scrolling through her photos. "This symbol looks familiar," she muttered, her eyes scanning the screen.

Finally, she found what she was looking for and handed me the phone. The image displayed was startlingly similar to the one on the disc—the same raven and crescent moon design, carved into a bloodstained wooden post.

"My cousin sent me this picture last year, after their settlement in the northern territories was attacked," Aja explained, her voice grim. "Days before the attack, they found these symbols painted on posts around their central gathering area. They believed it was a warning sign from the exiled shifters to stay out of the area."

As I zoomed in on the photo, a chill ran through me. The resemblance was too striking to be a mere coincidence. I passed the phone to Saige, watching as her lips pressed into a thin line.

"So, you think this means the outcasts have made their way to our territories, looking for revenge?" I asked, my voice tight.

Aja nodded, her hazel eyes glinting with a mix of anger and apprehension. "I'm certain of it. That's a Marauder's mark, no doubt about it. And based on the wood, it comes from the forests up north."

Nalani, usually the picture of serenity, now looked deeply troubled. "Our seers have been sensing dark energies gathering during the recent new moon rituals. This symbol confirms their visions."

Harper, however, seemed less convinced. She studied the disc with a critical eye, her brow furrowed in thought. "While this resembles a Marauder's mark, we shouldn't jump to conclusions about a larger conspiracy just because Cade has resurfaced."

She met my gaze, her expression serious. "It's more likely that Cade made this himself to unnerve us and retaliate for his exile. He probably hopes that by stirring up fear and paranoia, he'll be able to slip away unnoticed."

I considered Harper's perspective, realizing that perhaps we had been too quick to assume the worst. The appearance of the disc was undoubtedly concerning, but it didn't necessarily mean Cade had an army of outcasts at his back.

Harper, sensing my uncertainty, pressed on. "The fact is, we know from your own account that Cade has recently been spotted in town, and that alone is cause for concern. But let's not get ahead of ourselves by assuming he's brought an army of outcasts with him. We need to approach this situation rationally."

Turning to Nalani and Aja, I said, "Have your patrols

stay vigilant, but clarify that we don't know for certain if Cade has allies. We don't want to cause unnecessary panic." They both nodded, their expressions solemn.

Harper cleared her throat, drawing my attention back to her. "If I may, Ryder had a method for strengthening the inn's magical defenses during times of crisis. It might be worth exploring."

I was surprised by Harper's suggestion because it hinted at a level of familiarity with Ryder's abilities she'd not mentioned previously. Offering her a small smile, I said, "That's a good idea. I'll look through Ryder's records and see if I can find anything relevant."

"I believe he had an entire volume dedicated to warding magic," Harper added helpfully.

"Right, Less Than Welcoming Wards," I recalled, the image of the book's spine flashing through my mind.

She winked at me. "That's the one."

"Thanks, Harper. I'll dig into it."

I let out a slow breath, feeling a flicker of hope at the group's willingness to cooperate despite the obvious tensions. We still had a long way to go, but at least we were moving in the right direction.

With the meeting adjourned, I knew my next priority was to reinforce the inn's magical defenses. I retrieved the tome on warding from the library and returned to my quarters, determined to put Ryder's knowledge to use.

I lit some calming cedar-infused candles and sat down on the floor in a cross-legged position, surrounded by comfortable feather pillows. The ancient book fell open with ease, as if being directed by an invisible hand, and I could feel the profound enchantment emanating from its contents.

Closing my eyes, I focused on my breathing, visualizing a complex web of energy encircling the inn's perimeter. At first, my mind's eye showed only darkness, but gradually, shimmering strands of light began to appear, weaving together to form a protective barrier.

I poured my concentration into the task, willing the glowing filaments to grow stronger and brighter. The effort left me drained, but as I opened my eyes, I knew with a deep certainty that the wards were now more powerful than ever.

As I stood on unsteady legs, I glimpsed my reflection in the mirror. For a fleeting instant, the image of the shadowy figure from the woods seemed to loom over my shoulder. "You will not breach these walls," I whispered fiercely, and the apparition faded away.

Returning to my office, I immersed myself in the records of Crescent Crossing's past, searching for any mention of the raven symbol or similar omens. As I scanned the shelves of journals left by previous innkeepers, one volume in particular caught my eye. Its gilded letters were too faded to read, but as I opened it, the pages fell open to an entry describing the very same raven totem.

The passage spoke of a series of sinister events that had plagued the region decades ago, all preceded by sightings of the glyph near sacred sites. The unnamed author detailed their efforts to strengthen the inn's wards in response to the threat of marauding packs.

As I read on, a pattern began to emerge. The appearance of the symbol seemed to herald a coordinated campaign of chaos and sabotage, orchestrated by exiled shifters targeting places of spiritual and communal significance. Yet the ultimate purpose behind these attacks and the identity of the mastermind directing them remained frustratingly elusive.

I thought back to Harper's theory: was Cade acting alone, using the symbol to stir up old fears and unsettle us? Or did he truly have a network of collaborators, working towards some darker goal? The uncertainty gnawed at me, even as I knew I had to consider every possibility.

After days of chasing dead ends and waiting on pins and needles for a move from Cade that never arrived, the fragmented puzzle pieces suddenly clicked into place in my thoughts. I hastily gathered Hamish, Saige, and Briar in my office, scarcely able to contain my revelation.

"I've been a fool," I began, raking a hand through my windswept hair. "The signs were there all along. Malachi's deception runs far deeper than we realized."

Hamish leaned forward intently, his forearms braced on his knees. "Explain."

I started pacing as the words tumbled out in a rush. "Malachi pressed me for information on what I know so far about the investigation, and he got cagey when I mentioned that raven catchphrase."

I turned to meet their riveted gazes. "But we've had it backward. His poorly disguised prying reveals classic signs of an inside accomplice hoping to stay one step ahead."

Saige digested this silently before replying. "You believe

Malachi collaborated to kill Ryder? But I thought you'd pinned down Cade as the likely murderer."

I grasped her hands urgently. "Don't you see? All signs point to Cade as the killer. But banished from town, he needed a rogue operative working internally."

Understanding sparked in Hamish's eyes. "And loyal Malachi, his not-exiled friend, willingly obliged."

"Exactly!" I exclaimed. "Generating chaos serves Cade's bitter agenda perfectly. And manipulating events from the inside would be a perfect job for Malachi."

I expected doubts or debate. But Briar wore a triumphant grin. "By the moon, she's solved it!"

Buoyed by my friends' resounding support, I hastily outlined the next steps.

"We need tangible proof of Malachi actively assisting Cade if we hope to expose them," I said.

Briar's emerald eyes glinted cunningly. "Indeed. And I know just where to dig."

Before I could inquire further, she bustled off without another word, leaving me brimming with anticipation. Soon she returned, waving a leather logbook, nearly slipping on scattered papers in her haste.

"The delivery ledger!" she crowed triumphantly, tapping the cover. "I always record parcels received for guests in case valuables go astray."

Within moments, Briar had retrieved Malachi's records, eagerly spreading the papers across my desk. My brow shot up in surprise, noting the lengthy list of packages logged under his name, spanning many months, judging by the dates.

"I know we saw him after he picked up one box. From

what you said before, he does so with regularity. But why in the world was Malachi having so many heavy boxes delivered?" I muttered half to myself. "Was he stockpiling goods?"

"Look closer," Briar urged, jabbing her finger at the 'in care of' listings.

My eyes widened as understanding hit me squarely. "Several of these are listed for Wilder but 'in care of' Malachi, and Malachi signed for them. But Kai was mysteriously absent for some of that time..."

"...except we learned he'd secretly been sheltering Cade the last few weeks," Hamish finished grimly. "Even if Malachi was delivering package to Kai, then he still would have known Cade was staying with him."

I met his piercing gaze. "You see it now, too. Whatever these parcels contained, Malachi would have regularly been up at Kai's. Malachi had to be aware of Cade's reappearance, since he was picking up packages addressed to C. Wilder."

The damning evidence kept mounting, eroding the cunning conspirators' facade brick by brick.

I made calls to Aja, Nalani, and Harper, knowing I needed to circle them in on my findings.

A few minutes later, a brisk knock heralded Aja's arrival. I waved her inside my office, where the others had already gathered, their expressions ranging from intrigue to skepticism.

Aja inclined her head politely. "Apologies for my delay. I was just down the street at my clinic." She settled into the vacant leather armchair. "Your message indicated urgent news."

Wasting no time, I swiftly detailed my suspicion about Malachi assisting Cade, coupled with the delivery ledger showing proof that he'd been to Kai's home while Cade was hiding out there. My friends absorbed this bombshell intently, leaning forward with rapt focus, reflecting the gravity of the accusations.

When I finally paused, Harper wore a rare smile, touching her usually stern lips. "Well, well. She's cracked this egg wide open at last."

Aja nodded slowly, hazel eyes glinting. "Quite so. The fragments now take discernible shape. Your insights appear well-founded." She templed her long fingers. "Yet confirming suspicions beyond doubt remains imperative before implicating upstanding townsfolk publicly."

Nalani lifted an eyebrow, intrigued. "The alphas of each enclave should hear these allegations under the full moon at the sacred meeting site. Luckily, our next opportunity is tonight."

I considered this. "Where's the site?"

"It's up in the hills, straddling the boundaries of the Elk and Flat Tops territories," Harper explained. "It's a stone tower we call the Castle. At the base lies a natural amphitheater of stacked granite slabs. It's where we hold a lot of business, including all formal inquiries. In such a venerable setting, even the crafty charms of Malachi will be rendered ineffective."

Briar hesitated. "Should we not speak with Malachi first?"

Hamish cut her off gruffly. "And give him a chance to spin more lies? It must be the alphas who hear this."

I rested my chin on steepled fingers, turning the notion over fully. In a face-to-face interrogation here, Malachi might explain away the suspicious deliveries and probing questions. But if taken unawares at the Castle?

"You both make fair points," I acknowledged. "Publicly dropping revelations with the enclave alphas gathered could rattle his composure." I met their gazes in turn. "It could force mistakes in his narrative that we can exploit."

Nalani nodded thoughtfully. "And judgment held beneath that full moon may finally wring truth from his silver tongue."

Aja lifted her noble chin. "Convening all three alphas would add greater accountability against any rebuttal from Malachi or his ilk. Even cunning conspirators cannot stand before the united coalition."

Their arguments resonated with my own misgivings over Malachi and my fear that he'd evade justice behind closed doors. "Agreed. Let's summon the alphas to witness, along with whomever they deem appropriate." I met each of their resolute gazes. "We must ensure Malachi himself attends the gathering. But he's unlikely to arrive voluntarily."

"We must lure him there, unsuspectingly." Nalani's eyes glinted knowingly.

I leaned forward intently. "You're right. Make it appear innocuous, giving no hint of suspicion." I met her gaze. "Any thoughts on how we can convincingly invite Malachi to join us at the Castle without raising alarms?"

"Of course. An appeal to his ego and suggestion that the council requires his wisdom on a time-sensitive matter should do it," Nalani replied without hesitation. "But it should come from Harper. He'll be more likely to trust it coming from another Bittersweet."

I managed a thin smile despite the cloud of foreboding

hanging oppressively. Deceit still left a bitter aftertaste. But desperate times demanded it if we hoped to lure the killers right into our trap at long last.

In the hours that followed, I oscillated between conviction and doubt as the inexorable rising of the full moon crept closer. Harper had called and assured me her coded summons had been received, and our suspect took the bait readily, his insatiable pride blinding him to deception. Yet misgivings needled me.

I paced my office alone, my emotions seesawing wildly. Despite the evidence Briar had brought forward, exposing Malachi's duplicity publicly still felt daunting. In accusing a prominent townsman, even with suggestive proof, I risked igniting uproar and dividing already fractious alliances. Could the package log and my suspicions withstand Malachi's glib rebuttals and the alphas' piercing scrutiny?

A brisk rap interrupted my brooding. Briar stood, wringing her hands. "I know the shipping logs point to Malachi's betrayal, but it's still hard to accept."

Wordlessly, I drew my distraught friend close as muffled sobs wracked her slight frame. I had underestimated the emotional toll such deception from Malachi, a fellow Bittersweet, must be taking. This betrayal cut deepest for gentle Briar, who saw only the best in people, even when she herself had uncovered the damning package log.

When at last her weeping subsided, Briar slowly shook her head. "Even with the proof, I fear the repercussions of open allegations."

Though she clearly ached to believe in Malachi's innocence, I sensed her instinctual wisdom and recognized the troubling signs she felt bound to acknowledge after the night Ryder's blood pooled outside.

I drew back just enough to meet her anguished gaze. "Your heart is unusually pure, my friend. Of course Malachi's guilt strains credibility, even with the evidence you found." I hesitated before continuing gently. "Do you think we're mistaken?"

Briar's face crumpled as she gave the barest shake of her head. I clutched her hands. "We need more clarity on hidden issues to understand what's hiding in the dark. We need more evidence. That's why convening publicly is vital to settling doubts." I squeezed her icy fingers, willing my own flickering conviction into her wavering spirit.

"Whatever truths emerge, together we'll weather the storm." I brushed wayward curls back from her wan face tenderly.

At long last, Briar lifted her head, a watery yet resolved smile dawning again. After I'd sufficiently reassured my newest, dearest ally, we turned our focus toward making the arrangements for the climactic hearing ahead.

The silver dusk faded into the night, and I couldn't help but fidget with my moonstone ring, trying to ease the doubts that were consuming me. Accusing Malachi before the judgment of the esteemed enclaves based on mere assumptions and circumstantial evidence seemed like a reckless move. One that would either cement me as the innkeeper or have all three alphas calling for my replacement.

CHAPTER 17

I had never seen the sacred meeting grounds in person, and as I crossed the threshold of the Flat Top–Elk border, a shiver of awe ran through me. The Castle, an immense granite formation, rose up before me like a timeless sentinel, a testament to the countless battles and councils that had shaped this rugged land. Its weathered sides bore the scars of centuries, yet its rugged beauty remained undiminished. At the base of the Castle, a wide swath of level stone stretched out like a natural amphitheater, ancient and unyielding.

Earlier, my council advisors had briefed me on the evening's proceedings and the alphas I would face. Their words echoed in my mind, but they couldn't fully prepare me for the crackling energy that seemed to emanate from the very bedrock beneath my feet. The air thrummed with anticipation as scores of tense onlookers congregated before the three imposing alphas holding court at the circle's center.

Alpha Verell Silverpine, leader of the Elk enclave, stood tall beneath the moon's gentle light. His leathery features bore the etched wisdom of decades, his piercing blue eyes gleaming with uncanny intensity. Every line of his face spoke of his proud lineage, tracing back to the ancient Silverpine bloodline that had founded the Elk long before living memory.

Though distinguished silver now threaded Verell's chestnut mane, he carried himself with the vigor of a much younger wolf. As our eyes met, he gave me an almost imperceptible nod, a subtle acknowledgment of the momentous events about to unfold beneath the indifferent stars.

Flanking Verell stood the other two alphas: Talon Ironclaw of the Flat Tops and Oriole Dawnchaser of the Bittersweets. Even among his towering kin, Talon cut an imposing figure. Muscles rippled beneath his scar-traced skin, each mark a testament to the battles he had fought and won. His jet-black hair hung past his shoulders, partially concealing the ragged claw marks that raked one side of his chiseled face. The flinty gleam in his remaining eye fixed unerringly on me, assessing and calculating.

On Verell's other side stood Oriole Dawnchaser, the enigmatic alpha of the Bittersweets. Despite her reclusive reputation, Oriole's presence commanded attention. Nearly as tall as her male counterparts, she moved with a fluid grace that hinted at the latent power coiled within her statuesque frame. Feathers adorned her single long braid of light brown hair, falling past her shoulders like a cascading waterfall. Her arresting hazel eyes seemed to hold secrets beyond mortal ken, sparking whispers of her ties to ancient elemental magic and arcane solstice rites conducted deep within the Bittersweets' isolated mountain strongholds.

Regardless of the truth behind the rumors, Oriole's

unnerving focus and poised demeanor marked her as a dominant force to be reckoned with. Her steady gaze swept over the waiting crowd, taking their measure with an intensity that felt more penetrating than any shouted threat. Under that weighty scrutiny, even the boldest shifters seemed to shrink back.

Squaring my shoulders, I fought to master my escalating anxiety as I strode across the clearing. Each step carried me inexorably closer to the heart of the mystery I had so determinedly sought to unravel. A part of me still clung to the certainty that justice would prevail against Malachi's vile deceptions. Yet doubt gnawed at me, a growing fear that perhaps I had forced this confrontation too soon, dooming us all in my haste for answers.

As I approached the candlelit circle, my conviction warred with icy apprehension. The hour of reckoning had arrived, and there was no turning back now.

A hushed murmur rippled through the considerable throng encircling the ancient monument as we passed through their ranks. News of this unprecedented summit had spread like wildfire, drawing spectators eager for spectacle and resolution. Amid the sea of faces, I glimpsed Briar's wary expression and Kai's guarded stance, their eyes tracking my progress toward the waiting alphas.

As I scanned the crowd, I noticed that Kai's usual smug irreverence was conspicuously absent. Instead, a taut unease marred his handsome features as he hovered near the circle's shadowy perimeter. The gravity of the gathering had wiped away his customary cavalier smirk, leaving only apprehension in its wake.

Upon reaching the inner circle, a fierce surge of vindication coursed through me as I spotted Malachi standing with arms crossed, his posture radiating arrogance. For once, cracks showed in the pompous advisor's urbane facade, hints of unease bleeding through his steel mask of invulnerability. It was clear he sensed the unusual gravity of this gathering, even if he remained ignorant of the damning accusations about to be leveled against him.

My roiling emotions barely had time to settle before Verell Silverpine, the Elk alpha, stepped forward. His measured words effortlessly commanded the attention of all present. "Tonight, beneath the moon's watchful eye, charges of betrayal shall be weighed." His piercing gaze swept over the silent crowd. "The innkeeper will speak her piece."

With his solemn opening statement concluded, Verell retreated several paces before turning expectantly toward me. He inclined his head in a silent invitation. Drawing in a deep breath, I steeled myself, silently praying that my decisions would prove right in the end.

As I spoke, my voice rang out clearly across the glade, the amphitheater's natural acoustics amplifying my words to reach even the farthest edges of the gathering. "Faithful citizens of Crescent Crossing, I stand before you as your new innkeeper. While investigating the tragic death of the venerable Ryder Shadowfang, I have uncovered evidence of foul play that extends far beyond his murder. It has become clear that a cunning and coldly calculating faction has been operating in our midst, orchestrating chaos and sowing discord for their own selfish ends." A ripple of audible shock and disbelief spread through the crowd at my bold pronouncement. Centering myself, I pressed on, undeterred.

"The evidence clearly indicates that both Kai Wilder and

Malachi Sterling betrayed the trust of our community. Not only did they both aid Cade Wilder in returning to the community and staying hidden, but Malachi also provided supplies and information to the man whose goals we can only assume are nefarious." My words hung heavy in the air, the weight of their implication settling over the gathered crowd.

A chorus of angry cries erupted, overpowering the stunned silence that had initially greeted my revelation. Glancing at Malachi, I saw shock and disbelief etched across his face as he realized the depths of his own deceit had been laid bare.

I pressed on, detailing the extent of Malachi's lies and the web of deception he had spun. As the full scope of his betrayal became clear, the crowd's shock gave way to a simmering anger. Voices rose in a united call for justice, a resounding declaration that they would no longer allow evil to fester unchallenged in their midst. In that moment, I witnessed a community coming together, determined to root out the corruption that threatened to destroy all they held dear.

As the clamor died down, a tense hush fell over the assembly. All eyes turned expectantly toward Malachi, awaiting his response to the damning accusations leveled against him. Visibly gathering himself, Malachi stood tall, his golden eyes glittering with a dangerous light. When at last he spoke, his usually melodious voice dripped with scorn and contempt.

"Listen to yourselves, so eager to condemn without just cause!" He swept a disdainful glare over the gathered masses. "This fae upstart spins lies born of fear and envy, whispering only what you wish to believe against your own kin. How quickly you turn on one of your own, swayed by the honeyed words of an outsider."

Malachi's accusation ignited a spark of outrage within me, propelling me forward. "There is documented proof. We have shipping logs of received packages for the items you got for Cade," I declared, my voice ringing with conviction.

Malachi bared his teeth, his venomous composure cracking under the weight of my assertion. "Proof? No doubt conveniently conjured by your supposedly absent House Ash powers." He turned to Verell, his tone shifting to one of beseeching appeal. "Alpha, surely you can see that this fae newcomer seeks only to sow dissent with her wild claims."

But Verell silenced Malachi with a single, icy stare. "The evidence shall speak for itself, without further distraction." He beckoned Aja forward, his trust in her calm objectivity clear.

Composed, Aja held aloft the meticulously kept delivery logs. "For months leading up to the former innkeeper's murder, Malachi received many heavy boxes, all routinely logged under the name Wilder. On one particularly damning occasion, the records even specify 'C. Wilder.'" She fixed Malachi with a penetrating look of disdain. "How do you explain this?"

Malachi straightened, a cunning gleam entering his eyes as he crafted his response. "It was merely a courtesy extended to my dear friend Kai. I received those packages on his behalf and delivered them to him, nothing more. I knew nothing of his brother Cade's involvement." He shook his head, feigning dismay at the implication. "Had I been aware of the truth, I would never have aided the criminal Cade. My conscience would not have allowed it."

Frustrated murmurs rippled through the crowd at Malachi's slick evasion, their discontent palpable. I clenched my fists, my nails biting into my palms as I struggled to rein in the sharp words that threatened to spill forth. The audacity of his bald-faced lies was almost too much to bear.

Just then, Kai pushed his way to the front of the gathering, his face haggard, but his eyes ablaze with self-recrimination. "Enough with the lies, Malachi," he bit out, his voice laden with bitterness. "I confess, it was I who concealed my brother Cade." He held up a hand, cutting off Malachi's shocked interjection. "But you, old friend, were the mastermind behind it all. You counseled me to hide him, smuggled provisions to aid him, and even urged him to request a hearing despite his exile."

Kai met my stunned gaze, his eyes filled with remorse. "Forgive me for my cowardice in not speaking out sooner. But no more." He turned back to Malachi, disgust etched upon his handsome features. "Your lies end tonight."

A heavy silence followed Kai's damning confession, the weight of his words settling over the gathered crowd. Then, like a dam bursting, indignant cries arose, demanding justice for Malachi's treachery. Alpha Verell raised his hands, his commanding presence quelling the furious shouts. His sharp eyes bore into Malachi's pale countenance, seeking the truth behind the accusations.

"If what Kai says is true, what justification can you possibly offer for such treasonous deeds?" Verell's voice, though soft, carried the weight of a mountain. The judgment of the entire community seemed to hang upon Malachi's response.

Trapped by the web of lies he had so carefully spun,

Malachi's expression turned thunderous. Yet when he spoke, his voice rang out clear and defiant, refusing to yield even in the face of mounting evidence against him.

"Everything I did was in service of the greater good!" Malachi declared, his words dripping with righteous indignation. "Cade Wilder was wrongfully accused, a victim of the endemic corruption that you, alpha, so conveniently ignore." His scorn-laden accusation sent shockwaves through the gathered crowd, their eyes widening at his audacity.

Undeterred by their reactions, Malachi pressed on, his voice growing more impassioned with each passing moment. "Have you all forgotten the glaring injustices that stain our history, particularly that of the Bittersweets?" He paced, his golden eyes ablaze with fervor. "When my grandfather dared to challenge our alpha's unilateral rule years ago, demanding greater transparency and accountability, how was he rewarded for his courage?"

Malachi whirled to face Verell, bitter accusation etched into every line of his face. "Exiled! Cast out by a rigged council, cowed into submission by Oriole's predecessor!" He jabbed an incriminating finger at the impassive Bittersweet leader. "An upstanding man, destroyed for daring to question the high-handed rule of those in power!"

I felt a growing sense of unease as Malachi's words painted him in a sympathetic light, casting him as a hero fighting against oppression. The crowd's initial surge of anger now gave way to a sense of uncertainty, as murmurs replaced the previous intensity. Even Alpha Oriole remained inscrutable, her stoic features betraying no hint of repentance or remorse.

Seething with self-righteous anger, Malachi continued to

spin his tale, weaving a web of half-truths and twisted facts. "Yes, I helped the disgraced Cade seek justice against the corruption that plagues our packs. In the wake of Ryder's suspicious demise, drastic action was needed to force change." He lifted his chin defiantly, his eyes challenging those who would dare to oppose him. "I refuse to apologize for confronting tyranny. You may cling to your fragile peace at the cost of truth if you wish but know that judgment clouds all your eyes."

Despite the conviction in his words, I couldn't shake the feeling that Malachi's impassioned speech was nothing more than a desperate attempt to manipulate the crowd, painting himself as a tragic hero to mask his own selfish motives.

I stood in shocked silence as Malachi's words twisted the truth, weaving a narrative that cast him as a hero fighting against injustice. His accusations against the town and its leaders were powerful, and I grappled with the realization that I had no concrete evidence to prove his involvement in Ryder's murder.

Squaring his shoulders, Malachi turned slowly, meeting my dismayed stare with a look of pitying condescension. "What say you now, little fae?" he challenged, his voice dripping with disdain. "Do your flowery words of persuasion hold any weight against the cold, hard truth?"

I opened my mouth to respond, but no sound escaped my lips. The heavy silence pressed down upon me, suffocating in its intensity. My tongue felt like lead, uselessly glued to the roof of my mouth.

Malachi's cunning words cut deep, each barb more painful than the sharpest blade. I marveled at his ability to twist the revelations to his advantage, casting doubt on my intentions and obscuring the truth behind a veil of self-righteous indignation. A single glance at the agitated crowd confirmed my worst fears —his ploy was succeeding. They knew Malachi and trusted him, while I was still an outsider, an interloper in their midst. The once-unified outrage had given way to confusion, skepticism, and a simmering discord that threatened to tear us apart.

With a sinking feeling, I realized my overzealousness had led us to this precarious moment. By forcing a confrontation without irrefutable proof about the murder, I had played right into Malachi's hands, giving him the perfect opportunity to turn my cause against me.

In that moment, I could only hope for an unforeseen twist of fate, a miracle that would expose Malachi's lies and reveal the truth before it was too late. With each passing second and the escalating restlessness of the crowd, that initial hope began to dwindle, being replaced by a deepening sense of despair.

Just as I felt my resolve crumble, Drake shouldered his way furiously to the center of the circle, his eyes flashing with anger. "Why should we trust that you ever acted in good faith?" he demanded, his voice thundering across the gathered crowd. "A true martyr wouldn't hide behind pretty words and deception." He took a threatening step toward Malachi, his intentions clear, but Hamish's firm hand on his shoulder restrained him.

Malachi's lip curled into a mocking smile, unfazed by Drake's outburst. "Believe what you will," he sneered. "Your chronic suspicion only serves to highlight the need for change." His scornful gaze lingered on me, his words dripping with contempt. "Clearly, fate made an unwise choice in naming a starry-eyed outsider as the steward of alliances built over generations."

Each word felt like a knife, cutting deep into my skin and chipping away at my already fragile self-confidence. The doubts and fears that had been whispering in the back of my mind grew louder, threatening to drown out all rational thought. Despite my best efforts, I couldn't shake the feeling that I had failed the test, proving myself unworthy of the trust placed in me.

Just as I was about to succumb to the crushing weight of my doubts, fate intervened, altering the course of my destiny in a most unexpected way. My moonstone ring erupted in a brilliant light, pulsating with an otherworldly energy that demanded attention. As the light bathed me, visions swirled in my mind's eye—scenes previously concealed unfolded before me.

In the vision, I saw Malachi stealthily approaching the rear of the inn just moments after Ryder had stepped out for that fateful call. The faint echoes of Malachi's threats filled the air, his overconfidence rendering him careless. Ryder, ever the brave soul, confronted him, standing defiant despite the imminent danger. Malachi's reaction was swift and brutal, a calculated strike that revealed his true nature without a doubt.

As these vivid images cascaded not just through my mind but into the minds of all shifters present, a ripple of shock passed through the crowd. My lungs burned as I gasped for air, trembling with the intensity of the shared experience. A collective gasp arose, murmurs of awe mingling with the night air. Even Malachi recoiled, his eyes widening with a wary apprehension as he realized that the tide had turned dramatically against him.

Alpha Verell's gruff voice cut through the charged silence, his presence at my shoulder a steadying force. "The truth reveals itself at last, from realms beyond the reach of lies," he declared, his flinty gaze piercing Malachi, who seemed to visibly pale under the scrutiny. "Did we not warn you that the full moon's eye sees all in the end?"

For a moment, a silent plea for intervention flickered across Malachi's face, but it was quickly replaced by a mask of defiance. His lips thinned, pressed together in a bloodless line as he clung to his brazen arrogance. Though cornered and faced with undeniable evidence, he refused to surrender, his unbroken pride sealing his fate more decisively than any furtive conspiracy ever could.

The gathered crowd looked at Malachi with a mixture of anger and revulsion. No one would forgive the snake now that it had revealed its true nature, its deadly venom laid bare for all to see. Under the starry skies, the only path forward was to exact the punishment he so richly deserved. A shudder ran through me as I contemplated the fate that awaited someone who had so long pretended innocence, refusing to take responsibility for the horrific death of their beloved Ryder.

As the full import of my damning vision sank in, a chorus of furious cries arose, demanding justice for Malachi's crimes. All doubt had vanished, leaving behind a chilling certainty about the extent of his betrayal. He had callously exploited the trust placed in him, orchestrating tremors that threatened the very foundations of our peace, all in the name of his own selfish ambition. Not a single soul could now refute the blood that stained his hands and weighed heavily on his conscience.

"Murderer!"

"Exile him!"

"He butchered Ryder!"

The crowd's anger boiled over, their shouts of disapproval echoing through the night air. Kai quickly stepped away from Malachi, his former friend, as if trying to distance himself from the taint of his betrayal. Malachi stood alone, his face still set in a defiant expression despite the fury that surrounded him.

Remarkably, no trace of remorse or panic cracked Malachi's stoic facade, even in the face of the pack's palpable thirst for vengeance. They seemed ready to tear him limb from limb to make him suffer for his blackened deeds. His brazen lack of contrition only fueled their collective outrage, pushing them closer to the brink of violence.

I could feel the tension in the air—the barely restrained fury that threatened to explode at any moment. The crowd's anger was a palpable force, a violent wave that seemed poised to crash down upon Malachi, overwhelming any pitiful barriers of restraint or due process. The seductive call of primal vengeance tugged at their hearts, urging them to take matters into their own hands and mete out the punishment they believed Malachi so richly deserved.

"Silence!" Verell's commanding bellow cut through the din, his voice echoing with authority that demanded obedience. "Lawless vengeance dishonors everything Ryder stood for!"

Gradually, the raucous uproar faded to a low, menacing growl as the crowd reluctantly heeded the alpha's words. In the ensuing silence, Nalani's calming incantations could be heard, a soothing balm attempting to quell the simmering anger. With the reminder of their guiding principles, the fury of the people gradually settled, and a sense of tranquility filled the air.

Yet despite the temporary calm, the desire for Malachi's immediate removal from the pack remained a palpable force. None doubted his culpability for Ryder's death and the betrayal of their trust. He had willingly broken faith with his own kind, and such a transgression could not be easily forgiven or forgotten.

Alpha Oriole stepped forward, her shoulders squared and her voice ringing with immovable authority. Her smoky alto carried a weight that demanded attention and respect. "Malachi Sterling, the evidence against you is irrefutable. You were responsible for the death of Ryder Shadowfang." Her fiery gaze never wavered as she leveled her accusation, undeterred by Malachi's unwavering defiance. "There can be no doubt when faced with such clear evidence, and yet you still refuse to acknowledge the severity of your betrayal."

Malachi's face twisted in anger, his jaw clenching as he struggled to hold back a venomous response. But Oriole's cold pronouncement brooked no rebuttal, her words carrying the weight of an unassailable judgment.

"Hear now the just decree of the packs—henceforth, you are cast out, a wanderer without home or kin," she intoned solemnly, her voice heavy with the gravity of her proclamation. "For the wicked deeds that shall forever stain your honor, all privileges of heritage and homeland are hereby revoked. May the wilderness claim your tainted soul as penance for your crimes."

Alpha Verell then turned his piercing gaze to Kai, who stood with his head bowed, shame and remorse etched onto his features. "Kai Wilder, though your intentions may have been born of familial loyalty, your actions in aiding and abetting these criminals cannot go unpunished. As such, the council has decided that you will be placed under strict supervision, confined to a dwelling of our choosing with no contact permitted with your exiled brother. Should you violate these terms, you will face the same fate as Malachi—banishment from the pack and all its territories."

Kai nodded solemnly, accepting the council's judgment without protest. "I understand and acccpt the consequences of my actions. I only hope that, in time, I may prove myself worthy of the pack's trust once more."

Finally, Alpha Oriole addressed the gathered crowd, her voice taut with barely contained rage. "As for Cade Wilder, the council has reached a unanimous decision. His crimes against the pack and its allies are too grievous, and he has eschewed his previous exile. Should he be captured, he will face the ultimate punishment—execution. We cannot allow such a threat to roam free, endangering the lives of our people and those we have sworn to protect."

A murmur of assent rippled through the crowd, the weight of Oriole's words settling heavily upon them. The fate of the pack's enemies had been sealed, and there could be no mercy for those who had betrayed the sacred bonds of kinship and honor.

As the weight of Verell and Oriole's decrees settled over the gathering, Malachi remained eerily silent. No sound escaped his shuttered facade, but for a fleeting moment, I glimpsed something indefinable fracture behind those golden eyes. There was a brief glimpse of vulnerability, swiftly hidden by a resolute tightening of his jaw.

Squaring his shoulders, Malachi surveyed the sea of faces around him, each one a silent witness to his unanimous condemnation. Then, without a backward glance, he turned and strode into the liminal shadows that beckoned at the edge of the circle. The assembled crowd parted wordlessly, clearing a path for him to leave, their eyes tracking his every move.

Like the serpent banished from the garden, Malachi slithered into the unknown expanse beyond the reach of the pack. No one dared to follow as he disappeared into the uncharted wilderness, vanishing into the realm that awaited the downcast and forsaken. It was a fate he had brought upon himself —the price of his betrayal and the weight of his crimes.

CHAPTER 18

$\mathcal{I}$n the heavy silence that followed his departure, I swayed on numb feet, the enormity of what had transpired threatening to overwhelm me. But Saige was there, her presence a steadying force as she guided me away from the gathering. Hamish and Drake followed along behind us, ready to help shoulder the burden of the night's rough justice; their support a balm to my battered spirit.

The return journey from the Castle passed in a weary haze, the events of the night blurring together in my exhausted mind. I scarcely registered the lonely forest trails, the jostling ride in our vehicles, or the final winding approach to the welcoming lights of the Howl Away Inn. Every bone in my body ached with fatigue, the toll of the harrowing confrontation under the judging stars making itself known.

As the inn's glowing windows came into view, a profound sense of relief washed over me. The warm light bathed the familiar features of my steadfast allies, a beacon of comfort after weathering the storms of the night. Among them, I knew I would find the strength to face the aftermath of Malachi's exile and the challenges that lay ahead.

As I stepped into the inn's warmly lit common room, the heaviness in my chest eased. In such a short time, the inn already felt safe. Felt like home. Briar hurried over, her hands reaching out to grip mine with an urgency born of shared experience.

"When Malachi started weaving those horrid lies, I nearly lost all hope," she confessed, her voice trembling with the memory of that dark moment. "But your vision, Lydia, saved us all. It saved the night."

I squeezed her fingers, mustering a wan smile despite my weariness. "I'm just grateful that the moonstone's magic chose that moment to bring the truth to light. When words failed, it was the only thing that could cut through his deceptions."

Hamish approached, his firm hand coming to rest on my shoulder in a gesture of support. "Don't forget, Lydia; it was your determination that made this possible. Your unwavering commitment to the truth, even in the face of Malachi's lies." His eyes shone with quiet pride as he looked at me, a testament to the faith he had placed in my leadership.

I inclined my head, accepting his praise even as I struggled to process the night's tumultuous events. My desperate gamble had nearly ended in disaster, with the confrontation with Malachi pushing us all to the brink. It was only through the intervention of fate and the timely vision granted by the moonstone that we emerged triumphant.

Yet, even as relief and gratitude suffused the room, I couldn't help but feel a sense of humility. The magic that had saved us, the divine timing that had brought the truth to light

—it was a force far greater than me. I could take no credit for the way the moon had aligned in our favor.

Saige's gaze was intense as she turned to me, her voice low and thoughtful. "With Malachi gone and Cade still at large, you must remain vigilant. The threat to Crescent Crossing persists."

I nodded, my mind conjuring images of the chaos Cade could still unleash upon the unsuspecting residents of our town. "We'll work together to track him down and ensure that he faces justice for his crimes," I declared, my voice steady despite the unease churning in my gut.

Hamish's deep voice rumbled in agreement. "The safety of the community depends on it. We'll stand by you, Lydia, until this menace is eliminated."

"I'm grateful for your support," I said softly, looking between Hamish and Saige. "I know you'll need to return to your own pack soon, but your guidance has meant more to me than I can express. I'll carry the strength you've given me as I continue this fight."

Saige placed a comforting hand on my shoulder, her touch a reminder of the faith they had in me. "You've grown so much, Lydia. You're ready to lead this community through whatever trials may come."

With their belief in me bolstering my resolve, I knew that I could face the challenges ahead, even without their constant presence by my side. The bonds we had forged would endure, no matter the distance between us.

As the conversation lulled, I made a silent promise to myself. I would do what I could to help Kai, who had found the courage to stand against Malachi in the end. While I couldn't simply forgive his mistakes, I didn't want to see him suffer unduly for the crime of blindly supporting his family. There had to be a path forward, a way to balance justice with understanding.

Even as I grappled with these thoughts, my mind continued to churn relentlessly. The events of the night, the upheaval and its messy aftermath seemed to swirl in an endless loop behind my eyes. Though the memories I had recalled had exonerated me in the eyes of the crowd, I couldn't shake the stark image of hatred twisting Malachi's features in those last moments. The veneer of a lifetime's cultivated lies had been stripped away, exposing the ugly truth beneath with pitiless clarity.

Despite the support of my friends and allies, I felt a sudden, desperate need for solitude. Excusing myself from the others, I retreated to my room, my steps heavy with exhaustion.

The moment I crossed the threshold into my chambers, the full force of my emotions crashed over me in choking waves. I sank down onto the quilt, blinking back the tears that threatened to fall. I was still reeling, still trying to make sense of how quickly justice had nearly been warped into injustice and how close we had come to the brink of disaster.

A soft knock at the door startled me out of my thoughts. "Who is it?"

I heard the door swing open, and looking up, I saw Drake standing in the doorway, concern etched into the lines of his rugged face. Silently, I gestured for him to come in, profoundly touched by his unwavering backing. He crossed the room to join me on the bed, his strong arms enfolding me in a comforting embrace. For a long moment, we simply sat there, Drake's silent presence a steadying force as the storm of emotions gradually subsided.

As the minutes ticked by, I slowly regained a semblance of composure, my breathing evening out and the tears drying on my cheeks. I lifted my head from where it had come to rest against Drake's chest, suddenly self-conscious of the damp patch I had left on his shirt.

"Some victory this turned out to be," I rasped, my voice rough with emotion as I swiped the sleeve of my shirt across my eyes. "I nearly brought everything Ryder built crashing down around us, all because of my blind conviction."

Drake's hand came up to tilt my chin, forcing me to meet his gaze. "You had the courage to uncover the ugly truths that no one else dared to face," he reminded me, his voice firm but not unkind. "You can't blame yourself for the way things got complicated. Life's messy like that sometimes."

His thumb brushed across my cheekbone, a fleeting touch that sent a shiver down my spine. "Believe me, I know a thing or two about letting emotions get the best of you. My temper has brought its fair share of disasters." A rueful smile tugged at the corners of his mouth, a hint of warmth softening his gray eyes. "I thought your pure heart and your conviction would be enough to carry the day. But I guess I underestimated just how hard darkness can fight when it's backed into a corner."

I exhaled unsteadily, my breath shaky as I voiced the fear that had been gnawing at me. "I nearly played right into Malachi's hands by accusing him publicly like that."

Drake's hand tightened on my shoulder, a bracing squeeze that seemed to lend me some of his strength. "Maybe you did," he acknowledged, his voice gruff but not unkind.

"But in the end, your actions forced his deception into the light. Malachi damned himself the moment his lies unraveled." His intense gaze, brimming with a quiet passion, locked onto mine and stole my breath away. "It took a lot of guts to do what you did, Lydia. Face your fears head-on and be brave enough to venture into the unknown. Don't let anyone tell you otherwise."

I bit my lip, still wrestling with the doubts that seemed to churn endlessly in my mind. But as I sat there, wrapped in the security of Drake's embrace, I slowly began to feel a flicker of hope. His unwavering faith in me, his unshakeable loyalty... they were like a lifeline, giving me the strength to keep going even when the path ahead seemed impossibly dark. As the exhaustion of the night's events caught up with me, I felt my eyelids grow heavy. Secure in Drake's arms, I allowed myself to drift off into a dreamless sleep.

Sometime later, I stirred from my slumber, the events of the night still weighing heavily on my mind. Despite our triumph over Malachi, I couldn't shake the feeling that his vengeful shade still clouded everything, leaving a lingering unease in its wake. For so long, he had been spreading lies and sowing the seeds of deception. It would take time to fully root out the twisted ideas he had hidden in the shadows.

As I slowly blinked awake, I found myself tucked beneath the covers of my bed, still fully clothed. I had no memory of how I got there, but a quick glance around the room revealed Drake, slumped in the armchair beside the bed. He appeared to be sleeping, but even in his rest, the tension had not fully left his rugged features, a testament to the weight of the night's events. It was clear that he had stayed by my side, watching over me as I slept. Looking at him now, I couldn't help but feel that something had shifted between us. The vulnerable moments we had shared, the comfort he had offered in my darkest hour... they had redrawn the lines of our relationship, blurring the boundary between sentinel and shepherd. My despair seemed to have awakened a fierce protectiveness in Drake, a renewed conviction in his role as my steadfast guardian.

Slowly, I eased myself out of bed, moving with quiet reverence so as not to disturb his slumber. I knelt gingerly beside the worn leather chair, my heart racing at my own sudden audacity. Some intimate impulse had overridden my reason, compelling me to bridge the distance between us. With a tender touch, I brushed my fingers against the fabric of Drake's sleeve, privately marveling at how perfectly my smaller hand fit within his larger one, his palm calloused by the countless trials he had faced.

At the featherlight contact, Drake's eyes snapped open, a muffled snarl escaping his lips as he reflexively seized my wrist. For a moment, he seemed caught between the realm of dreams and the waking world. His grip on my wrist, though unyielding, lacked the bruising force of true aggression. As reality registered in those wolfish gray eyes, a look of recognition slowly dawned.

In one fluid motion, Drake tugged me forward, the sudden shift in balance sending me tumbling into his lap. A shocked gasp escaped my lips as I found myself nose to nose with him, his piercing gaze lucidly taking my measure. Our closeness, the warmth of his body enveloping mine, sent a jolt of excitement through me. I held my breath, my heart pounding in my chest.

"Sorry," Drake muttered, his grip on my wrist loosening

but not fully releasing. "You startled me." For a fleeting moment, his gaze dropped to my parted lips before meeting my eyes once more. "Trouble sleeping?"

I nodded slowly, my pulse quickening at his proximity. Drake made no move to disentangle us, his smoky scent and comforting warmth enveloping me. The intimacy of our position kindled a reckless desire within me, urging me to close the scant distance between us. Almost of its own volition, my body swayed forward, drawn to him like a moth to a flame.

As if sensing my intentions, Drake's hand slid up to cradle the back of my neck, his thumb brushing against the sensitive skin just behind my ear. The gentle touch sent a shiver racing down my spine, my breath catching in my throat. Slowly, tentatively, he angled my face towards his, his eyes silently seeking permission.

At that moment, the rest of the world seemed to fall away. All that existed was the pounding of my heart, the warmth of Drake's breath ghosting across my lips. I closed my eyes, surrendering to the magnetic pull between us as I leaned in, brushing my lips against his in a feather-light caress.

The contact was brief, almost chaste, but it ignited a spark within me, a heat that spread through my veins like wildfire. I felt Drake's sharp intake of breath, his fingers tightening almost imperceptibly against my neck. For a suspended moment, we hovered on the precipice, the air between us charged with unspoken longing.

Then, as quickly as it had begun, the spell was broken. Drake gently separated us, setting me back on my feet with a rueful smile. He took a step back, putting a more respectable distance between our bodies, though his gray eyes still smoldered with barely restrained desire.

Without a word, he turned and strode towards the door, leaving me standing there with my heart racing and my thoughts in turmoil. As the door clicked shut behind him, I pressed trembling fingers to my tingling lips, equal parts scandalized and thrilled by the brief taste of passion we had shared. I knew this moment had irrevocably altered the landscape of our relationship, blurring the lines we had so carefully drawn. What complexities would arise from this unspoken attraction? Only time would tell.

CHAPTER 19

In the days following Malachi's dramatic exile, an oppressive silence descended upon Crescent Crossing. Although his sinister presence no longer lurked in the tranquil valley, a lingering sense of unease gripped the remote hamlet. The upheaval of public confrontations and the justice meted out beneath the ever-watchful stars had left an unsettled quiet in its wake, casting a shadow across my once-peaceful haven.

Yet life had a way of moving forward, regardless of the turmoil that surrounded it. Seeking a quiet space to gather my turbulent thoughts, I found solace in the simple act of tending to the vegetable garden tucked behind a copse of spruce trees bordering the Howl Away Inn. There was a profound comfort in the rhythmic motions of twisting hearty carrots from the yielding earth, the sun warming my shoulders as I knelt in the dirt. For a fleeting moment, the shadows that clung to my spirit seemed to dissipate, chased away by the honest labor.

Harvesting ripe tomatoes, culling weed-choked patches, and turning over the soil for the next crop provided a welcome respite from the chaos that had consumed my life. The honest work left my hands pleasantly sore and my cheeks smudged with dirt, a tangible reminder of the simple joys that could still be found in the midst of uncertainty.

Though Malachi's sudden appearance and the news of Kai's disappearance had left me unsettled, I refused to let fear consume me. Instead, I drew in a deep breath of the mountain air, savoring the scent of overturned earth and the gentle melody of birdsong that filled the air.

As I knelt there, surrounded by the simple beauty of the garden, I clung to the spark of hope that had begun to flicker within me. Shadows would always linger, I knew, but even as one threat retreated, the dawn's hopeful rays pierced the horizon once more, a promise of brighter days to come. With a renewed sense of determination, I vowed to nurture that fragile light, to tend to it as carefully as I did the delicate seedlings that sprouted from the earth beneath my hands.

So lost was I in the soothing cadence of my labor that I failed to hear the approaching heavy footsteps until Drake's gruff voice shattered the tranquil silence.

"Lydia!"

I glanced up, shielding my eyes against the glaring midday sun. Drake's imposing figure emerged from the shadows of the spruce copse edging the garden, his usual intensity etched across his rugged features. I blinked in surprise, rocking back onto my heels as I took in his unexpected presence.

"Drake! I didn't expect to see you out here," I greeted

him, swiping errant strands of hair back from my face with a gloved hand. A flutter of anticipation stirred in my chest, a familiar reaction to his proximity.

As he strode forward, his piercing eyes tracked the surroundings warily, tension radiating from his powerful frame. I studied him curiously, stripping off my thick gardening gloves to buy myself a moment to observe the shifter who so often occupied my conflicted thoughts.

Though I knew Drake remained rattled by the wider threats still plaguing Crescent Crossing, there was something different about his demeanor today. A deeper disquiet and hypervigilance clung to him, evident in the way his slate-gray shirt stretched taut across muscular shoulders knotted with unease and the creaking of his worn leather jacket as he crossed his arms. It was obvious he hadn't simply been passing by when he glimpsed me alone out here.

Realization dawned on me then. Likely, Drake was still conducting regular perimeter patrols, his vigilance heightened by the knowledge that Malachi had vanished into the remote wilderness rather than being properly contained. The thought of further surprise attacks lingered like a specter in the back of my mind, a constant reminder of the dangers that lurked beyond the borders of our haven.

Rising fully to my feet, I regarded Drake openly as he paused a cautious distance away. "Was there something specific you needed?" I injected a note of gentle teasing into my tone, hoping to ease his concern with a touch of normalcy. I refused to be paralyzed any longer by nebulous dread when no obvious threat remained.

Yet the weight pressing down on Drake's shoulders whispered of darker premonitions yet to pass. "I just wanted to check that you were holding up alright," he replied, the words incongruous with his rigid bearing. They were delivered in his typical gruff manner, as I had come to expect from the stoic shifter. However, his eyes held a sense of urgency and warning that was impossible to ignore. Instinctively, I tensed, my senses heightening as they tracked our pastoral surroundings for whatever hidden peril had ratcheted Drake's alarm so high. But only the rustle of fir boughs in the gentle breeze reached my ears. No abnormal shadows staining the idyllic grounds in the midday brightness.

"Well, I appreciate your concern, but as you can see, all remains calm at the moment."

"Lydia, you need to listen closely." Drake enunciated each word with gripping emphasis, his smoldering eyes boring intensely into mine, devoid of his usual gruffness. "It's not safe for you to be here alone right now."

I blinked, my lungs suddenly forgetting their rhythm as a chill ran down my spine. Before I could demand an explanation for this change in his demeanor, an earsplitting explosion violently shattered the tranquil calm. Blinding heat seared my skin as the ground heaved beneath our feet, a deafening fireball erupting at the tree line. Fiery debris rained down upon us, accompanied by a choking cloud of pungent smoke. In a flash, Drake tackled me to the grass, his body shielding mine against the pulverizing onslaught. Blinded and gasping for air, I clung desperately to Drake's solid form until the avalanche of destruction finally ceased.

Dazed and disoriented, I struggled to rise on scraped elbows, Drake's brawny arms helping me to my feet. As the billowing dark clouds of smoke slowly dissipated, hazy forms emerged from the choking haze. My pulse stuttered wildly, a sickening realization dawning upon me. No, it couldn't be. But even as my mind grappled with the bitter truth, my heart knew with chilling certainty. Two brutish wolven silhouettes moved toward us, lethal intent blazing in their ruthless eyes. Malachi and Cade had returned at long last, hell-bent on reaping vengeance.

"Brace yourself and stay behind me," Drake commanded, his rich voice resonating with steely authority. Before my eyes, his imposing figure began a mesmerizing transformation, his human form giving way to that of a powerful wolf. Muscles rippled beneath his skin as inky black fur erupted across his suddenly colossal frame, clothes shredding into tatters as his features elongated and sharpened, taking on the sleek predator's build that was uniquely his. Within mere heartbeats, the formidable wolf that was Drake Frost towered before me, a low, blood-chilling snarl reverberating through the clearing, a warning to those who dared threaten what he held dear.

My breath caught in my throat, frozen by the bone-deep formidability exuded by Drake's primal incarnation. Only once before had I witnessed firsthand the true wildness possessed underneath Drake's human flesh. Beneath the feral exterior, I could still sense the profound intelligence and unwavering duty that continued to drive Drake's spirit. His deafening roar reverberated through my body, filling me with terror. He charged towards our stunned attackers without hesitation, his determination palpable in every stride.

Awestruck, I could only stare as Drake smashed into our would-be killers in a blur of snapping fangs and slashing claws, a display of savage power that left me both terrified and exhilarated. Howls of rage split the air as the three titans clashed in a frenzied explosion of primal violence, their battle playing out beneath the pristine mountain skies in a twisted mockery of the tranquility that had reigned mere moments before.

My knees threatened to buckle under the weight of the visceral, animalistic fury that bombarded my senses in waves as Drake fought relentlessly to protect me from further harm. Though outnumbered, even Malachi and Cade's combined mass and ruthless determination paled compared to the blistering onslaught unleashed by Drake. His shaggy coat ran crimson in places, though I couldn't discern whether it was his blood or theirs that stained his fur. Still, Drake pressed his assault, a whirlwind of snarling defiance and instinctive violence honed and focused by one all-consuming aim—to keep them away from me at any cost.

I longed desperately for some way to aid Drake in his valiant stand, but weapons were not my forte. Yet I could feel the power simmering through my veins, a latent potential waiting to be tapped if only I had the knowledge to channel it effectively.

As I grappled with ways to aid Drake, unable to seize upon a spell of intervention, a guttural shriek of agony jarred me violently back to the present. Cade's blood-streaked muzzle was clenched around Drake's exposed hind leg, razor-sharp teeth sinking mercilessly into the bone. A howl of anguish tore from my throat, echoing the agony that radiated from my beloved's stricken form.

With a pain-filled howl, Drake crashed to the earth, Cade's vicious jaws still crushing his mangled leg in a death grip. Sensing his adversary faltering, Malachi spun and began circling toward me, a demented glee alighting in his merciless eyes as he perceived my unprotected state.

Desperate panic gripped me then, a living thing clawing at my insides. With chilling certainty, I knew that no spell or ally could traverse the distance to my side before my assailant struck the killing blow. Even valiant Drake, still struggling to tear free from Cade's maw clamped about his hamstring, would never reach me in time. Horror clawed at my throat, rendering my futile cry for deliverance little more than a strangled gasp as the end descended upon me.

Malachi gathered himself, his haunches bunching as he prepared to spring for my vulnerable throat. In those last shuddering seconds, time seemed to elongate. The coppery tang of blood painting the air, the mottled fur bristling along Malachi's arched spine, the flecks of spittle dangling from gnashing teeth poised to rip tender flesh—every detail seared itself into my mind with terrifying clarity.

As my eyes drifted closed, feverish heat erupted in my palms, where I'd braced for impact. Perhaps a fitting finale, I mused detachedly—the awakened magic ever simmering within, manifesting one last defiant time. At least I would perish without surrendering utterly, my power a flickering beacon of resistance in the face of certain doom.

But rather than Malachi's fangs shredding through sinew and bone, only shocked silence greeted my grim acceptance. Tentatively cracking one eye open, my body was still tensed for annihilation. I glimpsed not the gory demise I had expected, but salvation.

Malachi hovered motionless, his snout mere inches from my throat, his advance suddenly halted by the brilliant white aura blazing wildly from my upraised palms. The intensity of the magical barrier continued to pulse between us, undulating with a life of its own as I stared in utter disbelief, flabbergasted by this unexpected surge of power. The force that had lain dormant since my last confrontation surged forth, a primal wave of protection and defiance in the face of looming death.

The searing barrier pulsated between Malachi and me, growing stronger with each passing second. I watched in astonishment as his expression shifted from predatory focus to incredulous dismay, the realization of his impending defeat slowly dawning on him.

Then, unexpectedly, a voice filled my head, Malachi's thoughts pressing into my consciousness as if the magic itself had bridged our minds. "What magic is this?" he snarled internally, his mental voice twisted with rage and disbelief.

A howl erupted from him, not voiced but echoing in my mind as blistering tendrils of white-hot energy engulfed his form, sending him yelping and thrashing to the grass. The acrid scent of burnt fur filled the air, overpowering any other smells.

I stared at my glowing hands, marveling at the power that had surged forth in my moment of desperation. "I... I don't know," I stammered, my mind racing to comprehend the incredible turn of events.

Suddenly, a thunderous barrage of pounding paws and feet shattered the stunned silence. I glanced behind me, seeing a group of shifters, both in human and wolf form, charging onto the scene. Among them, I spotted the familiar faces of Aja, Saige, and Hamish, their expressions a mix of determination and concern.

"Lydia!" Saige called out, rushing to my side. "Are you alright?"

I nodded mutely, my gaze drifting back to where Malachi had fallen. To my horror, the spot was empty, with only a trail of flattened grass and droplets of blood indicating his presence.

"He's gone," I whispered, a chill running down my spine. "But how? He was badly injured."

Hamish's brow furrowed as he surveyed the area. "It's not possible. We had the perimeter secured."

A fleeting thought crossed my mind, and I turned to Saige, my voice low. "Could someone be helping him? Someone from within the community?"

Saige's eyes widened at the implication. "I... I don't know. But we can't rule out the possibility."

As the adrenaline began to fade, the exhaustion of the battle caught up with me. I swayed on my feet, my vision blurring at the edges. Saige's strong arms caught me before I could fall, her voice urgent.

"Lydia, stay with me. Aja! Over here, quickly!"

The last thing I saw before the darkness claimed me was Aja's concerned face hovering over mine, her lips moving in a silent incantation. Then the world faded away, and I surrendered to the blissful embrace of unconsciousness.

I drifted in a murky void, neither fully present nor immersed in oblivion's embrace. Flickering visions swirled through my mind—Drake's mangled wolf form hitting the dirt, Malachi's fury morphing to dismay as mystical fire scorched him, and salvation arriving not a heartbeat too soon. I clung to that piercing image of Drake, broken yet unbowed in the grass, my champion falling only when certain that no further threat encroached upon me.

Gradually, the fog enshrouding my reeling senses lifted, and I awoke to muted chaos. Opening my gritty eyes, I found myself surrounded by shifters in both human and wolf forms. The lancing pain from the blast's countless cuts and bruises made me wince. A scarlet-smeared face filled my vision, concern radiating from familiar gray eyes as Drake's human form hovered over me protectively.

"Lydia! Thank the spirits, you're awake," Drake exhaled raggedly, one large hand coming to rest gently against my cheek in unconcealed relief, his touch a soothing balm amid the chaos.

I stared up at him mutely, still struggling to process the enormity of all that had transpired. My gaze tracked across the beloved visage I had come so close to losing, cataloging each fresh injury. Blood crusted along his hairline from a nasty scalp laceration, and his lips split and swelled rapidly even as I watched. What grabbed my full attention, however, was the hitch in Drake's movement as he knelt gingerly beside me, his face creasing with the effort of masking the red-hot agony that surely coursed through his veins.

"You're hurt," I managed hoarsely. This stoic man, I knew, would endure grave harm in silence.

Drake's thunderous features spasmed once more, but he waved off my concern with a dismissive gesture. "It's nothing serious. The leg will mend quickly enough once Aja works her magic." Despite his reassurance, I glimpsed a stark pallor beneath his usual swarthy complexion, belying just how much blood my self-appointed guardian had sacrificed in defending me.

As if summoned by his words, Aja appeared at Drake's side, her usual serenity fractured by brisk focus. She knelt beside him, her deft hands already reaching for the poultices and salves she carried with her. I watched as she tended to his wounds, her brow furrowed in concentration as she murmured ancient incantations under her breath.

The world around us seemed to fade away as I focused solely on Drake, my hand finding his and gripping it tightly. He turned his head to look at me, his piercing gaze locking with mine. In that moment, I saw a flicker of something in his eyes—a warmth that spoke of a bond deeper than mere friendship or alliance.

As Aja worked, I found myself pondering the nature of my relationship with Drake. We had grown close over the past few weeks, our shared experiences forging a connection that went beyond the simple roles of innkeeper and guardian. But was there something more to it? Something that neither of us had been willing to acknowledge until now?

My mind drifted back to the shattering kiss we had shared weeks ago, the memory of it still vivid and potent. In the chaos that had followed, we had barely had a moment to ourselves, let alone time to discuss what it meant. But now, with Drake lying injured before me, I couldn't help but confront the depth of my feelings for him.

Eventually, Aja leaned back on her heels, inspecting her meticulously applied wrappings with a critical eye. Though her mystical salves had worked their familiar wonders on his resilient shifter body, already beginning to knit muscle and skin back together, the leg would no doubt require time to fully rebuild its strength.

"How long before he can manage shifting fully?" I asked Aja.

Though unspoken, I knew that regaining Drake's more formidable wolf form was paramount until the remaining threat to us both had been resolved. As a shifter, his human body remained far more vulnerable to ruthless attack. Until Malachi and Cade were brought decisively to heel, none of us could truly breathe free, forever glancing over our shoulders in fear of the next assault.

Aja hesitated before responding judiciously. "Shifters have impressive resilience, but I must recommend holding off attempted shifting for at least a fortnight."

Drake's thunderous expression mirrored my shock at Aja's prognosis. Frustration and impatience warred across his features.

"I don't have the luxury—" Drake started, and then winced, pressing fingers to his split lip before continuing. "The luxury of taking time off when that villain Malachi is still hanging around town."

The healer pinned us both beneath her uncompromising stare and answered, her voice firm, "Then it's good you're not the only shifter helping guard the town. Further damage to your leg now could mean permanent impairment later." Then she turned her full attention to me. "Your mate would do well to exercise more patience during his convalescence."

My face flushed with embarrassment at her casual designation. "Mate? Surely you're mistaken, Aja. Drake's mate died years ago, and I'm not even a shifter."

Drake cleared his throat, his expression turning sheepish. "Actually, Lydia, there's something I've been meaning to talk to you about." He rubbed the back of his neck, avoiding my gaze. "In rare cases, wolves can have more than one mate. And lately, I've been suspecting that you might be mine."

I stared at him, dumbfounded. "But I'm fae, Drake. How is that even possible?"

Aja interjected, a knowing smile playing on her lips. "The ways of fate are often mysterious, Lydia. The bond between mates transcends all."

Drake nodded, finally meeting my eyes. "I know it's a lot to take in, but I can't deny what I feel. What I've been feeling for a while now."

I stared at him, my mind reeling from this revelation. A part of me wanted to embrace the idea of being Drake's mate, to believe that the connection we shared was something deeper and more profound than mere friendship. But another part of me, the rational, cautious side, couldn't help but question it.

"I... I don't know what to say," I stammered, my heart racing. "This isn't a possibility I ever considered. I mean, I'm not even a shifter. How can I be your mate?"

Drake squeezed my hand gently, his eyes soft with understanding. "I know it's hard to believe, but the bond between mates isn't limited by species. It's a connection that goes beyond the physical, beyond the rational."

I shook my head, trying to wrap my mind around it all. "But what does it mean to be mates? What would it change between us?"

"It doesn't have to change anything," Drake assured me. "Not if you don't want it to. I understand if you need time to process this and figure out what you want."

I nodded, grateful for his patience and understanding. But even as I tried to focus on the practical considerations, like how this would affect my role as innkeeper and my duty to remain impartial, I couldn't ignore the flicker of hope and longing that had ignited in my chest.

"I need time," I admitted, my voice soft. "Time to think, to sort through my feelings. And there's also the matter of my responsibilities as innkeeper. I can't be seen as favoring one enclave over the others."

Drake's jaw tightened, but he nodded. "Of course. I would never ask you to compromise your integrity or your duty. But know that I'll be here for you, no matter what you decide."

Aja placed a comforting hand on my shoulder, her eyes filled with wisdom and understanding. "Take all the time you need, Lydia. These matters of the heart are never simple, especially when duty is involved. But trust in yourself and in the bond that you and Drake share. Fate has a way of guiding us to where we need to be."

I offered her a grateful smile before turning back to Drake, my heart full of conflicting emotions. "Let's focus on your recovery for now," I said softly. "We can figure out the rest later."

He brought my hand to his lips, pressing a gentle kiss to my knuckles. "As you wish, Lydia mine. I'll be here, no matter what the future holds."

As I sat there, my mind reeling from this unexpected development, I couldn't help but feel a flicker of hope amid the uncertainty. Being Drake's mate was a possibility I had never dared to consider, but now that it had been laid before me, I found myself drawn to it like a moth to a flame.

But I knew I couldn't rush into this. I couldn't let my heart override my head. I needed time to think, to sort through the tangled web of emotions and responsibilities that bound me. Only then could I truly know if Drake and I were destined to be mates and if the bond between us was strong enough to weather any storm.

We were both wounded, but for the time being, I could only concentrate on tending to Drake's injuries and aiding in his recovery. The future would take care of itself. And no matter what happened, I knew I would have Drake by my side, a constant presence in the ever-shifting landscape of my life.

In the days following the violent confrontation, an uneasy pall lingered over Crescent Crossing. Though the immediate threat had retreated, the image of Malachi's ruthless visage continued to haunt my restless dreams. And despite the blossoming connection with Drake, my emotions roiled wildly in the aftermath—a tempestuous sea of grief, anger, and fear.

I set Drake up with a room at the inn so I could keep a close eye on him. As the days turned into weeks, Drake's pent-up restlessness finally overpowered lingering pain and prudence. I looked up from my book one evening to find him swinging himself gingerly to his feet, his temper flashing briefly across his craggy features as he caught sight of the instinctive protectiveness in my expression.

"Fret yourself gray if you must, but I'm taking a walk," he asserted gruffly, his voice brooking no argument. "These four walls are about to drive me mad."

I appraised his balance critically, ready to override foolish masculine pride if need be. But to my surprise, Drake's leg bore his weight steadily now. I knew he'd diligently followed the rehabilitation routine, which granted him this small freedom.

I set my book down with exaggerated care. "Would you like some company?"

Drake stepped closer to where I perched on the edge of the chair, watching him mutely. I scarcely dared to breathe when work-roughened fingers trailed whisper-light down my cheek, the touch so tender it made my heart ache.

"That'd be more than agreeable, Lydia." Drake's resonant voice held a vulnerability he seldom let show through his usual brusque facade. Almost of their own volition, my hands moved to cover his larger ones, pressing gently as if to seal unvoiced promises exchanged skin to skin.

At this moment, the approaching darkness of the night couldn't dampen the growing warmth of the fire between us. I leaned into Drake's touch, savoring the comfort and strength that his presence provided. But even as I allowed myself to be lost in the tenderness of the moment, I couldn't shake the nagging sense of unease that lurked at the edges of my mind.

Malachi's disappearance weighed heavily on me, a constant reminder of the danger that still threatened our community. How had he managed to escape, even with his injuries? And who, if anyone, was helping him? These questions swirled in my thoughts, refusing to be ignored.

I knew that we couldn't let our guard down and couldn't allow ourselves to be lulled into a false sense of security. Malachi was still out there, plotting his next move, and we needed to be ready for whatever he had in store.

But for now, in this stolen moment of peace, I allowed myself to draw strength from Drake's presence and from the unspoken promise of his support and protection. Together, we would face whatever challenges lay ahead, our spirits unyielding and our determination unwavering.

No matter what Malachi had in mind, no matter what darkness he sought to unleash upon us, I was certain that Drake and I would stand against it, side by side, ready to defend our community and each other with every ounce of strength we possessed. And so I let myself sink into his embrace, drawing comfort and courage from his touch, ready to confront whatever lay ahead, one step at a time.

CHAPTER 20

The golden rays of dawn filtered into my room, stirring me from a restless sleep. As I stood, a heavy sense of sorrow weighed down my chest. Today, Hamish and Saige would depart Crescent Crossing to continue on their journey to Hamish's home.

Though capable allies still surrounded me, the impending absence of their stalwart support and companionship filled me with a surprising sense of loss. We had braved so many harrowing challenges side by side since my arrival, and the thought of watching them leave this haven we had all fought so hard to protect gripped my heart with unexpected anguish.

At breakfast, I listlessly pushed the rapidly cooling eggs around my plate, struggling to contain the resentment and self-pity churning within me. Saige set down her coffee mug with an audible thump, her piercing green eyes seeing through my facade.

"We've stayed longer than planned," Hamish said, his

gruff voice soft. "The pack needs our report on recent events."

I kept my gaze locked on the tabletop, irrationally clinging to my last moments with these steadfast allies who now felt like family. A couple of weeks ago, when fortunes seemed to be improving, I had whole-heartedly endorsed their decision to leave. Yet now, the words congealed stubbornly in my throat as I warred silently against the volatile emotions within me.

"You've proven yourself capable of handling the challenges that come your way, Lydia," Saige declared. "Especially now that you have Drake by your side, and he's fully recovered. You're secure, with plenty of others to watch your back."

I flinched inwardly at her candid words, even as reason acknowledged the wisdom of her them. They deserved to continue on their journey home. I fumbled to conjure parting well wishes without revealing the cracks in my facade.

"You've both sacrificed more than enough for me already," I managed unevenly. "I can't begin to repay such loyalty."

I risked a glance up, my eyes suspiciously overbright. "Your pack must miss you deeply by now, Hamish." I attempted a smile that felt more like a grimace.

To my surprise, understanding shone from Saige's features rather than relief at her imminent liberation from my ceaseless drama. In that suspended heartbeat, I grasped that my odd malaise and irrational attachment had not gone unnoticed by my astute friends. Wordlessly, I clung to Saige's proffered compassion, the sole balm capable of soothing my conflicted spirit.

We finished our meal in brooding silence. As I walked with them to gather their belongings, my thoughts lingered on the times we had argued over my reckless decisions or when I had stubbornly ignored their wisdom. Perhaps they would breathe easier returning to pack mates who better respected their boundaries. I had relied heavily on their tireless support, but what had I offered in return?

As if reading my self-recriminations, Saige paused on the stairs, her blunt words laced with warmth. "You underestimate your value and commitment to this community."

Her lips quirked wryly. "Our journey was incomplete without this stopover at Crescent Crossing, believe it or not."

Hamish rumbled in agreement, his eyes glinting affectionately. "Never been one to shy away from a challenge either." His hand engulfed my shoulder, steadying me. "You'll manage splendidly on your own. Besides, the town is behind you now."

I blinked back tears, overwhelmed by gratitude for their faith in me. Our friendship had given me more than tactical support—it had reawakened my appetite for living when I felt too weary to continue. I silently vowed to honor that gift by embracing each new day, come what may.

As the noon sun glinted overhead, I stood beside their idling car, memorizing every detail—Saige's brown pixie cut tousled by the breeze, the crinkles fanning Hamish's eyes as he watched her fondly. This unexpected interlude had profoundly changed my life, gifting me with the family I had unknowingly craved. As they dwindled from sight down the winding road, I whispered farewell until we met again beneath the sparkling stars.

With their departure, the weight of all that lay ahead

crashed down, momentarily driving the breath from my lungs. I wandered back inside the Howl Away Inn, keenly feeling the void left by my strongest confidantes' absence.

As I settled into my office, my thoughts drifted to the aftermath of Malachi's banishment and the impact of his lies and deception on the community of Crescent Crossing. His actions had sown discord and mistrust among the residents, leaving a trail of broken relationships and shattered trust in their wake.

The catchphrase "A raven's shadow never fades" had become a sinister reminder of the conspiracy's influence, a dark cloud that had hung over the town for far too long. It would take time and effort to heal the wounds caused by Malachi's betrayal, to rebuild the bonds of friendship and loyalty that had been so callously severed.

Reflecting on the events that had transpired, I couldn't help but think of the wooden raven disc and the crucial role it had played in exposing the conspiracy. That small, seemingly insignificant object had been the key to unraveling the tangled web of lies and deceit, bringing the truth to light and rallying the community together in the face of adversity.

The banishment of Malachi and Cade was a testament to the strength and resilience of the people of Crescent Crossing, their unwavering determination to protect their home and their way of life. As the newly appointed innkeeper, it was my duty to lead them through this difficult time, to help them heal and rebuild, stronger than ever before.

With a renewed sense of purpose, I stood up and made my way to the window, gazing out at the town I had come to call home. Though Briar and Drake remained faithfully by my side, I still struggled to muster the self-assurance they exuded in the face of crisis. And the mundane tasks of running this sanctuary threatened to bury me.

I squared my slumped shoulders despite the oppressive weight of the unknown variables looming ahead without my familiar guardians. Neither falling apart emotionally nor shirking unpalatable duties was an option. I placed one leaden foot in front of the other until I reached my private chambers upstairs.

Upon entering that snug space which had become my sanctuary, emotion crashed over me with renewed ferocity, a riptide yanking me below remorseless waves. I sank to the quilt, blinking back tears over the irrational feelings of abandonment and inadequacy churning violently within me.

Intellectually, I knew I should celebrate their well-deserved departure rather than cling selfishly to the reliable pillars I had come to lean on too readily. But in that moment, it felt as though my anchors had abruptly given way, leaving me adrift and rudderless when so much still required minding. Would the disquiet plaguing Crescent Crossing linger unless I found a way to permanently restore unity? And if my best efforts splintered against the ancient wedge between enclaves, could fragile trust ever take root beyond these sheltering walls for a fae interloper like me?

Taking several bracing breaths, I dashed away the dampness on my cheeks. Wallowing in melancholy served no one. Hamish and Saige had reminded me that resilience still slumbered within, awaiting my beckoning. I simply needed to reignite my inner spark, though it seemed easier said than done.

A soft knock at my door jerked me from my reverie, my hands moving to smooth the creases in my bedding as I tried to collect myself. The feminine voice that called out, warm and cautious, through the sturdy barrier was a balm to my frayed nerves. It was Briar, her presence a steadfast reminder of the bond we had forged in recent tumultuous weeks.

"Come in," I called, my voice stronger than I felt, as I mustered a welcoming smile. Briar entered, her expression etched with concern and empathy, taking in my somber mood without a word of judgment.

"I thought you might need some company, especially today," she ventured, her gaze holding mine with an intensity that spoke volumes of her support.

Her presence, a beacon of warmth in my shadowed room, prompted a smile from me despite the ache in my heart. I gestured for her to join me, a silent invitation she accepted with a soft sigh, settling beside me with a comforting ease.

"What's on your mind?" she asked, her voice a gentle nudge, encouraging me to share my burdens.

As I opened up about the void left by my departed friends, Briar listened with unwavering attention, her responses laced with the wisdom and humor that had become her hallmark. She reminded me of our shared resilience, of the uncharted adventures that awaited us in Crescent Crossing, and of her never-ending support.

With the room dimming around us, time seemed to stretch, the conversation ebbing and flowing as naturally as the night outside. Briar's words, imbued with a quiet strength, began to mend the raw edges of my solitude, weaving a tapestry of solidarity and mutual trust.

"You're not alone in this," Briar assured me, her hand finding mine in the dim light. "Whatever comes our way, we'll face it together. I've got your back, always."

Her pledge, simple yet profound, pierced the lingering shadows of my heart, kindling a flame of hope amid the uncertainty. I realized then the depth of the bond we had formed, a partnership fortified by trials and cemented in the silent promises of the night.

"I can't thank you enough, Briar," I murmured, overcome with gratitude. "Knowing you're here, that we're in this together, it means everything to me."

"We're a team," she replied, her smile radiant. "And there's nothing we can't face together."

Our conversation dwindled to comfortable silence, the kind that speaks of deep understanding and shared resolve. In Briar's company, the weight of my worries seemed less daunting, the path ahead not as treacherous. Together, we watched the stars, a symbol of our united front against whatever Crescent Crossing might throw our way, fortified by friendship and a shared determination to thrive amid chaos.

THE END

***

Thank you so much for reading Hocus Pocus and Pinot Noir! It would mean a lot to me if you could leave a review. A single line or two makes a big difference for other people when deciding if a book is a good fit for them.

ACKNOWLEDGMENTS

Thanks to Chrisandra's Corrections their editing services.

And to my friends and family who've been a source of unending strength, laughter, and wine over the years: thank you for the inspiration.

And lastly, to my partner, Lee. Thank you for traveling alongside me in this journey. Your enduring support and candor mean the world to me.

A HUMBLE REQUEST

If you loved the book and have a minute to spare, I would really appreciate a short review on the page or site where you bought the book. Your help in spreading the word is greatly appreciated. Reviews from readers like you make a huge difference to helping new readers find similar stories.

Thank you so much for reading and supporting my work!

Candice

P.S. If you'd like to know when my next book comes out and want to receive occasional updates from me, then you can sign up for my newsletter at candicebundy.com. I promise I will never sell your email to the daemonic marketing hordes.

Twinned Shadow

Poisoned Shadow

Shadow Underground

<u>Other Works</u>

Ripples, a novella

Open Rack, a contemporary short

WRITING AS CR BUNDY

The Depths of Memory Series

The Dream Sifter

Dreams Manifest

For a list of my full catalog of available titles, visit my
<u>candicebundy.com/books</u> page.

ABOUT CANDICE BUNDY

Nestled in the sun-kissed and adventure-filled heart of Denver, Colorado, Candice thrives amidst nature's playground. Candice shares her abode with her partner and feline overlords who, quite frankly, aren the true monarchs of their cozy kingdom. A word alchemist at heart, Candice skillfully weaves tales drenched in angsty fantasy romance, exhilarating science fiction, and tantalizing paranormal spice. She likes to throw fierce, clever heroines off cliffs and into the arms of heroes who stand at the ready to catch them.

Her passion extends beyond the page, as she delves deep into the worlds of archeology and mythology, seeking the threads that bind our collective narratives. Not one to rest on her laurels, she's an advocate for habit hacking, ceaselessly striving to embody minimalist principles, promote holistic well-being, and infuse her everyday with an abundance of positive mojo.

Away from her writer's nook, Candice is either nurturing her garden—home to heirloom tomatoes and a symphony of jams and fermented delights—or quite literally tied to a wall. As a fervent sport climber, she eagerly tackles every new challenge, ascending to greater heights and mastering diverse landscapes.

Eager to embark on a journey through her literary realms? Subscribe to her newsletter here and be the first to uncover her latest creations. Should curiosity or inspiration spark within you, don't hesitate to drop Candice a line. Craving some delightful cat moments? Dive into her social channels, where enchanting feline captures await to brighten your day.

For more information:
candicebundy.com
candice@candicebundy.com